BEYOND THE SEA

Stories from The Underground

©2021

Dedication

One photograph - A single image - A lonely boat on the edge of sea

Is it adrift? - Was it abandoned? - Did it wash ashore? - Was anyone aboard?

Did someone leave it behind? - Is anyone coming back? - Who knows.

The sea has washed the footprints away.

Look at the vessel and think: "If that old boat could talk, what stories it would tell."

Wonder no longer.

Twelve members of Underground Authors all gazed upon the same image.

And to each the photograph told a different story. Same boat. Same image. Different genres.

From mystery and techno-thriller to romance and magical realism, from horror and historical fiction to fantasy and suspense with a little paranormal thrown in for good measure. These stories are presented in Beyond The Sea and are the handiwork of award-winning authors C.J. Peterson, Cindy Davis, Rox Burkey & Charles Breakfield, CW Hawes, Richard Schwindt, Ronald E. Yates, Kelly Marshall, N.E. Brown, Linda Pirtle, James R. Callan, Michael Scott Clifton, and Caleb Pirtle III.

The stories are all different as the boat had more than one secret to tell. It had a dozen.

The Underground Authors decided to dedicate the proceeds from 2021 sales of Beyond The Sea to a group that supports communities.
https://teamrubiconusa.org/

Team Rubicon serves communities by mobilizing veterans to continue their service, leveraging their skills and experience to help people prepare, respond, and recover from disasters and humanitarian crises.
The story of Team Rubicon and what they have accomplished is amazing. There are also volunteer opportunities with them if you wish to help. Enjoy the stories a bit more knowing you also contributed to a worthwhile cause.

Contents

Authors - Breakfield and Burkey

Breakfield is a 25+ year technology expert in security, networking, voice, and anything digital. He enjoys writing, studying World War II history, travel, and cultural exchanges. He's also a fan of wine tastings, winemaking, Harley riding, cooking extravaganzas, and woodworking.

Burkey is a 25+ year applied technology professional who excels at optimizing technology and business investments. She works with customers all over the world focusing on optimized customer experiences. Rox writes white papers and documentation, but found she has a marked preference for writing fiction.

Together these Texas authors create award-winning stories that resonate with men and women across the world. Their Enigma Series, TechnoThrillers, has twelve volumes and another in process. Additionally, they have four short stories available as eBooks on Amazon with more planned to release in 2021. They bring a fresh new view to technology possibilities today in exciting stories. Visit their website for more information and free stuff including suggestions on how to protect your security. You can reach out to them via:

Email: Authors@EnigmaSeries.com
Website: www.EnigmaBookSeries.com
Blog: https://EnigmaBookSeries.com/the-enigma-chronicles/category/blog-statement/
Connect and follow on Social Media:

LinkedIn: https://www.linkedin.com/in/charlesbreakfield and

https://www.linkedin.com/in/roxanneburkey

Twitter: https://twitter.com/EnigmaSeries

and https://twitter.com/1RBurkey

Facebook: https://www.facebook.com/TheEnigmaSeries/

YouTube: https://www.youtube.com/channel/UC6Vz4x5ctTnx3yUhZk1OJkw

Pinterest: https://www.pinterest.com/enigmseries/

Instagram: https://www.instagram.com/enigmabookseries/

Bublish: https://bublish.com/author/breakfieldandburkey

RRBC: https://ravereviewsbookclub.wordpress.com/about-breakfield-burkey-enigmaseries-rrbc-rrbc_community/

The Diving Bits

By:
Breakfield
& Burkey

The Diving Bits

Breakfield and Burkey

Xiamara bounced with dance-like steps tousling her curly copper-brunette hair, tugging Judith down the beach's packed sand.

"Slow down, Zee. I can't see where I'm going."

"You keep that blindfold on, Jude, or I'll clip that beautiful blonde hair while you're asleep. Relax. Feel the gentle warmth of the winter sun. Listen to the lapping waves. Inhale that fragrant salty air. And those breezes..."

"Are you taking me somewhere, Zee, or writing a travel brochure?"

Xiamara stopped her friend and whipped off the blindfold. "TADA! And for only three-quarters of our savings!"

Judith followed Zee's spread hands. "Ah...what is that? A boat?" A dark cloud covered them briefly as the breeze picked up.

Stunned for several moments in the shadow of the cloud, Judith stood stock still, hoping it was a mirage. Judith stomped her feet on the sand as her face reddened. "Zee, you bought this almost boat with our tuition monies? No, strike that. You got fleeced of our tuition monies."

"But listen, Jude..."

Judith fisted her hands at her side then lectured. "We agreed to pool our funds to go back to school in the fall. The chump change we make allows us a one-bedroom flat and almost two square meals each per day. That left us just enough to pay the tuition fees for those computer classes."

"I know, but if..."

Growing angrier by the moment, Judith crackled. "What is it with you, Zee. You enjoy our day and night jobs as booth babes and checkout chicks so much that you now sentenced each of us to a third job? Really?"

A grimace contorted Xiamara's sweet features. Trying to recapture her excitement, inserted, "You miss the point, Judy. We can use this boat to take tourists from the daily docking events out snorkeling. We know the entire San Juan shoreline, with its neat hidden places. I thought we'd advertise a modest touring service run by two geeky computer nerds trying to earn tuition monies. People love helping, especially for a cause like education."

Judith scowled. "Don't call me Judy. My mom's live-in, whatever he was, always called me that. I hated it. I got out of there when we agreed to live life on our own terms. Zee, you agreed when I said we'd have to hustle to make it. Here you are, conned out of our tuition monies it's taken months to scrape together. With no discussion. Tell me you at least got some magic beans to go with this deal. Maybe we'll bump into Jack and all climb the beanstalk together."

Xiamara opened her mouth, but Judith sarcastically contin-ued, "Exactly how did you think we would get this boat from here to anywhere without an engine? Were you counting you or me to row this tub full of passengers, gear, and refreshments to our target destinations? Wouldn't one of us have to steer? Argh."

Tired of the tirade, Xiamara faced her friend nose to nose. "Boy, you do have your panties in a wad. How 'bout letting me finish, alright? What you don't see yet is the sailing mast and jib that are also part of the deal. Ronaldo agreed to throw in his labor to add the rigging to our private ship. So, STOP calling it a boat." A dreamy, glazed expression crossed Xiamara's face as she continued. "We use our natural, free, wind supply to reach destinations. No one else sails so there is no competition."

Setting her jaw, Ziamara refocused on Judith with a grin. "Then we anchor in some nice coves so our guests can snorkel. I've got a line on some used gear, too."

Judith racked her brain for the right words, holding back frustrated tears. "Sailing? We know nothing about sailing." She added a weak argument trying to get Zee to be realistic. "We have challenges making the double mocha lattés infused with dandelion extract at the Coffee Shack where we at least get tips. Now you're talking about sailing a barely serviceable boat with some bolt-on parts?"

Xiamara sensed a shift and grinned. "I thought about that. I found some free how-to-sail-your-boat videos on YouTube. There's this cute hunk showing how to tack into the wind, how to use the jib sail, and steering techniques. We can both watch and take turns."

Judith closed her eyes, releasing her anger and considering the possibilities. "Okay, Miss I-Thought-It-All-Out, how do we snag tourists? You think we can persuade them to spend money with us? When you convince me that's solved, then we just take them to our *Lily of San Juan,* where we sail them to the first cove with some fish to watch."

Xiamara brightened and bubbled. "I like the name, Jude. Good one. I've already gotten permission to use the school printers and computers to make up some snappy brochures. We'll use these to hustle the local concierges to steer people our way. We can also stand at the disembarkation ramps and hawk our wares."

Judith patted her cheeks, nearly suppressing her grin. "How

is it possible that your harebrained scheme is starting to sound good? We need to hype up the fact that we're trying to put ourselves through school. It's like a crowdfunding exercise to the day-trippers. So, they can pat themselves on the back for paying more for the underdogs than the bigger services." With a smirk, she added, "We, of course, encourage tipping. And you can get your angelic smile on."

Xiamara cleared her throat and clapped. "Good one. Since we're planning some uniqueness, how 'bout digging out that cute bikini of yours? Isn't the color close to um..., your *Lily of San Juan?*" Mischievously grinning and gesturing to their new venture she added, "You still have it, right?"

Judith growled at her bestie. "Yeah, you mean the one that's a bit too tight in the boobs?"

"Yep, the one that makes guys trip all over themselves to get your attention. We both know I can't pull that off with my pear shape."

"Are you saying I get to be the head diver too? Isn't it a bit too revealing? We don't want to put off their wives or dates."

"Jude, I don't think it's immodest, just provocative. We'll add an elegant cover-up that doesn't cover all the way up to convince some of the male patrons. I mean, come on, Jude. Your long white, blonde mane, perfect complexion, sun-kissed skin, and ideal bod makes you a natural point person. I have the friendly smile and great chestnut curls but am far more suited to heavy lifting."

Remembering their friendship, Judith slightly hugged Zee. "You always make me feel special. You know I tend to hide beneath a shapeless dress except when I'm at work. I was annoyed 'til you consoled me when they insisted on fitted uniforms."

"You are my oldest friend. I never see the chunky, plain girl you always complain about. All I ever see is a person with a heart of gold and my friend. And gad, I wish I had those curls in my hair." Biting her lip, Judith scolded, "You could have talked this over with me before raiding our funds. It hurts, thinking that…well, you are becoming just another person conning me."

"I'm sorry. I was only trying to help get us ahead faster. I should have talked with you in advance," Zee grimaced. "But you were working a double shift. Ronaldo needed the funds badly, and I refused to lend him anything."

With a resigned look, Judith nodded. "Okay, I can see what you were thinking. Can you at least tell me you ran the business case?"

"You'll be glad to know I negotiated four months of free dock space while we ramp our business." Xiamara pulled out her notebook and moved to share the contents. "Then, I researched the tourist trade for several years and the annual income posted by the Chamber of Commerce for the last three years. If we can capture a modest seven percent of this business with lower prices and more personalization for seven months, we make our investment back and triple our tuition savings."

Judith grinned. This was where they'd always connected. "Even if we only capture four percent, Zee, we can make the tuition. Now what?"

"Now we just need a catchy name for the business so we can get the advertising started."

Getting into the spirit of the project that they can only move forward, Judith giggled. "Try this, Zee. We call it *Fall Snorkeling Bits* since we're hustling our fall tuition. I'll be the *Head Diving Bits,* and you're the *Sailor Diving Bits.* Your idea of a crowd-funding exercise with goals that continue to expand with each successful increment is brilliant."

Xiamara offered a high-five and hip bump as she as her excitement rose and she squealed with glee. "Jude, after our shift tonight, we work through those sailing tutorials. High tide is on its way, so I'll phone Ronaldo to help me get the *Lily of San Juan* into her berth to get ready for her maiden cruise. Can you work your magic and charm with those guys walking this on the beach to help push her into the water? The dock is only half a mile up the shoreline."

Judith immediately transformed into character, tossed her hair back over her shoulder, tied her dress around the waist, exposing her stomach and short shorts, with legs that went all the way up to meet at her curved bottom. "Like this?"

"Uh, let's not overdo it. Wow, those are tight short shorts, but you look great. I know you don't want charm on display that promises too much collateral in return. Lower the tie-up just a little."

Judith chuckled. "Point taken." She motioned to the three guys on the beach, who were only too happy to accommodate the two smiling ladies, flirting the whole time.

THE REST of the week was consumed with outfitting the *Lily of San Juan*. When the mast and sail were mounted, both girls daydreamed of non-stop business. As fresh glossy turquoise paint adorned the hull, the craft's name in white script gained oohs and aahs from other boat owners and the marina regulars.

They were nearly ready for the cruise ship due by the end of the week. The photo at the top of *Lily of San Juan* made a difference to the brochures. Positive comments, permission to distribute, and even contributions to their college funds boosted their confidence.

Every day they diligently practiced their YouTube training, with mixed results. By the end of day four, they were sore but competent sailors. The breezes on this side of the island were ideal for practicing. They scouted the coves that were deep enough, with minimal surf to allow them easy maneuvering. They rehearsed securing their position with an anchor and then releasing it until they felt efficient.

After the success with the small businesses, Judith was surprised by the response from the tour brokers. For them to promote to the shipping lines, they wanted positive reviews. When the first ship docked and passengers exited, they acted like carnival barkers to get attention. Finally, after Judith's umpteenth ten-second sales pitch, they snagged a single, elderly gentleman.

"Ladies," John Maling said, "show me your boat and perhaps a pretty beach where I can take a couple of photos. My visits before have mostly been in town."

Xiamara pulled Judith aside and whispered, "Is this guy okay? He's not a letch, is he?"

"Nay, he's okay. Besides, we can take him. Don't worry. Let's just be polite."

Turning back toward their first customer, she blurted, "John, I'm Xiamara; we are glad you decided to sail with us. But don't try anything funny. We know how to fight!"

John laughed uproariously for nearly a minute until they finally joined in. "You two are a hoot. No funny stuff, I assure you. You're too young for me, but your spiel was good. Show me the cove, miss."

Judith held out her hand. "I'm Judith, John." As they reached the boat, she handed him a life vest off the rack next to the dock then waved her hand. "Welcome aboard."

Judith hopped onboard after him while Xiamara secured the ropes. They snapped on their vests and made their way out of the slip, each with an oar in hand. Away from the other crafts, Xiamara unfurled the sail. They caught a nice breeze that propelled them toward their destination.

John pitched in to help as the wind shifted. "You know if you lean slightly in the direction you are headed, it will help your rudder get a better turn ratio."

Xiamara applied his suggestion. "You're right. Thanks, John."

Anchoring at the cove worked after the second try. John again made suggestions that proved correct.

"I work most of the islands in the Caribbean, setting up wind power for local governments. As many years as it has plagued this region with fierce storms, the idea of harnessing appeals to them. That is the part of your pitch that convinced me to try this little outing."

Judith beamed. "Yes, Zee had the original idea with the sailing aspect, and I'm glad she was right. Do you think we have a chance to gain more customers? The ship tour brokers want references."

John smiled like an indulging father. "You seem to want to work hard, Judith. A little more practice and your steering will get smoother, Xiamara. The spots you showed were good as they are hard to hike to and not in line with the cruise ships' path. Let's try some snorkeling, Judith!"

Judith turned into the instructor and showed John how to put on his gear. They went to a couple of rock formations below the surface she had previously scouted. John helped Judith get back on board.

Xiamara broke out the snacks and sodas. They all laughed at John's jokes. The girls explained a bit more about their school plans, then headed back to the docking point. John got out of the boat and saluted the two girls, then paid them.

"John, you made this trip a lot of fun. Thank you," Judith said with a grin.

"Come back soon, John," Xiamara added.

"Don't worry, I'll be back. Plus, I'll give your information to several of the tour brokers I know. Your business will pick up." Then he added with a grin. "So, I was a good first customer?"

The girls chorused, "Yes."

He laughed. "You'll do all right. See ya in a couple of weeks. I'll call the number on your card and leave a message about my next arrival date. Take care. And, oh, next time, have a little beer, wine, and rum for your guests. I like red, myself."

As they cleaned up the boat and stowed their gear, they talked about making the trips more enjoyable. John had suggested they point out landmarks for the tourists as a high runner that Judith did well. Xiamara spoke about practicing her sailing during any spare time. They picked up a tour a day over the next week. Each one improved, but they liked the idea of taking out a couple, so they focused on those targets. They started to get positive ratings on the website Xiamara had built for them.

Good to his word, John provided recommendations, and word of mouth worked in their favor. They added an additional tour per day to keep up with the demand when a cruise ship docked. They figured they could do three depending upon docking and departing times. Their scheduling and ratings steadily improved. The tour income began to dwarf their day jobs as cashiers. They quit those jobs, but the bar work tips were too good to give up at this point.

Sadly, their success did not go unnoticed. The Diving Bits became the target of another snorkeling tour operator. Disheveled and arrogant, Benjy swaggered toward their boat's berth one morning before the ship-of-the-day docked.

He kicked their cleaning rags into the water along with the bucket as he closed the distance to the girls. "You girls are in my space. Go find something else to do besides crowding my snorkeling gig here on the island."

Intimidated by the gruff overweight operator with his oily complexion and tobacco brown teeth, Xiamara turned pasty. She melted into the furthest corner of the boat as if to disappear.

Judith looked up with false bravado and confidently countered without a second thought, "Are you here to buy us out?"

"Nice try, sweet chops. Why would I pay for something I can run out of business? You ain't got the proper tour operator sticker displayed. I'm just gonna turn you in. I'll let the Shore Patrol do the unpleasantries of confiscating that joke of a boat." With that, he walked away, guffawing as he called over his shoulder. "See ya 'round, bitches."

Judith jumped up on the dock then shouted, "That's THE Diving Bits to you, Benjy. Don't underestimate us."

Benjy kept laughing while he walked away without a glance back.

Judith turned back to the boat to see the pained expression on Xiamara's face. "Don't you dare cry over this, Zee! Who the hell does Doctor Grimy think he's dealing with? You stay here and get us ready for our next group. I'm gonna go fix this." Judith stormed off like one of Poseidon's daughters hunting for the mortal who hurt her pet fish.

Zee swiped at a few stray tears and smiled at hearing Judith's favorite colloquial phrases used to reflect on someone's ancestry uttered at high speed coupled with highly animated gestures, echoing in her wake.

Xiamara worked non-stop getting the boat ready for the customer booked from the cruise ship arriving the next day. She had to finish at the dock before her second job shift at sundown.

Judith startled Xiamara as she jumped in the boat and handed over a packet.

"Judith, you scared me. What's this?" Zee carefully opened the packet; her eyes grew big as she thumbed through the contents. "How did you get these boat and snorkeling operator licenses? These normally take weeks, but you've been gone only a few hours."

Judith smirked. "Let's just say the Shore Marshal is fully on board with us being tour operators and promises to look into Doctor Grimy and his threatening statements."

"These aren't cheap, Jude. I know because I priced them when planning our adventure. That's why I didn't bother with it. We didn't have enough coin. I figured we'd be too small to mess with." Then she pointedly demanded, "You didn't promise him the *Pooty,* did you?"

Highly annoyed, Judith's face mirrored the are you kidding me look. "No, I didn't promise him the *Pooty.* I called our favorite gentleman, John. I asked if he could use his wit and gender to persuade the issuing official to grant us a temporary license. We are on the hook to make good. He said he'd extend it at the end of the season to next year, provided we show our tuition receipts." Sticking out her tongue, she added, "There, satisfied?"

Still bristling, Xiamara insisted, "Why would John do a favor like that? What do we owe him, or shouldn't I ask?"

"Zee, what is it with you? Why is everything about paying with horizontal refreshment? Remember when we dropped John off that first day, and he over-tipped us. He included a phone number and offered to fund our tour operation. He also plainly stated there were no strings attached. I just wanted us to try to make it on our own but appreciated his promise to tell folks we were a fun tour. He said our cause had merit."

"Are you saying he's wealthy? I thought he earned a living, but Jude, I didn't expect this."

"Duh. The second trip he gave us another great tip. No matter. I called and explained the situation. He even chuckled slightly. You know he told us he has connections in the Caribbean. He'll be here again next week and is already prebooked for both tours on that day. The one thing he wants is to have some relaxation with intelligent, determined ladies taking him out on snorkeling adventures when he's in port."

"Okay, it'll be his third trip. We can take him to that new spot we found."

"He mentioned the wine again for the return trip to shore. Apparently, the Boones Farm lacked something he wanted, so he said he'd arrange wines delivered before we set sail again. Apparently, he's a wine connoisseur. Who knew?"

Xiamara appeared dumbfounded. "He's wealthy, connected, and kind. I'm sorry I was so suspicious. I take it John leaned on the issuing official. Nice one, Jude. I'm not used to people offering to help for nothing. However, as a point of honor, we must pay him back at the end of the season."

"Agreed, Zee."

THE SUN REFLECTED off rippled water playfully dancing with the wind. Zee sang a silly pop song while Judith added the final supplies for their first tour of the day. They spotted the cruise ship easing toward the pier suggesting another hour before tourists touched the ground. Judith was cleaning the snorkels and masks when Zee stopped her song mid-line.

Judith looked toward her friend, who visibly shook and stepped back slightly. Gazing in the direction of Zee's eyes, Judith spotted an older pontoon boat with a faded canopy, motored to dock near *Lily of San Juan*. Not taking her eyes off the muscular guys, she positioned herself in front of Zee.

Zee's voice caught in her throat as she growled, "I've seen them before, Jude, never spoke, though. I recognize them from Benjy's outfit. I'm scared. This can't be good news or a social call."

Zee cautiously stooped, snagging both their sailor's bludgeon sticks, and handed one to Jude. They *whopped* loudly as each girl slapped them against their hands. Their eyes focused on the two men as they secured their boat near their berth.

The rugged guys looked at one another, then at the ladies, then back again. Recognizing that the wrong assumption was made, they smiled in unison and raised their hands.

Judith, feeling like a warrior princess, challenged, "Hold it right there. You both work for Benjy. The last time he swaggered by, he threatened to run us out of business."

Drawing courage from her bestie, Zee chimed in, "What's your business?"

The tall, lanky younger one of the pair grinned at his buddy. Looking back to the blonde, he replied, "Ah, the rumors are true. He threatened you to reduce the competition. Good, Mateo, we were right to quit that jerk-weed."

Mateo smiled broadly. "We don't work for him no more. Can we talk to you, please?"

Judith studied the two men, noting they were roughly the same age. Both appeared fit from working the water, though Mateo had some extra meat around the middle. "Sure, we can talk, but I'd rather you stay away from our boat. What's up?"

Adolfo moved an appreciative eye quickly over the feisty blonde, who raised an eyebrow in response. "Sorry, Ma'am. Give a guy a break for appreciating the scenery. We're here to ask for a spot with your group. Benjy is less than worthless to work for. He owes us a couple of weeks of wages."

Mateo added with a grin and quick glance over the brunette, "This here's our boat, free and clear. We work hard, and we like people. Plus, me and Adolfo knows the waters around here real good."

Xiamara wiggled her fingers in hello. "My name is Xiamara, this is Judith. I've seen you both around. Glad you aren't associated with Benjy now."

Adolfo set his jaw. "You ever hear the saying 'keep your enemies closer'? We hung close because he's a backstabber, which is why we came to you. We'll watch your back and handle any overflow business or larger groups. You ladies have a good rep growing with the brokers, whereas Benjy's is dwindling."

"Guys, nice as extra support would be, we're on a shoestring budget. We can't pay for employees, even if they come with their own boat," Judith said.

Xiamara blurted, "What if we partnered and split our earnings with Adolfo and the cute one only for what they contribute?

Their boat IS larger than ours, so together, we can carry more folks."

Blushing from his neck up, Mateo stammered, "What's the name of your business, Curls?"

Xiamara blushed at her outburst being heard, giggled. "Judith is the Head Diving Bits, and I'm the Sailing Diving Bits. But Curls works for me, too."

They all chuckled and visibly relaxed.

Adolfo recounted, "We've worked for Benjy for months and been paid piecemeal. The only thing we get is leftover food and drinks from the tours, which is usually meager. We do get direct tips from the customers, but we have to split them. We heard about you around town. People say you want to return to the tech school, and we think that's cool. Then Benjy bragged he'd run you two out of business."

Mateo nodded in agreement. "We don't want to work for that dump truck no more, so we quit yesterday. We want to compete fair and honest because that's who we are. Can we work together, ladies?"

"Uh, work for a dump truck?" questioned Judith.

"Yeah, Benjy, the dump truck. Always dumping on someone: his employees, his competitors, the cruise lines, or the suppliers. Always someone else. We don't want to catch his mental disease of being Teflon, so we came to you two. We heard your customers like you and recommend you. You also laugh and cut up. We seen you a couple of times at the bar, and you treat everyone fairly," Mateo said."

"Right now, Xiamara and I have to meet our guests at the pier. We need to talk about your offer and weigh our options. Let's get back together early in the morning and discuss it at the coffee shop."

Adolfo nodded. "Thank you, both. We'll see you around 6:30."

Resolutely the guys drifted back onto their boat. They sat on their deck and quietly talked. Judith became worried that they might be waiting for an opportunity while she and Zee were getting their passengers.

"Zee, you stay here while I go pick up our guests. If anything, funny occurs, yell for the guard on duty. I will ask him to keep an ear out as I go by."

Xiamara grinned. "Okay, I'll watch him, I mean them, like a hawk. I'm not worried in the least, though." She reached out and touched Judith's elbow indicating she had more to say. "Jude, ya know we can't just split our daily take in half because they'll be hauling more paying customers than us. That wouldn't be fair even if this is our operation."

Annoyed, Judith gazed at her friend. "There you go again with the honest and fair streak." She grinned. "But yeah, you're right. Let's talk later about it, please."

Adolfo startled Judith as he spoke right behind her. "Before you go, Ladies, let's approach this differently. Our boat is motorized, true, but yours is a sailing vessel with more panache. We would charge less per person for the motorized transport with the scruffy males. For a few extra shekels, they can sail with the two Amazon Warriors. We could also offer, as an extra service, pictures with the Sailor and Head diver as souvenirs. No one would pay for pictures with us unless we dressed up as Jack Sparrow, but I see good revenue with you two."

Xiamara blushed from toe to forehead. "Uh, no one would want to pay for pictures with me. I'm not..."

Judith turned on the two guys and pointed them toward their boat. "Timeout, all of you. You guys stay in your boat. I need to go grab our guests. Zee, watch our stuff."

"Geeze. Drama, I so don't like drama." Xiamara winked at the guys and watched her friend fume, knowing she'd think about it the whole way.

Judith stomped off at a good clip as the guys returned to their own boat. She knew Zee would be chatting it up before she returned. Quickly locating their guests, Judith was surprised to see the crowd.

"Mr. and Mrs. Marson, I'm Judith with The Diving Bits. Are you ready?"

Grinning like two lovebirds, Mrs. Marson gushed, "Yes, but the folks located on either side of our cabin would like to go too. I know there were no more tickets, but we thought we'd ask."

Dumbfounded, Judith looked up at the clouds and offered up a small prayer. Pasting on a big smile, she looked at the excited tourists. "We have a way we can make this work, but I need to collect the tour funds in advance. Since we are not on the ship, I have no way to let you do the auto-charge to your cabin. We can do cash or Zella if you have it. There is an ATM on the way to the dock if that makes it easier."

A cheer erupted from the group. Mr. Marson added, "Thank you so much we'll double your tour fee for helping us out." Marson quickly peeled off the cash and handed it to Judith.

They headed off to the boat, Judith mentally calculated the additional life vests and food needed. Judith breathed a sigh of relief that the other vessel was still there when she arrived with the crowd.

Looks of surprise from the three were quickly replaced with greetings listening to Mr. Marson explain what had happened. Judith grinned and motioned to Adolfo. Handing him cash, told him what she needed him to retrieve.

Xiamara smiled as she announced, "Great, I am Xiamara, the sailing lead. You already met Judith. The Diving Bits will lead the way to the first cove. Mr. and Mrs. Marson, you're with us in *Lily of San Juan,* and the rest of you will be with Mateo."

Mateo added, "Join me on the *Mini Black Pearl,* mates. My partner Adolfo will return shortly with our provisions and vests. Find your spots, and we'll take off shortly."

Adolfo returned less than half an hour later, pulling a wagon with vests and provisions. They stowed the gear. Adolfo secured the wagon to the berth.

All eyes centered on Judith, who stood on the dock in that teal bikini, demonstrating the proper use of life vests. Adolfo joined her to explain water safety and staying seated while moving. Xiamara led the way out of the harbor with Mateo right behind.

The San Juan day was nearly perfect, matching the cruise ship's advertising. Their tourists were delighted when pictures were taken. Photos featuring The Diving Bits was a hit, as predicted by the guys. After all the gear was cleaned, they agreed to go to dinner and discuss future possibilities.

They grabbed a patio table and sat to eat their drinks, burgers, and fries.

Judith started, "I want to know which of you guys has the crystal ball ability. If you hadn't shown up, we'd have lost some revenue." She counted the remaining funds after deducting the cost of the supplies. Judith counted out funds to each man, before Zee asked.

"This is a fair split for you guys based on the passengers you hauled. We do get a premium, as you kindly suggested, for those who snorkeled. Thanks for not being jerks."

Xiamara hip-bumped her friend. "We did great today. Now we can offer up to eight tour tickets and additional for snorkeling."

Clicking their glasses in a cheer, Judith added, "Better grab your pirate outfits. Adolfo, you'd be perfect playing the bearded Jack Sparrow."

Adolfo interjected with a gleam in his eye. "Does this mean...?"

Xiamara excitedly interrupted him, "Judith and I will draw up a contract tonight, and you can sign it in the morning. You are going to help advertise."

Judith rolled her eyes.

Mateo said, "I want a picture to mark this occasion, Curls."

"All right, group-selfie! Group-selfie!" Judith added.

Mateo changed the settings on his smartphone and propped it on the tabletop. They closed ranks and grinned as the timer pinged. They repeated the posing for each phone with Zee sticking out her tongue on the last one at Judith.

After several high fives with each other and a handshake agreement, Judith brooded, "What's Benjy going to do when he finds out we're working together?"

Adolfo's eyes flashed with anger. "Even if he pays us what he owes, we just agreed to be partners. We don't turn on partners. We won't let any harm come to you."

Judith smiled broadly and proclaimed, "You two are now dubbed *The Diving Bytes* since we are *The Diving Bits*. Let's make customers happy."

THE LITTLE COMPANY took customers snorkeling throughout the spring and well into summer. To keep everything fair, the team pooled everything, including the tips, then split it daily. It worked for paying the as-needed repairs. John Maling made the infrequent trip with the ladies and heartily approved the business expansion. After one trip, John had custom tee shirts sent for everyone.

Judith and Xiamara were making significant progress toward their tuition goals with school starting early October. Adolfo and Mateo were delighted with their earnings. Now and then, they saw Benjy glaring at them as they escorted their day passengers. They ignored him, even though he made annoyingly loud derogatory comments.

Things were running like a Rolex for the hardworking foursome, typically two trips a day. Toward the end of summer, the weather grew capricious and unpredictable.

One morning as they outfitted the boats, Adolfo suggested, "You know, Jude, for the rest of September, we will be hit with afternoon swells and rains. We might want to keep to our motorized boat and save *Lily of San Juan* for the first tour of the morning if the weather looks good."

Judith nodded, but Zee commented, "We talked about this last night. Remember we must secure the boat before we do any afternoon runs just in case the weather shifts. Ya know, like how we tie her up at night?"

Mateo indicated, "I'd like to be responsible for checking the weather every day. That way, we can do better daily plans."

Weather forecasting around Puerto Rico is an inexact science. Still, their planning worked for several days. The seas were a little rough, but they experienced safe returns. One group said it was like a rollercoaster ride, fun.

Then one morning, Mateo announced, "We can get the tour in today with both boats, but we got to return thirty minutes early."

Judith thought it a good omen with bright blue skies and whipped cream clouds when they started out with the life vest instruction. "Folks, isn't this a beautiful day?"

Adolfo added his safety speech. "No standing while the boats are moving. This is the season when the weather rapidly changes. If needed for safety, we may head back early."

Everyone nodded as they set off laughing, taking pictures, and snacking toward the snorkeling cove. Judith and four guests searched below the surface for sea creatures. Judith noticed the murky water was the worst she had seen. Signaling to her guests time was up, they returned to their respective boats.

One guest pointed toward the west. "Look how black the clouds are getting, and they're moving fast."

Mateo announced to his guests. "Folks, I need you to sit down in the bow of the boat. Make certain your vests are tight. We're going to race for the dock right behind *Lily of San Juan.*"

Then shouting over to Xiamara, "Zee, are you good or do you need help. It's going to get rough."

Xiamara smiled for her guests and swallowed hard. "I got this. Follow me."

Judith soothed, "The dark storm clouds are coming fast, which means the wind is increasing. Put your shoes on and hold tight to any bags you brought onboard. Our team is experienced, but it'll be a choppy ride."

The increasingly tormented seas set the stage for a test between wills and expertise. Passengers held onto one another with flashes of fear displayed in eyes and prayers whispered on their lips. Arriving at the marina, they secured their boats. The guests cheered the landing. The dock oscillated from the increasingly rough waters as the passengers scrambled toward their cruise ship. Both crews completed securing their crafts, along with every bit of supporting gear to avoid adding to the flying debris. Heavy rains assaulted the area, with the only thing good being the air was warm.

Judith hollered, "Zee, let's totally secure *Lily* and get to cover."

Adolfo and Mateo fastened their boat down and took off at a dead run toward the bar for cover from the pounding wind with rain plastering their hair and clothes to their bodies.

Finally, Xiamara tied the last rope, wiped the rivers of water from her eyes, and yelled, "Okay, she's secure! Let's go!"

THE STORM ABATED in the afternoon, and the team met at the dock. Slowly the four walked down the dock lanes in disbelief at the aftermath of the storm.

Mateo lamented, "This mess'll take weeks to repair. Some of these boats weren't tied right. Look how these two boats tore through the marina boards like a hot knife through butter. What a shame."

Judith said, "Oh my, the dock board sliced through that one's hull. I had no idea the wind was that strong. No wonder John wants to capture it for energy, but it's not clean." Then she stopped, and Xiamara nearly ran over her.

Xiamara rushed to the empty berth and knelt-down. Tears ran down her cheeks as she inspected the ropes, lax and dangling.

"Jude, I promise I triple-tied these like Mateo showed me. I pulled all ways, and these were tight when we left. Even in the driving rain, I promise, I did it right."

Judith studied the area in every direction, but there was no sign of their boat.

Then Xiamara exclaimed, "Look." She held up one end of the main rope, "Lily's mooring ropes were cut. It wasn't sloppy knots at all. Dammit, Lily is probably halfway to Havana by now. And we're out of the tour business."

Adolfo walked back and numbly stated, "Ours too. Gone."

Mateo noticed Zee's tears and wrapped his arms around Zee's shoulders and pulled her close.

Judith ground her teeth. "Were your mooring lines cut as well?" Both men nodded.

In a very disgusted tone, Adolfo suggested, "Come on, I've got a pretty good idea where our boats ended up."

They hiked down the shoreline before finding a small salvage party working to restore order to the damaged area. Small boats lined up like sacrificial lambs being claimed to facilitate clean-up. The four of them spotted their two vessels. Benjy was front and center with the local authorities pressing for ownership.

Judith marched up. "Hey, Benjy, you cut the mooring ropes on our boats. I bet you led them just far enough to claim salvage." Louder still, she added, " Is that how you treat everyone who works harder than you do?"

Overhearing the accusation, the shore official looked confused. "These are yours? Can you prove they belong to you? They had no papers on them and no registration plates. Sorry, but according to maritime salvage laws, anyone finding them can claim salvage rights if ownership cannot be established."

Benjy chortled in celebration of his obvious win.

Xiamara smiled sweetly at the official, handing him papers from her fanny pack. "These are our registration papers, sir. They'll match the plates under those seats."

Laughing at Benjy, she ridiculed, "Judith told me you'd try something like this, but I didn't believe her. Still, we removed the registration plates and fastened them into the wood under the left side seats of each boat."

All the color drained from Benjy's face before it was replaced with a crimson tone fueled by rage. He sputtered, trying to protest. The official simply motioned them all toward the boats. He searched both boats, then walked back and handed the papers to Xiamara. The official grinned as he faced Benjy. "Denied."

It took the four of them several hours to move the boats back to the water and finally get them to their mooring spots at the marina. They were tired but happy with how things had turned out.

A FEW DAYS LATER, Judith and Xiamara met with Mateo and Adolfo at the bar to celebrate. Adolfo brought the drinks over to the table.

Judith started, "To my best friend Zee for a wild plan that worked. We've paid next semester in full." They clinked glasses clicked and sipped. She added, "And here's to comping beers tonight for our new partners."

They toasted and drank again.

Adolfo chimed in. "To our business partners who will let us buy out their shares in the business."

"Yes," Judith said, smiling. "But only if we can work during breaks."

Glasses clicked again, and they took generous swallows.

Mateo grinned and hugged Zee close. "To some great girls we consider sisters. Congratulations."

They cheered and finished off their beers and asked for another round.

Zee wobbled a bit as she raised her glass toward Judith. "I promise the next wild idea I have I probably won't ask for your permission."

Glaring at Zee for a moment, Judith burst out laughing. "Agreed, if they all turn out this great, why not?"

Author - N.E. Brown

N. E. Brown is an award-winning author and has published over nine novels. Her lifelong interest in Texas history inspires her to create true-to-life fictional characters from the past. Galveston, 1900, Indignities is a six-book series that takes you on a journey through Texas history, as seen through the eyes of a young English woman.

Carson Chance, P. I., Over the Edge, Book 1, Unraveled, Book Two, and The Rain Man Murders are Mrs. Brown's latest Romantic Suspense novels and place you in the crossfires of solving crimes in the 1960s and 1970s in Dallas, Texas.

Mrs. Brown lives in East Texas with her husband and continues to write historical fiction. She believes that life is an adventure, and behind every experience is a story that waits to become her next novel.

Web-sites:

www.nebrown-author.com

http://amzn.to/2okITdv

h https://twitter.com/nbl276

ttps://www.facebook.com/nancy.b.larson.7

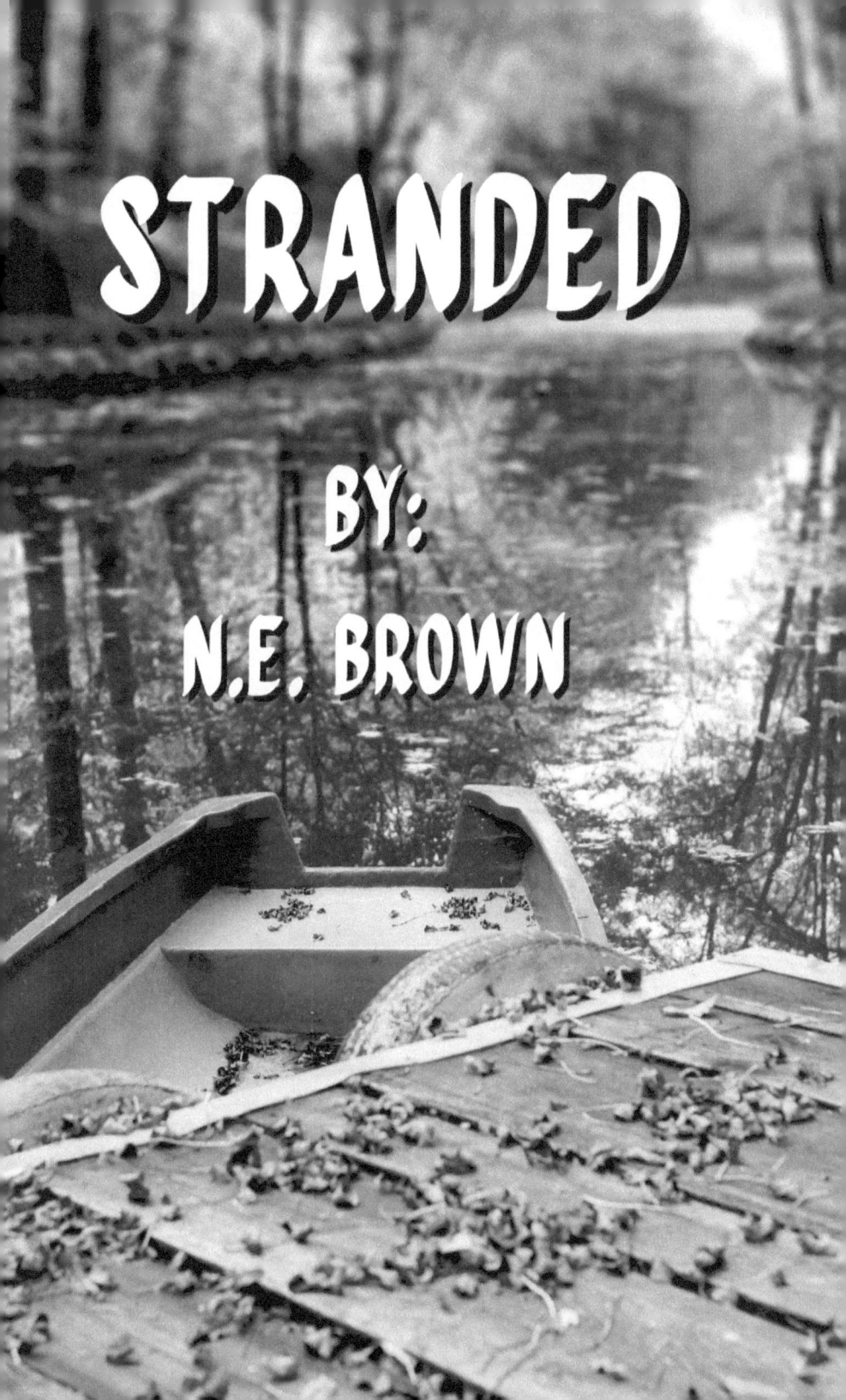

STRANDED

BY:

N.E. BROWN

2

Stranded

N.E. Brown

Friday, Six PM

Twenty-two-year-old Robin Harris pulled off the two-lane highway onto another side road that was almost as rough as the first. Having lost cell service at the last turn was terrible enough, but now feeling her way through a torrential downpour was making it impossible to find the cabin she'd rented for the weekend. *Another bad choice. What was I thinking?* A battered sign on the side of the road caught her attention. "Augie's Hide-a-way."

Breathing a sigh of relief, Robin turned her Toyoda SUV down the narrow path that led to the property. The road was thick with mud, and she pressed down on the accelerator as she crossed a rising creek. The tires spun several times before lunging forward. Almost losing control, she braked before hitting a small tree in front of the cabin. *Wow, that was close.*

Disappointment dampened her spirits even more, when she laid eyes on the cabin that was to be her home for the next three days. The gloomy weather didn't help the looks of it either. *I hope the inside will be more appealing.* Robin grabbed her overnight bag, tucked her purse under her arm, and made a mad dash to the front door.

She found the key under a flower pot as instructed by the Airbnb website. Robin pushed several times before the door gave way and opened. An uneasy feeling came over her when she glanced around the dreadful, sparsely furnished living room. Dropping her bag and purse on a nearby chair, Robin strolled into the bedroom. It was worse than she expected. Stained window shades, cedar paneled walls, and creaky wood floors added to the gloom of the day. The full-size bed looked as if it belonged in an attic, with a worn quilt thrown over ruffled sheets. *What did I expect, the Taj Mahal? You don't get much for $79.00 a night these days.* Robin returned to the living room, pulled out her cell phone from her jean pocket, and turned it on. *It figures, no cell phone service here either.* Her first impulse told her to grab her purse and bag and get the hell out of Dodge, but a loud banging on the front door caused her to drop her phone. Realization of her current circumstances forced her to step back. Frozen, she felt as if a magnet had fixed her to the floor. *Okay, okay, I can defend myself. Maybe it's just a neighbor.*

Thunder roared, and an explosion of rain pounded the roof as if tiny nails hammered into it. Another loud knock, and then the door handle rattled.

"Who is it?" she yelled.

"Augie, the caretaker," a loud voice replied.

Robin ran to the window and pulled the shade open far enough to peer out. A bulky man wearing a baseball cap and all-weather jacket crouched under the overhang on the small front porch. Long dark hair hung from under his hat, and he sported a beard.

"What's your full name?"

"August, August Fairchild. My name should have been on the information sheet you received when you got your confirmation."

Robin opened her purse and pulled out the paper. It took her a moment to find his name, but it was there. She sighed with relief. Now maybe she could stop shaking. "Okay, I'm coming."

Before she could open the door, the knob turned, and Robin was astonished at the size of the man lurking inside the door. For a moment, she wasn't sure what to say. His presence filled the room, and fear transfixed her.

"Please, don't let me frighten you. My car broke down in the mud, and I had to walk from the main road. I was hoping to be here when you arrived." Augie removed his baseball cap and ran his fingers through his wild hair. A sizable tattoo of a black panther appeared on his raised hand.

Stepping back, Robin inhaled a deep breath and held it for a moment before forcing it out. "Well, you're here now, and I hate to complain, but this house is not acceptable. It's in disrepair, and I'm canceling the remainder of my trip. My hundred and fifty dollar deposit should take care of my leaving."

"You might want to rethink that, Miss Harris. The water has blocked the driveway to the main road, and I'm afraid you'll get stuck just like I did."

Robin walked to the window and pulled up the shade. She could see the pools of water creeping over the road. "How could you let this happen? I can't stay here. I won't stay here."

"As I said, ma'am, when that inlet rises, it comes fast. The good thing is, when the rain stops, it drains out as fast as it came in. Then the road will dry out in a day or two."

"A day or two?"

"Now, don't get excited. I checked the weather report, and it's supposed to clear up by morning. You'll be able to drive out of here by Sunday."

Robin stared into the man's dark, cold, creepy eyes. Looking past his rugged demeanor, she could imagine that he would probably be handsome without all that long hair. "I'm sorry if I was rude, but I must admit your stature is a bit overwhelming."

When Augie removed his parka, a black t-shirt hugged his biceps in all the right places, and his tight jeans boasted the physique of a Cowboy's linebacker. "I played football in high school. I still work out from time to time. If you move aside, I'll put some wood in the fireplace and warm this place up a bit."

Robin stepped aside and folded her arms in front of her. Unsure of what to do next, she shuddered when she thought of being alone for the night with this strange man. Everything she'd brought from home was still in her car, along with her pepper spray.

"While you work on the fire, I'll get some groceries I left in my car." When she grabbed her car keys, a large hand wrapped around her arm and stopped her. Robin gasped.

"I'll get them. It's still raining." Augie swept the keys from her hand, pulled on his cap and jacket, and headed out the door.

Remembering her cell phone, Robin scoured the floor and found it lying under a chair. Even though there were no bars on her phone, at least it gave her a sense of hope. Maybe when it stopped raining and the cloud cover was gone, she might be able to pick up a signal. Robin put the phone in her back pocket. She was startled when the door flew open and Augie, dripping wet, walked past her into the kitchen to put the groceries on the table. When he came back into the room, she had a bad feeling that something wasn't right.

Robin glared at his wet face. Drops of water drizzled down his beard. Desperately trying to make conversation, Robin asked, "Do you live close? I mean, you aren't planning to stay here, are you?"

His cold dark eyes blazed back at her. "Do you think I'm stupid? You'd have to be crazy to go back out there. I don't want to alarm you, but we are under a tornado watch. Besides, it would be safer for you if I'm here in case a twister hits."

A streak of lightning hit close to the house. The lights flickered, and Robin prayed they wouldn't go out, but they did. She moved closer to the fireplace and swallowed the lump stuck in her throat. Augie lit the logs in the fireplace and then retrieved a kerosene lantern. "You don't have to be afraid of me. I'm not going to hurt you unless—" He stopped short of finishing his sentence.

"Unless what? You're scaring me. You're not August Fairchild, are you?"

Augie struck another match and lit the wick. He replaced the globe over the glowing flame, and the room once more came into view. Robin's piercing eyes demanded an answer.

"No. My real name is Bryan Hunt. My uncle is August Fairchild. When he's out of town, I help him rent out the cabin.

"Have you been staying here?" Robin demanded.

"Yes. Except when we rent it for the weekend."

"Where do you stay when it's occupied?"

"Truthfully, I usually rent to men that want to get away from their nagging wives. If you had clicked on the disclaimer on the website, you would have gotten a clearer understanding of what you were getting yourself into."

"You didn't answer my question."

"I sleep in a neighbor's boathouse on the other side of the bay."

Robin broke down, crying. "How could I have been so stupid? I was in such a hurry; all I wanted was somewhere close to Houston where I could spend a few days alone in utter quiet."

"Look, Robin, I'm not sure how you found this place. If you Google Airbnb's, multiple sites come up. What search words did you use?"

"Remote get-a-ways, no more than three hours from Houston, and nothing over eighty dollars a night." Robin sniffed as tears rolled down her cheeks.

Bryan shook his head. "I assumed you were a guy when you applied. Robin is a bisexual name." Bryan took a handkerchief from his pocket and handed it to her. "It looks like we both screwed up. As soon as the rain stops and the roads are usable, you can leave."

"Meanwhile, you'll have to stick it out with me whether you like it or not. I'll try to make you as comfortable as possible. I'll sleep on a pallet in front of the fire tonight. The bedroom has a lock on it. Don't worry. I'll return your deposit."

Robin wiped her eyes and slumped into an overstuffed chair. She dug her nails into the cushioned armrest and contemplated her next move.

"I'm curious. Why is a nice girl like you traveling alone to a place like this?"

"I broke up with my boyfriend a few days ago. We were supposed to take this trip together. It was his idea. Of course, I used my credit card, and it was too late to cancel. I thought it would be a good idea to come anyway. I'm always making bad choices."

"I'm sorry about that. I noticed a bottle of wine in the bag I brought in. Would you like me to pour you a glass?" Robin wiped her eyes as she nodded. "Mind if I pour myself one?"

"Help yourself."

A chill blanketed Robin's skin, and she wrapped her arms around her body. There was something about Augie that disturbed her. At times he had a predatory look. Nothing he'd said was mean, and in fact, he was doing everything to make her comfortable. Still, his eyes revealed something else. Something sinister. Her thoughts were interrupted when Augie returned with her glass of wine.

"Thanks. I don't mean to be so negative, but this is all so overwhelming. You're right. I should have read all the facts, but I was in a hurry to leave Houston. I wanted to get here before dark." Robin downed several gulps as the liquid caused a burning feeling in her throat. She felt a tingling sensation race through her body and felt lethargic. "Wow. I haven't eaten all day, and the wine is going straight to my head." It only took several more sips before Robin started to slump.

Bryan grabbed Robin's glass before she dropped it and led her to the small sofa. "Why don't you lie down? I'll fetch a blanket."

"What. What did you put in my wine? Did you drug me?" Those were Robin's last words before she passed out.

SATURDAY MORNING, Seven-Forty-Five AM

Robin blinked several times before her eyes flew open. Sitting up in bed, she noticed that her clothes had been removed and carefully folded over a nearby chair. Still wearing her panties and bra, Robin reached for her clothes and flew into them.

A slight headache hovered above her eyes, and she rubbed her forehead. The last thing she remembered was the glass of wine she drank before passing out the night before. Worry and fear crept through her, but it was important she kept her wits and try to reason with the insane man now holding her captive. *What if he is some kind of serial killer? Maybe he escaped from a mental institution. Wait. I'm still alive. I don't think he's violated me. Perhaps I can reason with him.*

Robin hid her apprehension as the door creaked opened and she peered out. Bryan was sitting in front of the fireplace, drinking what she assumed to be a cup of coffee. His gaze turned, and his cold, piercing eyes washed over her.

"Good morning. I trust you had a good night's sleep."

It took a moment for Robin to gain her composure. Clearing her throat, she asked, "Did you drug me?"

A low chuckle filled the room. "Guilty, but I want to explain. I'm not good with women, and I wasn't in the mood to deal with your hostility last night. I ground up a couple of sleeping pills and put them in your drink. When you passed out, I removed your outer clothing and put you to bed. That's all."

Robin was not only angry, but she was bleary-eyed and out of sorts. *I have to keep my wits and concentrate on finding a way out of here.* Robin moved to the front window and looked out. "Thank goodness. The rain has stopped, and it looks like the sun is trying to come out."

"The road is still mushy but should be passable tomorrow. There's coffee. Want a cup?"

"I'll get it myself." Furious, Robin was glad to have an excuse to leave the room. The kitchen was nothing more than a small counter, a refrigerator, and a two-burner gas stove, where an antique coffeepot simmered. After pouring a cup, Robin smelled it first before taking a few sips. She walked to a small window over the sink and looked out. There was a clear view of the canal and a small wooden fishing boat resting in the water. *I suppose I could row a boat if I had to.*

The brown paper bag was still on the small kitchen table, and she rummaged through it, looking for the package of powdered donuts she packed. Tearing open the bag, Robin stuffed two of the mini donuts into her mouth. Remembering her last meal was over thirty-six hours ago, she ate four more before closing the bag and downing the remainder of the back coffee. The sugar rush gave her a renewed strength. *What am I doing? I have to get out of this place. There is no way I'm spending another night with this monster.* Robin rushed into the front room, where Bryan was still sitting.

She steadied herself as she stood beside the fireplace. "How far is it across the inlet? It doesn't look that far."

His cold gaze lifted to meet hers. "About a quarter of a mile to the landing. You have to paddle against the current."

"I could make out a few piers that look closer."

"Most of the people on that side are part-timers. They put locks on everything. You won't be able to get past the property lines. It's all private property, and most of them have guns. Fishermen use the public landing about a half-mile to the North. You aren't thinking of paddling over there, are you?"

Robin's knees nearly buckled, but she corrected her stance. "You could row me there."

"Not a chance. That old boat probably won't hold two people. I was planning on repairing it when the weather clears up."

"You know what I think?" Robin placed her hands on her hip and glared at Bryan."

Her anger seemed to amuse him. "Let it out. I know you are dying to tell me."

Fear gripped her senses, canceling out what was really on her mind. Instead, she said, "I think this place is a sham, and I'm going to give you minus five stars on the internet."

"I don't give a damn what you do."

"You. You're a monster, and I hate you."

"I've had enough of your foul mouth and slander. Do what you got to do. I'm out of here." Bryan grabbed his parka and hat and headed for the door.

Robin scowled at him. "Just how are you going to get out if you are stuck?"

"I've got four-wheel drive." Bryan was out the door before Robin could respond. It closed with a loud bang, and Robin tugged hard, but the door was stuck.

"Wait. Please don't leave me here alone. I need help getting my car out. Hey, come back." Robin struggled, giving one last heave before she fell back on the floor. Jumping up, Robin ran out the open door. "Bryan, please come back." She screamed his name several times, but he was nowhere in sight. Robin shivered as she stared out at the muddy road. There were no footprints. No tire tracks. *Where could he have gone?* Robin returned to the kitchen and stared out the window. The small boat was gone. Fear inched up her back. She was alone now, and for some reason, it terrified her.

"Anybody there?" A gruff voice called through the front door. "My name is Sheriff John Sutton."

Robin ran back to the front room and stared at the stranger. "You. You're the sheriff?"

Sheriff Sutton was a stout man in his late forties. He looked legitimate with a holstered gun and a shiny badge pinned to his brown uniform. "Yes, I am, and who are you?"

"Oh. I'm so glad to see you. I'm Robin Harris, and I rented this place for the weekend. The owner just left a few minutes ago."

"The owner, August Fairchild? I'm sorry, ma'am, Mr. Fairchild was murdered two days ago. We are still looking for the person that murdered him."

Robin felt faint, closed her eyes, and passed out.

When Robin woke, the sheriff was standing over her, patting her face and calling her name.

"I'm sorry I upset you. You mentioned a man you thought was the owner?"

Robin glanced around the room as she sat up. "At first, he said he was the owner of the property. Later he said his real name was Bryan Hunt and August Fairchild was his uncle. He knew a lot about the property."

"Ma'am, I need you to look at this picture." Sheriff Sutton removed a sheet of paper from his pocket.

Robin took a step back. "That's the man. Who is he? Did he kill Mr. Fairchild?"

"His name is Bryan Jeffreys. He escaped from the Huntsville prison a week ago.

Robin began trembling, and tears flowed from her eyes. "Oh my God. I can't believe I spent the night with a murderer."

"You spent the night with him? Were you two intimate?"

"No. No. Of course not. We met when I arrived the night before. He drugged me, and I passed out. I feel so stupid."

"You are lucky. Things could have turned out very bad for you. About how long has he been gone?"

"Maybe thirty or forty minutes. I think the man left in the boat by the pier."

"You've been a big help. I would appreciate you staying here while I go to my car and call this into the station. I may be gone for a while. Here is my card in case he comes back or you get scared."

Robin watched from the front porch as Sherriff Sutton spoke to someone on his police radio. Minutes later, the red lights blinked on top of his car. When the cruiser sped away, Robin realized she was in danger. *What am I thinking? I've got to get out of here.* Robin ran back inside, collected her things, and rushed out to her SUV. Clicking her key fob, she threw her belongings in the back and jumped into the driver's seat. Robin turned on the motor and drove to the main road without hesitating another minute.

The thought of staying one more night in this horrible place was terrifying. Besides, what if Bryan did come back? *Okay, calm down. You've got this.* Robin began to relax for the first time in two days as she turned onto the main highway. There was nothing in her future that could be worse than the last two days.

Feeling a sudden push on her seat, Robin tensed. After checking the rearview mirror, there didn't appear to be anything in the road behind her. *What could it have been?*

Robin stared into the mirror once more. A moment later, the stranger's face appeared. "Hello, Robin."

Author - James R. Callan

After a successful career in mathematics and computer science, receiving grants from the National Science Foundation and NASA, and being listed in *Who's Who in America, Who's Who in Computer Science* and *Two Thousand Notable Americans*, James R. Callan turned to his first love—writing. He has had four non-fiction books published. He now concentrates on his favorite genre, mystery/suspense/thriller. His fourteenth book released in February, 2021. In addition, he speaks at conferences and gives workshops on various writing topics such as character development, dialog, audiobooks, plotting, and the mystery/suspense/thriller genre. He and his wife split their time between homes in northeast Texas and Puerto Vallarta, MX. They have four children and six grandchildren.

Website: www.jamesrcallan.com
    Blog: https://www.jamesrcallan.com/blog/
    Author Page: http://amzn.to/1eeykvG

I'D RATHER DROWN

BY:

JAMES R. CALLAN

3

I'd Rather Drown

James R. Callan

His hand shot out and before Darcy had a chance to duck, her head snapped back.

"Don't you ever contradict me again."

Darcy rubbed her cheek with her left hand. "Contradict you?"

"I said the ball was in and you called it out. That's a contradiction."

This had been a mistake. She was clearly better than Donald. She was sure she could beat him serving underhanded. But she now realized, he did not like to lose. In fact, she was beginning to understand the whole thing with Donald was a bad idea. She needed to get out of this. And the sooner the better.

"I've got a terrible headache. Maybe we'd better call it quits for today." She turned and started off the court.

"Get back out here. We said we'd play a set. We haven't finished. Fifteen all. Serve."

Darcy hit a slice that kicked up a bit of chalk.

"Out," he called.

She opened her mouth to object, but quickly clamped her teeth together. She served him a soft ball and when he hit it to her backhand, she faked a slight stumble and didn't get to the ball.

"Fifteen thirty," he yelled.

Next, she double faulted. She couldn't remember the last time she'd double faulted, but it was the right play today.

Last night, when he said he was a pretty good tennis player, she thought maybe they could have a fun match. A dozen tennis trophies graced her apartment in Oklahoma, a fact she did not mention. She smiled as she thought, Donald's best shot is one that is out and he claims is in. She hit an Australian twist serve and Donald hit it into the net.

She walked back to the baseline. What to do? If I hit a decent serve, he'll probably miss it. And that will prolong the game. With careful precision, she smacked the first serve a tad wide. The second serve she placed a few inches deep.

"Game," he yelled.

Thirty minutes later, she had managed to throw enough points that the set mercifully ended.

"You played very well, Donald. I just couldn't keep up with you. I think I'll just shower and then head back to my hotel."

"Nonsense. You'll shower at my house." He grabbed her hand and jerked her up beside him.

She pasted a smile on her face. "I'm awfully tired. You really wore me down."

He continued to pull her along. "A quick shower and then we can relax in bed for a bit before dinner." The leer on his face almost made her gag.

"I probably won't be much fun tonight. Maybe we should—"

"Oh, I'll have fun, don't worry. We'll eat and then hop in bed early. More fun."

"My clothes—"

"Already in the car."

THE NEXT MORNING AFTER BREAKFAST, Darcy gave him a big smile and said, "Thank you for a good match yesterday, and an excellent breakfast. I think I'll go do a little shopping. Can someone drive me into town?"

"Miguel will drive you and Rosa wherever you want to shop. Take as much time as you want. He'll wait for you."

The smile slid off Darcy's face. "No need for him to wait. I'll just grab a taxi to the hotel."

"I've already closed out your hotel. And not to worry, Miguel has already brought all your stuff from the hotel here. It's all taken care of." He gave her a toothy grin. "So, go do your shopping. No need to hurry. I've got a lot of business to attend to. Have lunch out if you'd like. See you at dinner." He leaned over and gave her a pat on the bottom, then turned and walked out of the room.

If he had slapped her in the face, she wouldn't have been more shocked. Or frightened. She opened her mouth, but nothing came out. It didn't make any difference. He was gone. And she had the unnerving feeling that what she said would make no difference. None.

Moved my stuff out of the hotel? Doesn't the hotel protect my possessions?

They had brought her clothes from the tennis club, but that was his club. It might make some sense that he or one of his men could retrieve her stuff there. But the hotel? Her hotel? An international chain hotel? How did he do that?

"He is very powerful man." Rosa stood in the door. "Many men under his…" She thought for a moment. "His control."

Darcy's head jerked up. Did I say that question out loud? No, she reassured herself. She had only thought it. But, I've got to get away from him. Now.

"He expect all loyalty. Do not make him think you unloyal. That not be good."

Darcy looked at the Mexican woman. How was she … what?

Basically, verbalizing her side of a dialog. She knows what I'm thinking and she responds to it. She stared at Rosa, who looked completely innocent, as if she was just answering Darcy's questions.

The solution suddenly appeared in her mind. Rosa has seen this before. I'm not the first one to have these thoughts, to wonder how to escape.

"Rosa, why don't we go shopping in about an hour?"

"Yes, ma'am. I tell Miguel."

Five minutes later, Darcy called Rosa to come upstairs. When she arrived, Darcy asked, "Rosa, have you seen my cell phone? I'm sure I left it on the dresser, but I can't find it now."

Rosa looked down at the floor and half turned away. "I can not say, Miss Darcy."

Can not say. Does that mean she doesn't know, or she's not allowed to tell what she knows? "Rosa, I don't want anyone to get in trouble. I just need my cell phone. I use it for everything."

Rosa did not look at her and her voice was soft. "I am sorry you no have your phone. But, I no can help." Without looking at Darcy, Rosa turned and left the room.

For nearly a minute, Darcy just stood there staring into middle space, seeing nothing. Her clothes were moved, her hotel room cancelled, and now her cell phone had disappeared. She had not misplaced it. Someone took it.

Like ice water slapping her in the face, a sudden realization hit her. She turned and grabbed her purse from the dresser. She had rifled through it when looking for her phone. Now, she dumped everything out on to the bed and began checking each item.

Her money was gone.

Her credit cards were gone.

Her passport was gone.

She sat on the bed and put her face in her hands. Think. After a moment...What's to think about? I'm a prisoner.

Her inclination was to cry, complain, scream. But that was not her way. She was thoughtful, level headed, not prone to panic. She almost laughed. Those were all true, but she had never been kidnapped before. This was a new experience. And she was close to panic.

———

HER THOUGHTS TRAVELLED BACK to the first time she met Donald. He had picked her up at a beach bar not far from her hotel. And now that she thought about it, that's exactly what it was—a pick-up. She'd been out with two women she'd met at the hotel. After a couple of drinks, the other two women left to attend a theater production. They had invited her to come with them, but she declined.

As she reached into her purse to retrieve money to pay for her potent Mexican drink, this handsome man stepped up and laid a bill on the counter. "A beautiful woman should never have to pay for a drink."

She objected, but he insisted. Then he invited her to come sit at his table and meet two of his friends. It seemed innocent enough. After another drink, the musicians switched to a dreamy selection from a movie. She couldn't remember the name of the song, but when he asked her to dance, she accepted. After two more songs, the musicians went back to a salsa and Donald begged off from trying to keep up with the saucy Cuban music.

The other couple was gone. Darcy decided it was time to return to her hotel. Donald offered to drive her, but she refused, saying it was only two blocks and the walk would be good for her. She hadn't played tennis in a few days. She needed the exercise.

Donald grew excited. "Let me at least walk you to the hotel and you can tell me about your tennis experience. I love to play, but often I have trouble finding a good opponent. I'm pretty good."

Darcy smiled. She had been number one on her college tennis team and since graduating had played in many tournaments. She had a number of trophies from the tournaments she'd won. She did not share that with Donald. By the time she and Donald reached her hotel, they had agreed he would pick her up at the hotel tomorrow and they'd play a set at his club.

SHE SHOOK HER HEAD. That was stupid. I thought a tennis workout would be good for me. Hadn't played in two weeks. Mistake.

She walked into the bathroom and splashed cold water on her face. Do not panic. When you design systems, you always consider the worst-case scenario. Do that now. They were going shopping in town. Maybe she'd just disappear. Forget about her suitcase.

SHE AND ROSA had shopped for an hour or so when Darcy said, "Let's have lunch at the Sundowner on the beach."

In the past hour, Rosa had never been more than five feet away from Darcy. Even when she went to the restroom, Rosa stood inside the room, combing her hair, washing her hands, watching. When they bought something, Miguel appeared instantly and paid for their purchases. He was never far away.

She considered racing over to one of the security men and telling them she was being held against her will. Then she thought of her limited Spanish. That would never work. Miguel and Rosa would convince the guards she was crazy.

Lunch was a disappointment.

Her friend Joe visited the Sundowner almost every day.

He did not show this day.

There is always tomorrow, she told herself.

On the way back to the house, she thought about the situation and whether she wanted to get Joe involved or not. Already she had decided that Donald and his crew were dangerous. She had seen the vicious knife that Miguel always had with him, though it generally was hidden. She needed someone's help. Joe was the only person she felt could and would come to her aid. But it must be done in such a way that he would not be suspected. Clearly, I need to give this more thought, create a better plan.

She didn't see Donald until dinner. He smiled a lot, laughed when he told her about some funny incident that happened to him that afternoon. The chef had prepared a special dish whose name she could not even pronounce, but was surely the best meal she had had in years. Maybe ever.

After dinner, they danced on his terrace which overlooked an impressive and massive garden and beyond that, the beautiful blue Banderas Bay. He was a good dancer and the music was to her liking. But she couldn't stop thinking about being a prisoner.

"You dance very well," he said, "but, you are very tense. Relax. I won't bite."

"I'm sure you won't. I've just been feeling sick all afternoon. I'm sure I'll be okay tomorrow."

"Do you need a pill or something? We have any kind of pill you need. Or want."

"No. I don't need a pill. I just need to lie down and rest, maybe get to sleep early. I had a hard time getting to sleep last night. I'm sure I'll be fine in the morning."

"I slept like a baby," he laughed. "Of course, I was completely relaxed."

Because you're not being held a prisoner. "I'll see you in the morning." She turned left, heading for her bedroom. I have a lot of thinking to do. I have to plan an escape.

THE NEXT MORNING she spent a long time fixing her shoulder length, honey blonde hair before going downstairs. She didn't relish any more time with Donald than necessary. When she entered the dining room, he was not in sight.

Rosa was setting orange juice on the table. "Oh, Miss Darcy, Mr. Donald had meeting. He already gone."

Darcy was careful not to smile or look excited over Donald being gone. She had an excellent breakfast, then announced that she wanted to walk around the property.

"Is okay. Be careful. To keep bad guys out, there is electricity wire around property. It hurt you if you touch it."

Of course. It keeps the prisoners in.

AROUND ELEVEN, she asked to go into town to shop. Miguel drove her and Rosa into the city. As they passed a small mercado, Darcy asked Miguel to stop and let them out to do a little browsing. At one shop, Darcy picked up a liter bottle of water and further along, she found a nice turquoise cloth bag to hold the plastic bottle. Miguel had simply double-parked and was always close by to pay for her purchases. Darcy again suggested they have lunch at the Sundowner.

They had ordered and while waiting for their drinks, Joe came in. When he saw Darcy, he rushed over and gave her a hug. She hugged him back and pressed a piece of paper into his hand. She hoped her keepers did not observe the transfer. Neither seemed to take any notice of it.

"Rosa, this is Joe, my friend."

"Coma esta?" Joe said to Rosa.

"Bien," she answered.

Darcy looked around. Miguel had risen from his chair and

watched Joe carefully. Darcy did not introduce Miguel and Joe. Darcy sensed Joe was about to ask if he could join them. Quickly, she said, "It was good to see you. Maybe we will see you again—in a couple of days."

Joe frowned, but as he looked at Darcy, he nodded slightly and said he hoped so. "Nice to meet you, Rosa. You two have a good lunch." He turned, glanced at Miguel, and left.

After lunch, they shopped. Darcy found a blouse and a bulky jacket she liked and Rosa selected a simple, inexpensive blouse.

By mid-afternoon, they were back at the hacienda. Again, Darcy wandered the grounds and gardens, being careful to drink from her water bottle often. Coming back in and filling the bottle, she said to Rosa, "The only time I've ever been in the hospital was right here in this town. I was badly dehydrated. So now I am careful to keep hydrated."

LATER THAT NIGHT, as she lay in her bedroom, she said, "Donald, this is a beautiful place. The gardens are wonderful. But I need to get out and see some of my friends in town."

He pulled the sheet down and kicked his legs out of the bed. "Nonsense. We are your friends. And if any of the staff is not friendly to you, just let me know and I'll get rid of them."

As he got up from the bed, Darcy said, "But I need to see my girlfriends."

Donald laughed. "You've got Rosa. And she loves to shop with you. She'll do whatever you want. This is your home. These are your friends." Then he gave her a leering smile. "And you've got me for fun."

She knew better than to say what was in her mind. Instead, "Thank you for an exciting evening. I'm sure I'll sleep well tonight."

Fortunately, he left the room before she gagged.

TWO DAYS LATER, she and Rosa went shopping. Lunch was again at the Sundowner. Half way through their paninis, Joe appeared at their table, and once again Darcy got up and received a big hug from him.

"Can't stay," he said, "but saw you two in here and wanted to just say hello."

"Glad you stopped. Enjoy your meeting or whatever you're off to."

"I will. Good to see you again. And you, too, Rosa."

LATER THAT AFTERNOON, Darcy was again wandering through the gardens on Donald's estate. She had checked them out and knew where her best spot was. She could not be seen or heard from the house, and she could see anyone coming near her well in advance.

She pulled out the phone Joe had slipped to her at the restaurant. "Hey. I need to be brief. I am being held a prisoner."

Joe tried to interrupt her to say he would get her out.

"No. Don't even try, Joe. These are dangerous people. Miguel has a vicious looking knife with him all the time. And even if you did, Donald would have his people hunt me down and bring me back. Or worse."

"But—"

"No. I have a plan, if you can make it happen."

For the next five minutes, she told him what she needed, and when she needed it. "It could be dangerous, and I don't want you to get hurt. So, tell me if you'd rather not get involved. I wouldn't blame you. These are dangerous people."

"Do you think you can pull it off?"

"I think so. I've got to try. Otherwise, I'll slit my own throat.

I can't stand this. I wouldn't last long as a prisoner. But I worry about you. I don't want—"

"Stop right there. I will do whatever I can. And if this doesn't work, I'll think of something else. You're sure I couldn't just grab you and take you away from the Sundowner?"

"I'm sure. And please do not call this number. If it rings, someone will hear it and it will be taken away from me. I'll check in with you in—how much time do you need to get this set up?"

Joe was silent for several seconds. "Give me two days. Can you make it that long?"

"If I think there's a chance we can pull this off, yes. If you think it's getting too risky, or something doesn't work out, tell me. I'll come up with a different plan. Oh, and remember, Rosa gave a hint that maybe a number of the police are on Donald's payroll. So, I don't think we can ask any of them for help."

"Call me tomorrow."

"If I have any problems, and can't call you then, I'll call the next afternoon."

"Call when you can. I'll try to get it set up ASAP."

"Thank you, thank you. I'll owe you big time."

"No you won't."

TWO DAYS LATER, Darcy sat in her favorite calling spot, eyes scanning to see if anybody came out of the house. When Joe answered, it sent a chill through her. "What's the story?"

"Slight change of plans."

Darcy's smile evaporated.

"It's supposed to rain tonight. A heavy rain."

Her brows crowded together. "But, what—"

"The river will carry a lot of silt down and spread it in this end of the bay."

"And I care about silt because?"

"Makes the water cloudy. Provides cover."

"But what if nobody wants to get wet in silty water?"

Joe laughed. "Get on the end. Then you can make it happen yourself, and at the optimum time."

"Okay. I'll make it happen."

"Good. Then we're on tomorrow morning. Now once there, make certain that the man with a bright colored toucan embroidered on his shirt fits you with the lifejacket. He'll also have a blue bag and he'll switch it for yours."

"My bag is turquoise."

"Whatever. I have a boat and it's the same color, more or less. I just call it blue-green. But let the man with the toucan fit your lifejacket on you. He'll take care of the details."

"What time?"

"This end will be ready at eleven. Will that work for you?"

Her smile had returned. "Oh yes."

"If something comes up and you can't make it, call me as soon as you can."

JOE HAD BEEN RIGHT. It rained all night. In the morning when Darcy looked out the window, the sun was shining and it was a beautiful day. But, the bay was indeed murky.

After breakfast, she announced that she wanted to go into town later in the morning. Donald had had a good night. He called Miguel into the breakfast room. "Take Darcy into town today."

"¿Donde?"

"Wherever she wants to go. Rosa will go with her. Pay for whatever she gets. Just be back here before five. I want her to meet some friends of mine after six."

About ten-thirty, Darcy came downstairs and said she was

ready to go. She had on a spandex bathing suit with a light cover-up, her water bottle in its cover in her hand.

When they neared town, Darcy said she wanted to go ride on a banana boat. Rosa and Miguel both objected, but Darcy reminded them that Donald said to take her wherever she wanted to go. Miguel tried to call Donald, but the call did not go through.

Darcy let out a long breath. "What is the problem? You can watch me all the way. They don't go out very far." She turned to Rosa. "You can ride with me." She certainly did not want Rosa to go along, and she didn't think she would. She was certainly not dressed for it.

"I no swim," the Mexican woman said, shaking her head.

"I don't either," Darcy said with a grin. "But you'll have on a lifejacket."

"I no like any boat."

Darcy checked their position. "Miguel, turn here. There is a banana boat place over on the beach—right across from here."

He pulled over to the curb. But he did not unlock the doors.

"Find a place to park and come with me, Miguel. You and Rosa can watch, and see the boat all the time."

Miguel and Rosa chattered back and forth in Spanish, too fast for Darcy to catch any of the Spanish words she knew. Finally, as a few tears slid out of Rosa's eyes, Miguel pulled across the street, parked the car and got out.

Darcy jumped out, reached in and practically yanked Rosa out of the car.

"Rosa ride with you," Miguel proclaimed.

At the beach, they found the banana boat. Darcy scanned the various men, trying to find the toucan. She began to panic. There was no one with a toucan stitched on his shirt. Had she missed the right place? She looked right and left, trying to find another banana boat. But as far as she could see in either direction, there wasn't another one.

She turned, ready to tell Rosa they would do this tomorrow, when Rosa could wear other clothes.

"Are you ready for an exciting ride? We need just one more rider to start the next trip." A young man had walked up to her. On his left sleeve was a brightly embroidered toucan.

"Yes, yes. I am ready. And my friend, Rosa, if you have room for both of us."

Her response seemed to startle him. Darcy didn't know what to say. Why was he hesitating? Of course, he wasn't expecting there would be two. Did he think she was the wrong person? She reached into her cover-up pocket and pulled out her water bottle in its turquoise cover and took a big drink.

He smiled. "I think we can accommodate both of you." He turned to one of the men by the boat. "Oscar, will you help Rosa with her lifejacket? She can take Juanita's place." He turned back to Darcy. "It's okay. Juanita is my sister. She can ride any time."

Oscar took Rosa's hand and led her to the middle of the boat, as Juanita got off the banana. Oscar almost had to drag Rosa up, but he expertly fitted the lifejacket on her, and spoke in a quiet voice, reassuring her.

"My name is José," said the man with the toucan on his shirt. And then as a whisper in Darcy's ear, "I am José for today only." He straightened up and resumed his loud voice. "I will help you with your jacket, and show you how the buckles work. You will get the seat at the end. It is the most fun seat."

"Thank you, José. You speak perfect English, with hardly an accent at all."

"I spent eleven years, from the time I was five until I was sixteen, living in Los Angles. I do know English. Sometimes my Spanish is not too good, though."

As José replaced her cover-up with the lifejacket, Darcy scanned the area. There was Miguel, focused on her and José. She didn't think he could hear everything, still she decided to say nothing at all. But she worried that José might not get the water bottle switched.

"Okay. Now, you sit across the banana. Then you hold on to this strap. Use both hands. Sometimes, the women like to have their hands around the strap, one coming down from the top and one coming up from the bottom and grasping each other on the other side."

Darcy looked over where they had been standing. There on a small wooden bench was her water bottle in its turquoise cover. Or was it? She hadn't seen or felt anything. But checking, now she could feel something in the lifejacket. Was it what she needed? Or was it a bottle of water?

She turned to Jose. "My water?"

"Is okay, over there on the stool."

When she looked concerned, he added, "All is good. You are ready. Do not worry. Your lifejacket will keep you safe." He pointed at her water bottle in its cloth bag. "And that color is very beautiful."

The woman sitting just in front of her turned her head and said, "It's very safe, and fun. I've ridden the banana many times."

Darcy looked at her and said as clearly as she could, "I'm not worried. And I'm not afraid of drowning. In fact, I'd rather drown than be locked up as a prisoner."

"Well, don't think about that. Just enjoy the ride."

And before anything else was said, the boat took off with the yellow banana trailing behind.

ON THE RIDE OUT, Darcy could feel that the cloth bag nestled under her arm seemed a bit heavier and harder than her water bottle. The shore quickly receded from her view. Rosa seemed to be holding on tightly, and was not screaming, thank goodness.

She felt the banana slowing, getting ready to make a turn. She scanned the water and spied a boat, a turquoise boat. José said it was a beautiful color. The only occupant was a man, who appeared to be fishing.

Got to be the one.

That's a long way out!

Was it too far?

How long would…

Don't think about that.

Just do it.

You can do it.

Slowly the boat pulling the banana turned and began to swing the banana around, ready for the return trip. Now the banana sat perpendicular to the rope. Darcy started to rock the banana. The rope pulled more to the side. She increased her motion. She leaned over, her right arm dragging in the water.

She gave a giant jerk, swinging her whole body to the left.

The banana turned over.

Everybody was dumped into the water.

Darcy wasted no time. She grabbed the turquoise bag from her jacket.

She unbuckled the lifejacket and slipped out of it.

She went completely under water and let herself sink deeper into the murky bay. She could hear the screaming, yelling and laughing of the other riders. She knew the screaming came from Rosa. Darcy hoped she would be fine. But she couldn't worry about Rosa now. She needed to save herself.

ON THE SURFACE, the boat slowed and swung around. All of the riders, save Rosa, were laughing and yelling at one another, enjoying the "usual" dump into the water when riding the banana. It was a game for them. The driver repositioned the boat and drew the banana near the orange lifejackets bobbing in the water. Several minutes passed before the first woman managed to climb back on the banana.

Everybody was having fun, except Rosa who was screaming and terrified.

ANOTHER WOMAN TRIED to help Rosa, who was thrashing around, swinging her arms in all directions. She struck the helping woman in the face and drove her away. A man came over, was able to protect himself and managed to get Rosa halfway on the banana. At that point, two other women came in and pulled and pushed, finally getting Rosa completely on the banana.

A man yelled, "We're missing one."

A minute later, one of the women pointed and called out, "Mike, I see a lifejacket."

Mike swam over. "There's no one here. Just the jacket." Immediately he dove down in the water. A minute later he came up. "I can't see anybody."

By now, the operator had brought the boat back alongside the banana. He stood up and scanned all around. "No puedo ver a nadie moviéndose."

"What'd he say?" asked a woman.

Another translated, "I can't see anything or anybody moving."

He very slowly turned in a complete circle, his focus on the surface of the water. After another careful survey, he yelled something in Spanish.

One of the women translated for the others. "He said there is nobody, nothing, on the surface of the water as far as he can see."

Mike called to all the banana riders. "If any of you feel

comfortable doing it, let's dive down, under the banana or the boat. Any place. She must be there somewhere."

Several of those on the banana slipped off into the water and dove deep. When one woman came up she said, "It's so dark down there you can't see two feet in front of your nose. I'll try again, but it's really hard to see anything."

A man surfaced and said to the others, "There's so much silt in the water. It's thick and heavy. Impossible to see anything."

Mike took off his lifejacket, put it on the banana, and made two more plunges, trying to see anything below the surface. Without his jacket, he stayed under water much longer.

Finally, he swam up to the boat, put his lifejacket back on, and spoke to everybody. "Let's all be very quiet and see if we can hear anything. Maybe she'll call for help, or we can hear splashing, or even her heavy breathing." To the boat operator he said, "Apague el motor."

Quickly, the motor was silenced.

Mike swam up beside Rosa, who was still crying. "Please try to be very quiet. Everybody."

For several minutes, no one made a sound. Gulls called to one another. A jet-ski zipped by, much closer to the shore, but its noise quickly faded. Again, silence. Several of the people closed their eyes, focusing all their attention on listening for any sound.

"All right, I take it, nobody heard anything," Mike said. "Let's all scan the water systematically. First, let's study the water between here and the beach. See if we can see anybody, or any splashing, a ripple in the water, anything even the least bit unusual."

Eight pairs of eyes studied the water, looking for even the slightest unexpected movement.

"Okay, now let's all look in the opposite direction. Holler out if you see anything the least bit unusual in the water. A piece of cloth. Anything."

Now that the boat had stopped, the surface of the water

around the boat was very smooth. Any movement should be picked up by one of the group.

"Once more. This time, let's study the water in the direction we were headed when we got dumped," said Mike.

And finally, Mike asked all to study the area they had just come through, now behind them.

Nothing.

When everyone agreed there was nothing else they could do, they got on the banana and headed back to the shore. Donald was there, yelling in the face of the head man of the banana boat operation. He turned his attention to Rosa, who was once again crying. "How could you let her get away?"

Rosa could not talk, but just kept on sobbing.

Mike walked over to Donald and held out the lifejacket. "Sir, you can see the lifejacket buckles are open. They cannot come open by themselves. They are strong. It looks like she took it off herself."

"What do you mean she took it off? Are you crazy? And who are you anyway?"

"I was a rider on the banana, along with my girlfriend. We found the lifejacket pretty quickly and immediately started searching."

"Then why is it my man called me after everybody got dumped in the water and I was able to drive here before you got back?" Donald was shouting at the top of his voice and people on the walk stopped to see what the commotion was about.

"That's because we all were looking for her, probably for thirty minutes. I and several others were diving down, trying to see what happened to her. We spent some time scanning the surface of the water in all directions, looking for any sign of a person in the water. Everybody tried to find her."

"Well, you failed!" Donald screamed. "Was there another boat nearby?"

"No," Mike said quietly. "There was a fisherman in a boat farther out, but I'd say it was nearly a kilometer out in the bay."

The driver of the banana boat nodded. "Si, un kilómetro de distancia de nosotros."

Donald scowled at them, a vein pulsing in his neck.

"Sir, we did the best we could. It was almost as if she wanted to disappear. But where could she have gone?"

One of the women joined Mike. "I don't know what was going on, but just as the ride was starting, I heard her say, 'I'd rather drown.'"

Donald turned an angry face to her. "What did that mean?"

Another woman stepped up. "Yeah. I heard that too. Something about being a prisoner and she'd rather drown."

His face turned even redder. He glared at the women, and muttered, "Are you crazy?"

Rosa did not raise her head, but quietly said, "She say she no can swim."

Donald turned his attention to the man who appeared to run the business. The muscles in his face were tense and he shook a finger at the man. "I'll have your license torn up. My lawyers will rip you apart in court."

The man held the lifejacket. "You and all can see, this is the lifejacket she had on. It is in perfect shape. You can test the buckles." He pulled and jerked on them, but they did not open. "They are strong and will not come open without the wearer opening them on purpose. They cannot come open accidentally. And I have many witnesses here who will tell that it was put on her carefully, and tested before anyone goes out on one of my boats. I am not afraid to present my case in court."

Miguel had walked up. "Mr. Donald. I saw man test straps and buckles. I think they no open unless Darcy open them."

Donald turned on Miguel. "Get out of here. Take the sniveling Rosa and go home. I'll deal with you later."

For another ten minutes, Donald continued to harass the

group. He yelled, clenched his fists and shook them at the people he tried to intimidate. Several of the women turned away and walked off even as he yelled after them. One woman muttered, "I can see why she'd rather drown, if she had to deal with him."

Donald had turned to accost another member of the operation, when he saw a beautiful woman step off the walk and onto the sand. She was looking over at the group. Donald's angry face morphed into a smile and he walked over to speak to the woman. "Hello. I don't think I know you. My name is Donald. Would you like a nice, cool drink in the bar over there?"

The woman smiled at the man she had just witnessed terrorizing the banana boat workers. "Yes, I would."

Donald's smile widened. "Well—"

"In fact, my husband is ordering me one right now, so I think I'll join him." She turned and headed for the small bar.

Donald just stared as she walked away.

———

IT WAS two days after the banana boat incident. Two women in a VW were breezing along a road by an inlet to the bay. The driver said, "That's a beautiful boat over there on the beach. What a pretty color it is."

"Yes it is. A near match to my turquoise bag. Maybe a little darker."

"Okay. Just how did you manage to escape? Didn't anyone see you swimming away?" Darcy laughed. "Nope. I made sure of that. As soon as I went in the water, I slipped out of the lifejacket, grabbed the Smarco, opened the valve, and stuck the mouth piece in my mouth. I dove deep, and headed away from the shore, toward that lovely turquoise boat."

Rita, Darcy's close friend asked, "Nobody saw you?"

"Nope. They were all laughing and yelling and having fun. By the time they realized I was missing, it was too late; I was gone. The water was not clear. You couldn't see very far under water. In fact, I'm sure they could not have seen me ten seconds after I got the lifejacket off. And with the Smarco, I stayed deep until I got out to Joe's boat. In fact, I swam under it and came up on the side away from the banana boat. I just rolled over into the boat and lay flat on the bottom. Joe stayed far out in the bay until we were pretty much out of sight."

"How did you swim holding the smar thing?"

Darcy laughed. "Smarco. It's a tiny scuba device. I just pulled the top of my spandex suit out and stuck the bottle inside. It was only a liter, but it gave me plenty of air for the swim."

"By the way, I like you as a brunette. And while that's a pretty severe cut, on you, it looks cute."

"Thank you. At least it will dry quickly."

"You think Donald will be looking for you?"

Darcy laughed. "I doubt it. He thinks I drowned. But I'm taking no chances. He won't be looking for a short haired brunette."

"You said he kept your passport. We're almost to the airport. How are you going to get on a plane and into the U.S. without one?"

"I keep a copy of my passport on my father's computer. I called him. That's the email I got on your laptop and printed last night. It will get me back into the states. Then I'll have to get a new one." She giggled. "Think I should send Donald the bill for replacing my passport?"

"Maybe not."

"You know what really gripes me? I mean, now that I'm away from that psychopath. Having to let that lousy, cheating Donald win that tennis set. It should have been mine—six love."

THE END

Author - Michael Scott Clifton

Multi Award-Winning Author Michael Scott Clifton, a longtime public educator as a teacher, coach, and administrator, currently lives in Mount Pleasant, Texas with his wife, Melanie. An avid gardener, reader, and movie junkie, he enjoys all kinds of book and movie genres. His books contain aspects of all the genres he enjoys...action, adventure, magic, fantasy, and romance. His fantasy novels, *The Janus Witch* and *The Open Portal*, received 5-Star reviews from the prestigious Readers Favorite Book Reviews. *Edison Jones and The Anti-Grav Elevator* won a 2021 Feathered Quill Book Award Bronze Medal in the Teen Readers category. He has been a finalist in a number of short story contests with *Edges of Gray* winning First Place in the Texas Authors Contest. Professional credits include articles published in the *Texas Study of Secondary Education Magazine. The Open Portal*, won The Feathered Quill Book Finalist Award, and launches the fantasy book series, *Conquest of the Veil*. Michael's latest release, *Escape From Wheel*—also a 5-Star Readers' Favorite Review—is Book Two in this fantasy series. Visit Michael's official website https://michaelscottclifton.com/ or google him @ authormsclifton.

Facebook (personal): https://www.facebook.com/
Facebook (Author): https://www.facebook.com/authormsclifton/

LinkedIn: https://www.linkedin.com/in/authormsclifton/
Twitter: https://twitter.com/authormsclifton
YouTube: https://www.youtube.com/feed/my_videos
Instagram: https://www.instagram.com/authormsclifton/
Website: https://michaelscottclifton.com/

Regi Vitam

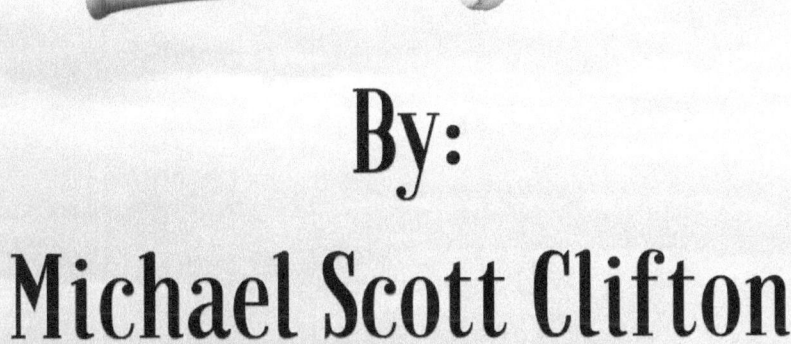

By:

Michael Scott Clifton

4

Regi Vitam
Michael Scott Clifton

Frankie Sicotto reclined in his beach lounger and watched the college kids on spring break drink, play beach volleyball, grope each other, and pretty much engage in every extreme activity their alcohol-fueled minds could conceive of.

He shook his head. When he was a kid, his parents had taken him to the Barnum and Bailey Circus in Jersey City. The clowns, trapeze artists, and wild animals couldn't hold a candle to these kids. They were a circus all to themselves. At eighty, while he no longer appreciated the lush, scantily clad bodies of the young women, the entertainment value of the crazy 'breakers provided plenty of free theater.

And he had the best seat in the house.

An old boat lay on the beach. Peeling paint decorated its sun-bleached hull, the keel partially buried in sand. The stranded boat proved to be an immovable object. All he had to do was set up his umbrella and chair next to it, and the beached boat did the rest. The undulating mass of students was forced to go around the vessel, giving Sicotto his own little island of serenity to view the world.

He sipped a cup of pineapple juice, wishing it was something

stronger. His doc, however, had prohibited alcohol and cigarettes, along with any food group whose taste didn't resemble
wicker furniture. Said his ticker, lungs, and liver were already
past their shelf life, and stress to them should be avoided at all
costs.

Sicotto sighed. What was the point of living if you couldn't
enjoy a cold beer, a good smoke, or a Cuban sandwich?

In his younger days, he'd washed out as a minor leaguer for
the Chicago White Sox. His dream of making it to the big
leagues crushed, he took up a second career when one of the
Sox's scouts took him under his wing. As a major league scout,
his travels took him all over the country, and later, all over
Central America and the Caribbean. Back then, he could drink
any man under the table, and eat anything he damn well pleased.
He'd visited every dive, greasy spoon, and taco stand from east
coast to west coast, drank tequila straight up, and never suffered
anything more than a mild hangover and noxious farts.

Now look at him. Reduced to fruit juice and pudding, and
watching the future leaders of the country behaving like brain-
dead fools. At least he wouldn't be around when that particular
shit hit the fan.

He placed his hand on the gunwale of the old boat, its wood
rough, dry, and the colors faded. A bitter chuckle escaped Sicotto's lips. He and the boat were much alike. They were both old,
dried out husks that had outlived their usefulness. The boat
would never float again, and he would never discover another
promising major league prospect.

When old age and his failing liver finally caught up with him
ten years earlier, he was forced to retire. Forced from the game
he loved and doing what he loved, he led a rudderless existence
until finally settling in a small house near a Florida beach. To say
it was a fixer-upper was an understatement, and he used much of
his meager savings to repair the leaky roof, warped doors, and
corroded plumbing.

Since many of the major league teams had their spring training in Florida, his initial plan was to attend as many of the grapefruit league games as possible. After just one game, however, he never attended another. He saw a few faces he recognized, touched base with a handful of old friends, but the looks he received told far more than their words ever could.

He was yesterday's news, the old pair of pants so hopelessly out of style you wouldn't be caught dead wearing them. Like the old boat, he had run aground, never to float again.

Life had pretty much seemed pointless since then. With no family to speak of, and many of his old friends dead or living far away, all he had left were his memories. Even they began to fade as each colorless year passed to be replaced by another. That he was reduced to watching twenty-somethings prance about like mindless idiots, showed just what a low point his life had reached.

The sun had risen far enough that even with the beach umbrella, the heat made Sicotto uncomfortable. With a groan, he struggled to his feet. The next few minutes were spent straightening his arthritic back, popping old joints, and loosening stagnant tendons and muscles. The more challenging task lay ahead: getting his umbrella and chair to his car. He had to position the chair or umbrella under his arm while holding on to his walker. Then came the hardest part of all. Pushing, or rather *lifting* his walker and advancing a few feet at a time. Since he couldn't carry both of his beach items at once, this required two trips.

By the time Sicotto got to his car, he was exhausted. For the hundredth time, he asked himself if all the effort was worth it just to have a distraction. For the hundredth time, the same answer came to mind. When the alternative was to sit alone at home and watch four walls, any trip that got him out into the fresh air was worth it.

He put the car in gear, backed out, and slowly made his way back to his home and the same dreary walls.

CRASH.

The baseball landed on the living room floor amid a shower of broken glass. Rolling across a threadbare rug, it finally came to a stop at Sicotto's feet. Seated in an ancient Lazyboy, the arms covered in stains and cigarette burns, his eyes shot open at the abrupt interruption to his nap. He blinked at the broken window, his shoe brushing against something.

"Well, well. What do we have here?"

Sicotto reached down with liver-spotted hands, and picked up the ball. Struggling to his feet, he grabbed the walker next to his Lazyboy. With ball in hand, he pushed the walker to his front door, opened it, and shuffled outside.

The day was bright, and birds were singing in the trees. A soft, warm breeze ruffled leaves as puffy white clouds scudded across the blue sky. He closed his eyes and took a deep breath. Exhaling, he prepared to find his favorite rocking chair on the porch. Sicotto pushed the walker ahead of him like a shopping cart. He stopped in mid-step.

At the bottom step of his porch, a boy stared at him.

Fear shone in the boy's eyes as he looked at the baseball in Sicotto's hands. "I'm sorry, Mister. I was playing catch and the ball—and the ball just got away from me! I'm-I'm not very good."

Sicotto grunted. He looked past the boy and asked, "Who are you playing catch with? I don't see anyone else."

An embarrassed look played across the boy's face. Looking down, he mumbled, "It's just me. I was playing catch with myself. Like I said, I'm not very good."

Grunting again, Sicotto pushed the walker to the rocking chair. He placed the walker beside the rocker, then sank grate-fully into the chair. Sitting back, he studied the boy. He looked about ten or eleven years old with brown, curly hair forming an untidy mass on the boy's head. He had a dark complexion and brown eyes, and kept his eyes downcast as he shifted nervously from foot to foot.

"What's your name, kid?"

"Devin Ramos. Are you going to tell my mom, Mister?" he blurted.

Sicotto ignored the question. "*Hmm.* I'm guessing Puerto Rico. Your family is from Puerto Rico. Am I right?"

Devin blinked. "Well, um, my dad is. My mom's from Texas. How did you know that?"

Sicotto laughed, exposing yellowed, nicotine stained teeth. "Kid, I was scouting Latin American baseball players before your parents were even born—maybe even before your grand-parents were born. You do that long enough, you get to recognize the surnames of the country the players are from. Ramos is a common Puerto Rican name."

Devin's eyes grew wide. "You are a baseball scout?"

"Was, kid." Motioning to the walker beside the rocker, Sicotto said, "As you can see, those days are long behind me."

His fear forgotten, Devin darted up the steps. "You think you can teach me how to play baseball?"

Sicotto chuckled, a wheezing sound that escaped from his lips much like leaking air from a balloon. "Slow down, kid. Why don't you get your dad to teach you?"

Devin's face fell, his cheeks turning red. "I-I haven't seen my dad since I was five years old. Mom says he went back to Puerto Rico."

Sicotto shook his head. "Tough break, kid. I'm sorry to hear that." Saddened, he watched the boy's face grow longer and longer. "Tell you what, kid. You do some chores around the house and yard for me, and I'll do what I can for you. We'll consider that payment for the broken window as well."

Devin's eyes lit up and he hopped up and down. "You bet, Mister! I'll work hard! What do you want me to do?"

Sicotto smiled and held up his hands. "Whoa, kid. First things first." He thrust out his hand. "Name's Frankie, Frankie Sicotto."

Taking Frankie's hand, Devin shook it. "When can we start?" he gushed, barely able to contain his excitement.

"We start," Sicotto answered pointing at the broken window, "by *you* getting a broom and dustpan and cleaning up this mess."

———

SICOTTO SOON DISCOVERED the only baseball-related thing Devin owned was the single baseball that shattered his window. Fortunately, Sicotto's garage was full of boxes of baseball equipment that had been retired for as long as he had been. Digging through a box of old mitts, he finally chose the smallest one he could find. It still swallowed up Devin's hand like a pillow, but it would have to do.

The glove was old and wrinkled, much like Sicotto, and he showed Devin how to rub soft-soap into the leather to bring back its pliability. The small boy's brow was wrinkled in intense concentration as Sicotto demonstrated. Satisfied, Sicotto gave the boy the glove to take home. A warm feeling bloomed inside Sicotto as he watched Devin cradle the old, scarred baseball mitt in his arms as if it were made of gold.

Starting the next day in Sicotto's backyard, he sat on a padded bucket, his walker beside him, while Devin threw to him from a bucket of baseballs as yellowed with age as Sicotto's teeth. At first, the boy was all over the place, his throws wild and unpredictable, and Sicotto was obliged to wear an old catcher's mask and pad for protection. Over time, however, Devin's control got better, and soon the *pop* of a baseball landing solidly in Sicotto's own mitt became the norm.

———

WINCING from the laser Devin threw into his mitt, Sicotto remarked, "That's good, kid. I think it's time to move on to something else now."

Breathless, Devin ran over to where Sicotto was sitting. "What? What's next, Frankie?" His eyes glowing in eager anticipation, Devin could barely contain his excitement.

Picking up an old wooden bat lying at his feet, Sicotto pointed with it toward a corner of the backyard.

"Fielding. I'm going to hit you some grounders and you pick them up and throw them to me."

"Yes!" Devin cried. Waving his arms over his head, he sprinted toward the corner where Sicotto pointed.

Still seated on the padded bucket, Sicotto picked a ball up with the glove in one hand, tossed it in the air, and then hit it with the bat in his other hand. Dribbling on the ground toward Devin, he scooped it up and threw it to Sicotto all in one motion.

The baseball sailed over the fence into the alley.

The screech of a startled cat echoed from the alley, followed by a *bang* as the ball ricocheted off a garbage can. Sicotto looked over his shoulder and then back at Devin.

"Kid, it looks like we are going to need to work on your fielding."

The next few weeks were spent working on Devin fielding and throwing. Sicotto explained to Devin that a good player had to field *and* throw while on the move. Soon they relocated to a nearby park, Devin pushing Sicotto in his wheelchair while he held a bucket of balls in his lap. As best as he was able, seated as he was on the padded bucket, Sicotto included fly balls in the mix of grounders he hit to Devin.

Nodding in approval at Devin's vastly improved catching and throwing, Sicotto said, "Kid, we have one more area to work on...your batting. Tomorrow, we'll get started."

DEVIN FOUND it hard to sleep that night he was so excited about finally getting to bat. The next morning, he rushed over to Frankie's house and found the old scout waiting for him on the porch.

"C'mon, kid," he said.

Leading the way down the wheelchair ramp adjacent to the porch, Sicotto stopped in front of his garage. It was a wooden structure, the white paint covering the exterior peeling in numerous places, exposing the grey, weathered wood beneath. Dusty, single-pane windows formed a line across the garage door, and Sicotto had Devin grasp the handle on the door. Together they heaved the garage door open with a noisy, torturous screeching.

Inside was a single car almost as long as the garage itself. The car was black with fins like those on a rocket ship thrusting from the rear end.

Lovingly, Sicotto ran his hands alongside the car's dusty exterior. "1959 Cadillac Coupe De Ville. The best car ever made."

Handing Devin his walker, Sicotto slow-walked his way to the driver's side door and slid in. He turned the ignition, a throaty growl erupted from the Caddy as Devin got in. The seat was so large it swallowed up his small frame, and Devin looked around in wide-eyed amazement at the car's interior.

"It's as big as my house."

Sicotto patted the seat. "They don't make 'em like this anymore, kid."

He backed out, and they rolled down the street, Devin's head barely above the car window. A short time later, Sicotto pulled into a sports annex with coin-operated pitching machines. Rows of batting cages lined with green nets were arrayed alongside each pitching machine. Devin retrieved Sicotto's walker, and together, they made their way to the nearest batting cage.

"Nothing beats live pitching, but my pitching days are long

behind me, kid," Sicotto explained. "So, we'll have to go with pitching machines. Got this for you to use," he added handing Devin a wooden bat.

Sicotto shook his head when he saw how large the bat looked in Devin's hands. "Ain't got any of those new-fangled bats made of space-age materials, and that's the smallest bat I could find. You'll have to choke up considerably on it."

Showing Devin what he meant, he shuffled back a step, eyeing the boy's stance. Several times, he adjusted Devin's grip on the bat as well as the placement of his feet. Then he had Devin take several swings, making more adjustments after each swing. When he was finally satisfied, he pointed to the back end of the batting cage.

"Batter up!"

Beginning at the lowest velocity possible, Sicotto fed balls one after another into the machine. Devin swung wildly at the first ball, missing badly. Devin kept swinging and missing, and with each miss, Sicotto would have Devin make small adjustments to his swing. Frustrated, Devin's face grew redder with each successive miss.

Thwack!

After almost thirty minutes of swings and misses, Devin finally connected on a pitch.

Thwack!

The next baseball lined past Sicotto like a frozen rope and rebounded off the net. Soon, Devin was spraying pitch after pitch all over the batting cage. Sicotto finally called a halt, and Devin walked out of the cage, a huge smile across his face.

"You did good, kid," Sicotto said nodding.

For the next several weeks, Sicotto drove the boat-like Cadillac to the batting cages, with Devin growing more proficient as Sicotto changed pitching speeds on the machine.

After a batting session, they pulled up into Sicotto's driveway and he stopped short of the garage and put the car in park. Turning to Devin, he tapped the boy on the shoulder. "Kid, ya' got talent. I've done everything a broken old man can do for you. You gotta take it from here."

Fear seized Devin's heart. "You mean you won't help me anymore? I won't be able to come over?"

Sicotto chuckled. "Of course you can, kid. You live next door, remember? What I'm saying is you need to take it to the next level. You need to get on a team, join a league. You need to start playing live ball."

"It won't be the same without you, Frankie," Devin whispered, tears leaking from his eyes.

Sicotto ruffled Devin's hair. "I'll always be with you, kid. A part of me got ya' to where you are now, right?"

Devin nodded, his eyes swollen.

"Tell you what, kid. Ask your mother if you can come over for dinner tomorrow evening. We're gonna have a celebration."

Devin perked up. "A celebration? Of what?"

Grinning, Sicotto said, "Your graduation from the Frankie Sicotto Baseball Academy."

The next day couldn't come fast enough. As the sun lowered into the horizon, Devin sprinted over to Frankie's house, banging on the front door.

"C'mon in, kid!"

As Devin walked in, his eyes widened at the sight of a table set with a large cheese pizza in the middle. A single candle was placed in the center of the pizza. Seated beside the table was Sicotto. Striking a match, he lit the candle.

"Happy graduation day, kid! The pizza is what we Italians call an 'Italian Cake'. All you need is tomato sauce and cheese. Now blow out the candle."

Grinning, Devin puffed his cheeks out and blew out the candle. Sicotto served him a slice of the pizza. As Devin was eating, he slid a box tied with a bow toward him.

"From me to you, kid."

The pizza forgotten, Devin picked up the box. It looked like an old shoebox, and he untied the bow. Looking inside, he saw a collection of photographs, most of which were in black and white. As he went through them, he saw a much younger version of Frankie with a succession of baseball players of all different nationalities.

"That's my life, kid. That's who I am. I want you to have it."

Devin looked up, confused.

"You know, kid, when I was in school, they made us take Latin. It's a dead language and no one uses it anymore, but I remember one phrase from all those years ago. It's *Regi Vitam*, or 'The King's Life'. And for all these years, that's what I've done. I've led a King's Life. I've done what I wanted to do, lived my life as I wanted, and if I could do it all over again, I wouldn't change a thing."

Sicotto handed a picture to Devin. It was of Devin, his face a mask of concentration as he waited for a pitch at the batting cages.

"I took that with an old Polaroid, and wonder of wonders, it still worked. I want you to add that to my collection."

Sitting back, Sicotto said, "I'll be checking into the hospital tomorrow. I got diagnosed a couple of months ago with the big 'C', and as the old saying goes, 'It don't look good for the Gipper'. But I want you to know, teaching you baseball these past six weeks has made me very happy. My wish for you, Devin, is to find your dream, your own *Regi Vitam*. That would make me happiest of all."

Sicotto put on a contented smile. "One day, when you make a great play, get that big hit, pull out that picture and look at it."

Remember me then, Frankie Sicotto—the man who led The King's Life."

"RAMOS!"

Devin looked up from tying on his cleats. The manager of the Las Vegas Rattlers, Roger Hammonds, was waving at him. He trotted onto the field. "Yes, sir?"

"Go clean out your locker."

Devin froze. "What? But I've been batting a ton! I lead the team in average, RBI—"

"Its not that, kid," Hammonds said chuckling. "You've been called up. You're going to the big leagues."

Devin whooped and hopped up and down. Hugging Hammonds, he raced into the modest fieldhouse. He pulled open the door to his locker and emptied it. He paused at the sight of a single photo he had taped to the back of the locker. He had kept it with him for the past fifteen years, from little league, high school, and now the minors. The picture, taken by his mother with Frankie's old Polaroid, showed Devin with a broad smile on his face and an ancient wooden bat in his hand. Next to him stood Frankie, the old scout's arm across his shoulder.

"I made it, Frankie. I made it to the Bigs," he whispered.

Author - Cindy Davis

Cindy Davis was born in Massachusetts. In 2014, to avoid any more cold weather, she sold everything and moved south where she met her future husband on a dating site. Rick is also from the Boston area; they find it humorous that they had to come all the way to Florida to find the perfect relationship.

Together they have written a number of self-help books and visionary fiction. They study all aspects of the metaphysical world; have seen past lives, do self-healing, and even became certified Master Healers and Hypnotists. He must love her a lot; he's taken a half-dozen courses on book promotion and brought a number of her mysteries to Top Ten status.

They have become energy vortex chasers, finding some in the most unexpected places, like Bok Tower Gardens in Lake Wales, Florida. This year they are going to Hawaii to chase down yet another one.

You can find her online at:
 www.fiction-doctor.com
 www.cindydavisauthor.com

www.cindydavisauthor.com/blog
https://podcasts.apple.com/us/podcast/meet-the-author-the-carters/id1554282854

The Perfect Future

By:

Cindy Davis

The Perfect Future

Cindy Davis

Zipacna heaved his school bag into the corner of the bedroom. From under the mattress he snatched his journal and headed outdoors. The sun would be shining for another hour. He didn't want to waste it doing homework...or yard work. The idea made him chuckle. Couldn't exactly do yard work in the dark. But no matter, the grass would still be there tomorrow. The fact that he'd be in trouble for not taking tending to chores went in and out of his head. Something amazing had happened and he couldn't be distracted right now.

He traipsed along a well-worn path to the water. A leaf from high above wafted and twirled in the air performing an intricate dance toward the earth. As it neared his nose, he snatched it between thumb and index finger. The dull green surface of the sea grape leaf was laden with fingerlike veins. Brown speckles marred the underside; the drought on the eastern Mexico shore was affecting the gnarled and ancient tree. This time of year it affected everything, including humans, because it meant temps were over a hundred with a humidity to match or even exceed. Never had the intense weather been a bother for him. It was as though he was part of it.

Waves slapped the shore, rougher than usual today due to a severe thunderstorm that roared through the countryside before dawn, breaking the intensity of the drought. The water tick-ticked against the sides of a dilapidated canoe. Zipacna stood savoring the breeze and watching the irreverent water eating away at the innocent hull. Most people just smelled salt water at times like this. But there was so much more to absorb: the mildly sweet beach pea, pungent driftwood, the seemingly ever-present sargassum seaweed the ocean-surge had pushed high up on shore, and…wait, what was that? He lifted his nose to the air. Yes, sweat. Someone, probably a woman jogger, had passed here within the hour.

He tugged his own canoe from the dense shrubbery and laid his journal on the bench seat. He tucked the oars into place and climbed in, holding carefully to each gunwale to keep from tipping. Not that getting wet was a problem; that happened more often than not, but he didn't want water spots on the journal. Zipacna rowed a ways from shore. For a while, he paddled close to the overhang of branches whose leaves rattled with each smack of wave. Juvenile redfish swarmed as one unit in the inch-deep water. An enormous Portuguese man-o-war skittled around the oar tip barely seeming to notice the alien object in its path. A curly-tailed lizard waddled away as the canoe's shadow passed.

Zipacna dropped the small anchor about ten feet from the beach, making sure neither he, nor the canoe, was visible from shore. For a short time, he leaned back taking in the afternoon serenity. He pulled the journal—warmed by the sun—into his lap and let his fingers caress the mandala design etched into its boar's hide cover. Six months ago, he'd used a small sharp knife to carve the elaborate pattern. Thin bands of strapping bound cover and pages together. At home, stowed under his narrow bed were dozens of journals, begun when the *voice* first came into his head. He chuckled recalling the fear he'd felt at that time. That was years ago.

He placed his forearms on his jeaned thighs, palms open and turned to the sun. There was much to think about today—decisions to make. Decisions he hadn't expected to make on his own. He lifted his chin to the sky. Far above, just a small speck right now, a peregrine falcon circled in graceful seemingly choreographed motion. While the boat bobbed in an arc around the distended rope, Zipacna prayed for rain that would bring everything, including people, to life again. Practically overnight crops would sprout; birds would splash and flutter in puddles; flowers would bud and bloom as if by magic. Not everything was positive about rain. Rain meant mosquitos appeared in droves, almost angry in their intensity. At least they provided food for bats and other flying creatures. The cycle of life was as important to the earth's survival as breathing was for humans. Earth's survival was what a shaman lived for—what kept him breathing from one moment to the next.

Rain-meditation complete, he turned his attention further inward. Deep, deeper inside himself, he focused. Breath slowed, the thump-thump thump-thump of his heart the only sound. Soon the too-familiar voice in his head began.

"I thought I'd find you here."

Zipacna popped his eyes open. "What are you doing here?" He cursed under his breath and squinted at the face poking between the sea grape branches. How had Chaahk gotten through all that underbrush undetected? It couldn't have been his size; he stood six-foot-four with wide shoulders and huge feet. It took all Zipacna's willpower not to haul in the anchor and row away.

Chaahk splashed, barefoot as always, into the water and made his way toward the boat. It lurched and jerked as he climbed aboard. Once settled, he shot Zipacna a level stare, holding it for several uncomfortable seconds. He had something on his mind and Zipacna wasn't anxious to learn what it was. Chaahk picked up a stone from the belly of the canoe, brushed dirt from the smooth round surface, and held it up to the sun. His blue eyes gazed with admiration at the spiderweb obsidian embedded into the quartz. He lowered the stone and stabbed Zipacna once again with his dark eyes. "This would make an amazing pendant."

Zipacna didn't bother glancing at the stone; he'd brought it here yesterday…when he was alone…without his half-brother's interruptions. The intrigue for him was in the stone's energy, not the intricate weave of the obsidian through the quartz, or possibilities for it being made into jewelry. Of larger interest to him: since when did Chaahk have interest in jewelry?

Chaahk spoke, almost as if addressing the stone, "You said you wanted to talk to me."

"That was three days ago."

Chaahk flung the stone into a thicket of wild sage, sending a spray of water everywhere, and rousing a scourge of mosquitoes from under the leaves. Zipacna used his shirttail to dry the journal's cover before the water spotted the leather.

"Do you think I have nothing else to do but come when you call?"

Actually, no. At twenty-seven, Chaahk should've been out on his own with a job, family, a home. It was never right to voice that type of thought so Zipacna let it fly away from his mind.

"I don't have to come running every time you beckon."

So, he wasn't letting it go. Zipacna pulled in a breath and pushed it out between his teeth, but still said nothing.

Chaahk changed tacks. "Is this about the school?"

Zipacna gave a benign smile. "No, actually. It *was* about our store."

"Our parents said we couldn't do it. Case closed."

Zipacna grinned. He brought his fists together in his lap, knuckles touching. "When did their saying no ever stop us from following our hearts?"

"I get that. The trouble this time is we need their help financially."

"No, we—"

Halt!

The word resounded in his head as his mouth added, "—don't."

The shouted warning came again. *Halt!*

Zipacna tried to suck the explanation back down his throat, but it was too late. The words came anyway: "Actually, we don't need our parents' help." Damn. The damage was done. He was committed.

The voice in his head went quiet. Too little too late.

"No?" Chaahk's single word response was spoken with distrust and scorn. "Do you expect money to just rain down from the sky? Yes, of course, a dreamer like you would think that."

Hesitation and doubt struck Zipacna like a physical force. Not because of Chaahk's unkind words. Why was he being warned against bringing in his half-brother? For years they'd talked about opening a spiritual shop in downtown Tulum. They would sell charms, gems, dream catchers, and cards—the traditional wares. They'd also offer readings and workshops of many kinds. Events that would help open people's awareness and spirituality. He and Chaahk had spent months drawing plans, and even going so far as to build display units. It was all they talked about.

But now, for some reason, Universe wanted to stop it. Which meant something had happened to change the course of the planned cycle. But what? He waited, silent. No answer came. It would, though. All he had to do was be patient. For now, there remained a problem: how to stop this situation from moving forward until he learned the reason.

Chaahk unfolded his left leg and kicked him in the shin with a soaking wet sneaker. "I asked you a question. Why don't we need to worry about money?"

What to say? He couldn't just renege on this. Not after he'd thrown out the lure about the financing. So Zipacna gave a sly grin, and improvised. "Because, when you voice your intentions to Universe, you have to let go and trust that what you want will appear."

For a moment Chaahk appeared to accept the diversionary words. Then he reared back and kicked Zipacna harder. "What the hell kind of crap are you feeding me? *Everyone* knows that!" He flew onto his knees and leaned into Zipacna's face. The pungent scent of jalapenos puffed up his nose.

Think! he told himself. Hurry before—

Chaahk thrust him backwards. His head hit the canoe floor with a thud that ricocheted back and forth in painful waves inside his brain. Chaahk knelt on Zipacna's seat between his thighs. The stench of jalapenos came again when he shouted, "Just how much money did you get? And why didn't you tell me about it?"

Zipacna pushed the big body away. He wrestled himself into a sitting position. Then to his knees. He placed his palms on Chaahk's bony chest and heaved him back. The boat wobbled. It threatened to dump them both in the water. His brother tumbled to the side with a feral growl. Before he could launch a new attack, Zipacna leaped onto the bench seat. Although a dozen years separated the two, Zipacna was far stronger. He had to admit, though, Chaahk had a mean streak. And meanness produced powerful adrenaline rushes. Every other time, as long as Zipacna kept his head, he won every battle. For the time being, he decided to relate the entire story. Universe would have to figure another way for the business relationship to implode.

Zipacna climbed down, prepared in case Chaahk yanked him by an ankle. When no further attack came, he resumed his original position, only this time kept his hands clenched in his lap just in case; the journal sat safely, for now, on the seat at the bow. Though Chaahk was lazy, he never shied from a battle. Why Zipacna ever considered going into business with him—*two* businesses at that—he couldn't recall.

Zipacna began the story with, "I went to a cleansing ceremony the other night." It was something he did monthly in preparation for his upcoming shaman initiation.

Chaahk moved to sit with his back against the seat. Zipacna relaxed—a little. No way could Chaahk get up from that position fast enough to attack without plenty of warning.

Contrary to his usual impatient nature, Chaahk waited. So Zipacna replied with, "I met up with Mr. Martinez afterward."

"Luis Martinez? He's Papi's good friend, right?" Interested now, Chaahk cllimbed on the seat opposite Zipacna.

"Yeah, but I was so excited I forgot about that at first. I told him everything we talked about doing. When I mentioned how the perfect shop just came available, he said there was no time to waste and we should jump on it."

"That's when you told him our parents refused to give us any money."

"Right. And I told him how that pretty much killed the plan." Zipacna laughed. *"That's* when I remembered he and Papi were friends. And I got to thinking I shouldn't have said anything because it would get back to Papi."

Chaahk shrugged. "You didn't say anything wrong—nothing Papi doesn't already know."

"No." He definitely hadn't thrown any of their parents under the bus. Hadn't lain blame on anyone. He'd just stated the facts, that if they wanted to open a business, they would be responsible for financing it themselves.

"So, what happened with Mr. Martinez?"

"Happened?" Zipacna wrestled himself back to the present moment.

"Obviously, you got the money." This was said with a bit of exasperation. "How did you do it?" These words were punctuated with the same exasperation but now emphasis was placed on each syllable.

"Zipacna! Where are you?" came a new voice.

Chaahk made a gurgling sound in his throat. "Bad timing."

Zipacna shot to attention. He swung around on the seat. Their father stood on the beach, water splashing his work boots, arms crossed in the familiar *I'm irritated* stance.

"I'm over here, Papi!"

"Why aren't you mowing the lawn?"

He took hold of the anchor rope. "I am just getting to it."

"Good. It'll be dark soon."

Chaahk helped wind the wet rope and stow the anchor at the stern. Zipacna paddled toward shore, not in a hurry since Papi was striding across the road toward home.

"Then what happened with Mr. Martinez?" Chaahk asked.

Zipacna restrained himself from heaving a sigh. He'd hoped Chaahk would forget their conversation. "He was quiet a while." Zipacna climbed onto solid ground. "I guess he was thinking what to do. Then he asked how much money it would take. I told him we needed about ten thousand for the down-payment and inventory." He held the boat for Chaahk.

"How'd you come up with that amount off the top of your head?" Chaahk wrinkled his cheeks and waved his hand to erase the question. "Don't answer. You always know shit like that. But he agreed to give us the money?"

Zipacna yanked the boat up the gritty sand and shoved it under some overhanging bushes, safe from thieves and weather. Then he faced his brother. "There are what he called *conditions*."

Chaahk waved again and started home. "That's no big deal. This is fantastic news."

News he could've heard three days ago. Zipacna didn't bother adding this information. Their father stood in the porch doorway, his shoulders taking up most of the space in the frame. Zipacna handed his journal to him, said bye to Chaahk, and headed for the shed in the backyard.

"What are you up to today, Chaahk?" His father laid the

journal on the stair railing and ran a hand through his thinning hair.

"Nothing much. Just going home to do our lawn."

This made Zipacna laugh out loud. The sound echoed inside the overcrowded shed. *Really funny, Chaahk, really funny.* More often than not, Zipacna was the one mowing his stepmother's grass.

It was uncanny how alike Chaak and Papi looked. Not just the height and physicality; they carried themselves in identical self-confident ways. Funny too how the same father produced two entirely different specimens of humanity. Zipacna wasn't short, by any definition, but he lacked the muscles and, he chuckled to himself, the giant feet. As for the self-confidence, he didn't lack anything there, but he didn't wear it on his outer being like his half-brother.

As he poured gasoline into the funnel, he mulled over the situation. Most of what bothered him was Universe's sudden decision to keep Chaahk out of things. More than likely, it was due to the fact that Chaahk never seemed to be able to hold a job. He'd work a few weeks and find something to fault the company, the owner, or his co-workers. Whenever Zipacna asked about it, Chaahk said he felt sure that when the time was right Universe would present him with his perfect future. Right now, he needed to work for himself, to make his own rules, which, now that Zipacna thought about it, might be the exact problem—something he'd missed. When it came to compromising, even on something as trivial as drinking soda or lemonade, Chaahk wasn't flexible. It was generally—what did Americans say—*his way or the highway.* Was this the reason Universe decided to intervene? Because he hadn't figured it out on his own? Probably.

The mower chopped a swath toward the house. Papi and Chaahk were still talking, Papi now with the journal clutched against his chest, Chaahk leaning on the stair post. Both were at ease, which was nice. Too often their discussions ended in shouting. Papi was strict, but he wasn't unreasonable. He had high standards for his two sons, and one kept falling short of expectations. Chaahk confided once that he felt guilty over this, but said he had to follow his path, not the one set out for him. This made Zipacna laugh. Sure, Papi tried to carve a path for Chaahk, because Chaahk needed guidance.

He turned the mower left and passed near the porch. Papi and Chaahk were still talking. Even up close, he couldn't hear what they were saying. But the mood was still positive.

Way back when Chaahk graduated from high school, Papi tried to bring him into the business. His plumbing company did quite well. Papi would've loved for his eldest son to follow in his footsteps. But, like all the other jobs, it lasted only a few weeks.

Gradually, Zipacna made smaller and smaller rectangles until the backyard was smooth and neatly cut. By the time he finished, Papi and Chaahk were gone. He swiped the sweat from his forehead and neck with a towel hanging on the rail. *Thanks for leaving it, Papi.*

It wasn't hard to realize that Chaahk's inability to hold a job was probably the reason Mr. Martinez put conditions on the ten-thousand-dollar loan by leaving Chaahk's name off the paperwork. But that raised another question: did Zipacna want to be responsible for repaying all the money? If—no, when—Chaahk bailed on him, could he manage on his own? Could he handle payroll, employee scheduling, and ordering inventory? He felt pretty sure he could. He had spiritual abilities; he had the desire, was smart, and he worked hard. Sure, Chaahk's spiritual talents were more developed, but his own were growing daily, he made sure of it.

The front yard took longer to do. The house was set far back from the road and the lawn contained lots of obstacles: trees and shrubs, statues and flowerbeds. They were his mamá's pride and joy. Zipacna took satisfaction in keeping them looking nice—not for his mother, for himself. Which was another reason he would be a success. He cared intensely about things, most especially for himself. Which made him a better person to be around—so Mamá said.

One thing was for sure: Universe's decision to omit Chaahk from the deal hadn't been spontaneous or random. There must have been other messages, ones he'd totally missed. But, actually faced with the money that would make things a reality, Universe had acted abruptly. Unfortunately, it came several seconds too late. He had no doubt something would happen to squash things —that was how Universe worked.

Feeling vindicated for having missed the message's timing, he continued on his task. By now, his shirt was soaking wet. Sweat dripped from his hair and ran into his eyes.

Deeper analysis of the situation produced two answers as to why he kept including Chaahk in his plans. First, he felt bad his brother was twenty-seven years old and had nothing to show for his life. Not that it was Zipacna's problem or responsibility in any way, shape, or form. It was part of his personality to want things to go right for everyone, most especially family. Second, each time he lost a job, Chaahk claimed one of these days the exact right job would show up. Zipacna believed in this with all his heart. All you had to do is voice your desires and Universe would set the path in front of you. Whether you walked down the right path was up to you. Zipacna couldn't help thinking that if he at least pointed Chaahk toward the path, his brother would slide into his destiny without further assistance.

It was nearly dark by the time the lawn was done. Dinner waited on the table. His parents had finished eating. They were in the living room talking. He couldn't make out what they said and didn't bother trying to listen in. He picked up his journal from the counter where Papi left it and went to the back porch. The screen would keep the bugs away. The homemade sage scented candle—that he made from the homegrown herb and would be sold in the shop—would provide light so he could write.

Zipacna slipped the pen from the binding and penned the words as they entered his mind. He wasn't sure what to call what happened during these moments; the voice was inside him, as if it was his thoughts, but the ideas were nothing he'd consciously considered. Yet he was compelled to write what came to him.

She looks like an angel. Her name is Jade. She carries the traditional Mayan looks even though her mamá is a blonde-haired blue-eyed American. Her father is my son, Menye.

Zipacna smiled at the words. His son Menye. His grand-daughter Jade. He was only fifteen and his family tree was already mapped out. Not just the family tree...his destiny.

The weird and quite inconvenient thing was the messages didn't come in chronological order. Today he was being told about Jade as a child, yet other messages had included intricate details of how she would someday take over his school.

His school.

Merely thinking the words popped goosebumps all over his body. He already knew what he'd call it: *Centro de Educación Espiritual Avanzada.* Center for Advanced Spiritual Education.

The school was the second business he and Chaahk discussed owning together. Odd though. In all his journal writings, not one word had come regarding he and Chaahk working together. As a matter of fact, it was quite the opposite. Just last week, he'd written—through whatever powers stimulated what he'd come to think of as automatic writing—that Jade would eventually run the school. No mention whatsoever of Chaah. To Zipacna, that meant his brother would somehow be out of the picture by the time the school dream came to fruition.

Something he hadn't learned yet was why Jade was to be his protégé rather than Menye. In most families, the son carried on the work of the father. It had been that way throughout history. Particularly in shamanism, as it had a strictly male-oriented hierarchy. In all the cleansing ceremonies, initiations and certifications, Zipacna had never seen a female. He had learned not to stress over the answers to questions that arose in his writing. He'd found that, as time passed, all answers became clear. He just wished things could be more sequential. Then they would definitely make more sense.

The screen door opened. His father stepped onto the porch. "Am I interrupting anything?"

Zipacna shut the journal and replaced the pen in the binding. "No, I was getting ready to take a shower. Did you and Chaahk have a good talk?"

His father sat in the adjoining chair, shaking his head and wearing a small grin. "I don't know where I went wrong with that boy."

"He's not a boy anymore."

Papi gave a chuckle. "Hard to tell much of the time. I wish I could help him find something he wants to do."

"I've tried too." Zipacna shrugged. "He'll be ready when he's ready."

His father leaned forward, placing his forearms on his thighs. Clearly, he intended to say something serious. "He mentioned you two were opening a shop."

Gosh, couldn't Chaahk keep his mouth shut for a single minute? Zipacna didn't reply. It wouldn't be long before Dad expounded with his thoughts on the matter.

His father leaned back against the flowered cushion. He sighed. "You know why your mamá and I had to refuse to give you the money to open the store, don't you?"

Zipacna didn't want to give energy to negative words—any words—against his half-brother, so he kept silent.

"It has nothing to do with you. I have no doubt you'll be a success at anything you attempt throughout your life. Just to double check, I'm assuming you have no interest in coming into the plumbing business with me."

"Sorry. No. I couldn't be cooped up indoors all the time. I'd be miserable."

"Kinda figured that."

"Sorry, Papi."

He slapped Zipacna's knee. "I'm not the kind of father who insists his sons follow his footsteps. The offer was mostly for Chaahk, to try and give him a focus."

Long ago, Zipacna had experienced a twinge of guilt over his refusal to join the business. Thankfully, Papi's words chased away the emotion.

"When things implode with your brother, you realize you'll be responsible for repaying Luis all on your own?"

"I've given it a lot of thought. I'll be okay. The town needs our kind of store. It can do nothing but become a success."

"I know I don't tell you often enough how proud I am of you." Before Zipacna could respond, he added, "There was a time your abilities confounded me no end. But I've watched you develop into an amazing young man."

Not entirely comfortable with the praise, Zipacna rushed to add his brother. "Chaahk's talents are stronger than mine."

"The trouble is, he doesn't take them seriously." He laughed. "He doesn't take very many things seriously."

That was the truth. As a matter of fact, Chaahk often referred to his abilities as burdens.

Papi slapped his knee again. "It's late. I'm going to bed. If it's okay with you, I'd like to sit in on your next meeting with Luis."

"I think that's a good idea." He didn't say the next words that came into his throat—*I'm not sure how Chaahk will feel.*

"You coming to bed?"

Zipacna picked up the journal from his lap and followed Papi inside. After a shower, he spent some time writing in the journal, this time expanding on what happened during the day. As he was closing the cover, preparing for sleep, the now-familiar voice returned to his head. He hurriedly opened the journal and began to write.

Jade's spiritual abilities will not blossom until her thirtieth birthday.

Zipacna did some quick math and realized he would be long gone into the other world before this time. This was unfortunate because he dearly would have loved working with her. Different from his father, he *did* care if blood relatives entered into the family business. But, it was not to be. He wrote further:

She will come into her talents as suddenly as a tornado forms across flat, dry land. They will perplex her at first. But she will embrace them even more completely than I did. She will go to great depths to educate herself, to perfect herself.

Pride flowed through him at the thought. Sure, he wouldn't be able to watch her as a physical being, but he could do so from his place on the next plane. For as long as he could remember, song lyrics and mental images came to him—as if Universe knew a child could better interpret them. It hadn't been revealed to him yet whether Jade would experience the same sort of messages. No matter, if she did, he'd be there to help her interpret and mentally handle them.

The information seemed to have dried up for tonight, so he stowed the journal under the bed, cramming it between the others. Soon, he'd have to find a new place for them—there were too many.

Later, lying in bed, staring out the uncurtained window, he watched the moon move across the sky, and thought about the messages he'd been receiving since he was a small child. They came in bursts that sometimes fed through so fast, he couldn't write them all down. For a long time, this puzzled him. How was he supposed to learn if he couldn't interpret them all? Finally he realized that literal interpretations weren't what mattered. Nor did he need to recall every word. The important thing was what the messages meant to him personally. Right now, he wished he'd received the information about Chaahk before blurting out about the financial windfall from Mr. Martinez.

Just then, the little voice in his head—his real mental voice, not the intrusive one—reminded him that he'd known all along and chosen to ignore the signs.

———

ZIPACNA AND CHAAHK worked hard setting up the shop. The sign was attached to the front of the building. Inventory had been set onto the display units. Advance advertising already had workshops, readings, and healing sessions almost filled to capacity.

Three months passed. Things were going amazingly well. Chaahk showed his immense knowledge about healing stones and the books they carried on the shelves in the far corner. He interacted with customers, even had them laughing and joking with his sociable personality.

One morning he wasn't waiting by the door at opening time. Zipacna didn't phone to find out where he was. Nor did he stress over it. He was grateful Chaahk had been a dedicated worker for three months.

His half-brother sauntered in the door after lunchtime. Zipacna greeted him with a friendly welcome, as if it were ten in the morning instead of two-thirty in the afternoon. He never mentioned there had been a line of customers practically out the door all day.

The next morning, the same thing happened. Zipacna phoned a woman who'd applied for a job when they first opened. Thankfully, she was still available. He hired her to cover Chaahk's hours.

Again, Chaahk strolled in, this time fifteen minutes before closing. Again, Zipacna greeted him with a cheerful attitude. Chaahk laid a black velvet cloth on the glass countertop. With reverence, he unfolded the edges to reveal several pieces of the most beautiful jewelry Zipacna had ever seen: pendants with jade stones, malachite, and identical pearls; a pair of bracelets strung with perfectly matched cowrie shells; and a ring bearing the most amazing piece of chrysocolla in a silver filigree setting.

Zipacna gripped the ring tightly in his fist, the stone's calming energy so strong it made his fingers tingle. "Wow. I didn't know you had it in you, brother. How much do you want for these?"

Between customers, they settled on a fair price for the pieces. Zipacna tucked the bills into his half-brother's hand. "Bring me more when you can. You do amazing work." Then he chuckled. "I bet you wish you had that spiderweb obsidian you threw in the bushes last summer."

Chaahk broke into a wide grin. "I poked through the bushes and found it almost immediately."

Zipacna stopped talking to ring up a customer's purchase. After she left, he fingered the ring once again, still amazed at the energy emitting from it.

Chaahk, obviously confused as to why Zipacna behaved so calmly, frowned, folded the now-empty velvet cloth, slipped it into a pants pocket, and left the store. On the way out, he held the door for a tall thin man coming in, never noticing it was Luis Martinez, their benefactor.

Lips pursed, Mr. Martinez tore his gaze away from Chaahk's retreating backside and faced Zipacna, still holding the gorgeous ring.

"Wasn't that your brother?"

"Yes. He brought this." Zipacna handed him the ring.

Mr. Martinez wasn't well versed in stones and their healing abilities, but it was clear this one affected him strongly. Lots of white teeth soon showed in his wide mouth. He reluctantly set the ring on the counter and examined the other pieces Chaahk had left.

While Zipacna wrote out price tags for the new items and arranged them in the glass display case, Mr. Martinez wandered around the space. "I have to say, I am very impressed with what you've done here. You've got a nice variety of inventory. It is different each time I am here." He poked the tummy of a bronze Buddha.

"Thank you, sir."

At that moment, two customers entered. Mr. Martinez approached Zipacna and spoke softly while the women browsed. "I am a bit baffled to have seen Chaahk leaving the shop. Is he up to his antics again?"

"Sir, I'm not sure what you're talking about. My half-brother is the same wonderful person he's always been."

Mr. Martinez broke into a wider smile than earlier. "Son, I admire your attitude. There isn't a stitch of animosity in you, is there?"

"Anger is a wasted emotion. It does no good for anyone. Today, I hired a woman to replace him."

"Good for you."

Zipacna gazed through the glass at Chaahk's jewelry pieces thinking maybe Chaahk had finally achieved his perfect future.

Author - CW Hawes

CW Hawes is a fiction writer and award winning poet. His interests are wide ranging and this is reflected in both the genres and the contents of his books. He writes in the post-apocalyptic, mystery, alternative history, and horror genres at present. His love of fine food, interesting locations, philosophy, music, art, books, and history can be seen in each of his tales.

Born and raised in Cleveland, Ohio, CW spent 49 years in the Land of 10,000 Lakes (aka Minnesota), and now proudly hails from the Lone Star State (aka Texas).

He hasn't met a pizza he doesn't like (okay, he detests pineapple), is something of a tea snob, and rocks out to Handel and Vaughan Williams.

Website: https://www.cwhawes.com

Twitter: https://twitter.com/cw_hawes

Facebook: https://www.facebook.com/CWHawes1

Amazon Author Page: https://www.amazon.com/CW-Hawes/e/B00PGAIQ2S

Mailing list signup page: https://www.cwhawes.com/lp/

THE BOAT

A TALE OF
THE ROCHEPORT SAGA

BY:

CW HAWES

6

The Boat - A Tale of the Rocheport Saga

CW Hawes

1 November

All Saints Day. Forty-six days after That Day. The day the world as we knew it came to an end. Forty-six days of grief, fear, fighting, scavenging, and trying to make some sense of what remains and how we move forward.

Although with our current leader, I see no real hope for our group of survivors moving forward. Kenny has far more brawn than brains, still thinks he's captain of the football team, and only thinks about his stomach and his crotch. His day consists of scratching one itch or the other. Usually both.

I've stayed with the group because some of the people were my neighbors in the before time. But mostly I stick around because there is relative safety in numbers.

But with winter staring us in the face I don't think I want to stick around too much longer. Best to get out while the getting is good. Because with Kenny not willing to listen to good advice, the group is headed for disaster. How the majority thought he'd be a good leader beats the heck out of me.

Not being able to get any direction out of our fearless leader, this morning I said to hell with it and decided we needed supplies. And a fine day to go scavenging it is. No snow on the ground, and the temp is a balmy thirty-seven degrees. No one wanted to go with me, so I'm on my own. Probably not the wisest decision, but I did just fine by myself in the first couple weeks after That Day. Today should be no different.

I don't want to brag, but the fact of the matter is that I know more about survival and how to handle myself than the whole group put together. And I'm well aware of the lessons of London's "To Build A Fire".

Back in October, because we can get snow in October, I put snow tires on the van. Haven't needed them thus far, but who knows about tomorrow? I haven't quite got the hang of old-time weather forecasting.

The stores and houses close by our development have been cleaned out. What it's like further out is unknown. Although one thing we do know for certain is that to our south, the inner suburbs and the urban core are a war zone. Gangs and survivalist paramilitary groups battle for supremacy. It's a place you don't want to visit.

Therefore, for today's excursion, I decided a trip to the north was in order. In our brave new world, ignorance is definitely not bliss. Knowing what lay to our north would be good intel.

The group I'm with is located in a housing development on the northern edge of the suburban ring. Twenty minutes further out is the beginning of farm country. Far fewer people to contend with. Fewer people also increased my chances of returning home in one piece, and possibly returning at all.

I drove up Highway 65, also known as Central Avenue, for a half-hour before turning off the highway onto a side road. Anything along Central has probably been cleaned out by now. Off the main road, is where I'll probably hit the jackpot. Mostly because most of my fellow Homosapiens missed getting the sapiens part at birth.

I've found people to be lazy and many are not overly bright.

Consequently, I've made some great finds off the beaten path. Stuff the others missed.

The land out this way is flat and dotted with rows and clusters of trees. Houses are well-spaced. Probably sitting on five-acre lots.

After turning off Central, and after a couple miles on the county road, I noticed the road up ahead making a Y. The main branch curved south. The other fork of the Y curved north and was the main route into a small housing development. I slowed down, and as I got closer to where the road divided I saw the reason for the split, and why there was a housing development in the middle of nowhere. There was a sizable lake, and everyone in Minnesota loves lakeshore property.

I turned into the development. The houses on my left backed up to the lake and had probably been very expensive before That Day. Now they were vacant shells of siding, two by fours, and sheet rock, with shingles on top.

To make for a quick exit, should I need to make one, I turned the van around and parked it on the street. My dogs, Bob and Bobbi, were with me and I left them in the van to protect it from intruders. Their presence also allowed me to leave the driver's door unlocked. I didn't want to waste time unlocking the door on my old van if someone was after me.

The houses looked to be on half-acre lots, which gave them a decent yard for kids to play in. After looking them over, I chose the fifth house from the corner and walked to it. I was carrying two revolvers, a knife, slungshot, and a prybar.

The front door of my chosen house was locked. I walked around to the backyard. All the windows in the front and on the side were intact. This could be virgin territory, I told myself.

The backyard sloped gently to the lake, which was roughly circular and covered about twenty acres by my guesstimate. In the middle was an island.

Off to my right, as I faced the lake, was a sandbar and a boat beached on it. I walked over for a closer inspection. From the boat to the grassy shore were shoe prints, and that meant I wasn't alone. The boat was empty, and I guess whoever owned it had arrived about the same time I did.

I turned around and there she was standing by the corner of the house next door. And in her hands was a rifle.

As sure as snow in Minnesota in the winter time, I was dead meat if she decided to pull the trigger. And she could pull it faster than I could get to one of my revolvers.

I put my hands up and said, "You mind pointing that thing in a different direction? I already have enough holes in my body."

"Are you alone?" Her voice had a certain music to it, and the pitch was neither too high, nor too low.

"If I said, yes, would you believe me?"

"Maybe."

"And if I said, no, I could still be lying. In fact, right now, my buddy might be sneaking up behind you." I smiled at her.

She turned her head to take a quick glance behind her, and in the second it took for her face to point back in my direction, I had my revolver pointed at her.

"Very clever, Mister, but I have a rifle and I'm a good shot."

"Okay. One for you. I have a three-fifty-seven magnum revolver and I can hit a bulls-eye where you're standing."

We looked at each other for an eternity that was probably three seconds long. I held up my left hand, and said, "I'm going to put my gun down." I squatted, set the revolver on the grass, and stood back up. "Now, if you want to kill me, go ahead. My life is in your hands."

"Where are you from?"

"Circle Pines."

"What are you doing way out here? That's, what, an hour drive?"

"Something like that. I'm doing the same thing you're doing: looking for stuff to take back to my group."

She nodded.

"How many are with you?" I asked.

There was a long pause before she said, "There's just me. My friends were killed a month ago."

"I'm very sorry. Very sorry to hear that."

"Are you with a good group?"

"No. The leader, and I use that term loosely, is a real dick. That's why I'm out here all alone. I take it you live on that island."

She nodded.

"And let me guess, you took care of any boats around here so no one can go out there."

"You're pretty smart, Mister."

"That's why I'm still alive."

"I could kill you, Mr. Smarty."

"You could, but I'm wagering you won't. So why don't you point that rifle in some other direction, and I'll be off and let you be."

"How do I know you won't be back?"

"You don't. But I do my best to live by the Golden Rule. You know, do to others as you'd have them do to you."

"So what does that mean?"

"If I was living on that island and you came here, I wouldn't like you intruding on my turf. So, if you don't mind, I'll pick up my gun and leave you to your scavenging. I'm sure there are plenty of other places that haven't been picked over."

"What's your name?"

"Bill. What's yours?"

"Milana."

"That's an unusual name."

"It's not my real name, but I like it."

"If you say it's your name, then it's your real name. Nice to meet you, Milana. Hope you find lots of good stuff."

She hadn't lowered the rifle, but I was pretty sure she wasn't going to kill me. I slowly knelt down, retrieved my gun, put it in my waistband, and slowly stood up.

She blurted out, "Do you want to help me? I mean we could work together. It would go faster."

"You're still pointing that cannon at me."

"Sorry." The rifle went to the crook of her arm, muzzle pointing at the ground.

"What makes you think you can trust me? I might be a homicidal maniac."

"Like Hannibal Lector?"

"Yeah. Any good chianti around here?"

She laughed. "I think my dad would've liked to you."

"Why do you say that?"

"He had a screwy sense of humor."

"I take it he didn't make it."

She shook her head. "My mom, too, and my little brother."

"I'm very sorry, Milana."

"Yeah, thanks. Are you married? Do you have kids?"

"My wife died, and I don't know if her daughter survived. I don't have any children."

"I'm sorry she died."

"Thanks. Me, too. I miss her. Miss her a lot. Probably like you miss your parents."

She nodded.

"Well, Milana, how about we get to work. The day isn't standing still."

"No. It isn't."

⊷

WE SPENT the rest of the morning and early afternoon loading supplies into the boat. I learned that she was twenty-four, had graduated from the University of Minnesota with a degree in product design, had spent a year working on a ranch in

Wyoming, and was looking for a job when That Day hit. Her dad was something of a prepper, loved paintball, camping, and fishing.

I told her about my interest in philosophy, political theory, and the shooting sports.

Her boyfriend, James, lived for skeet and trap. He was the one who died a month ago. She, James, and two other friends were ambushed. She was the only survivor.

"That's when I moved to the island," she said. "I feel safer there."

When her boat was half-full, she said, "Do you want to come over to the island and have supper?"

"I have two dogs and I can't leave them. I also have my van, and I don't want to leave it on the street."

"You have dogs?"

"Yes."

"Oh, I love dogs!"

We went to the van and she oohed and ahed over Bob and Bobbi. "We can take them in the boat, and I know a garage you can put your van in. I'd really like the company."

"Okay, I'll have supper with you."

"Thanks, Bill. You've made this such a wonderful day."

We shifted things around to make room for me, the dogs, and a few things from the van that I didn't want to leave. Then it was off to Milana's island.

The two of us paddled across the lake and docked on the opposite side of the island because there were fewer chances for people to see the boat.

We unloaded the goods we'd found, while Bob and Bobbi checked out the acre-sized island, and when everything was put away she made supper for us. Into a pot went canned beef, canned potatoes, canned carrots and peas, and canned onions.

"You would vary your diet and get fresh protein if you trapped squirrels and rabbits," I volunteered.

"That was James's job," she replied. "I just can't bring myself to kill animals. And cleaning them?" She shuddered.

"I know what you mean. The first time I started skinning a rabbit I threw up. I still don't like doing it, but canned food isn't very nutritious."

"I know. But I just can't kill them."

I didn't say anything, but I knew that if she didn't change her mind she wouldn't last long in our new world.

When we'd finish the stew and the cracker bread, she broke out a can of fruit cocktail and we split it.

The meal over, I got out my pipe and asked if she minded.

"No. Go ahead. My grandfather smoked a pipe and I always liked the smell."

So I filled it, lit it, and puffed away.

"Do you want to stay the night? Taking the boat out at night isn't very safe."

I smiled. "In other words, I'm kind of trapped here."

She looked down at her feet to hide the sheepish grin on her face.

"I'll stay."

"I'm not looking for sex. I'd just like the company."

"I understand. I'm not looking for sex either. But the company would be nice." She was, after all, a pretty young woman. And easy to talk to. A big change from the group back in Circle Pines. There, I was alone in the midst of a couple dozen people.

After a pause, she said, "This is it, isn't it? There's not going to be any help. The government isn't going to do anything."

"As I see it, yes, this is it. This is now our world. In fact, I'd wager there probably isn't a government anymore. Which means there's no one to send help. Anyone who survived is too busy trying to go on surviving. We're on our own, I'm afraid."

"That's what I think. Millie and Rob kept saying the government would be arriving soon. James didn't say much, but I think he, too, thought this was it. And for them it was. They're all dead. And there's no help coming. We have to help ourselves."

I nodded.

After a lengthy pause, she said, "But I don't like it. I had a good life, you know?"

I nodded again.

She went on. "I had good parents. An adorable kid brother." She swiped her hand across her eyes. "I had a good car and friends and I was going to get a good job. I just know I was. I was a vegan and ate organic. I cared about people and justice."

"And now?"

A bitter laugh burst from her lips. "I'm eating shit out of cans and trying not to get raped or killed. This isn't living, Bill."

"No, it isn't. It's surviving, so some day we might be able to live again."

"Do you even think that's possible? Living again?"

"Yes, I do. That's why I get up every morning and do what I can to help myself and others to make it through the day. Without hope, we perish. And right now, I don't want to perish."

"You're a dreamer."

"Perhaps. But if we don't have our dreams, what do we have?"

She didn't give me an answer. Just put another chunk of wood on the fire, and stared at the flames.

Milana had a very nice cabin. It was one room, but there were three movable room dividers. A fireplace was on one end and a wood stove on the other. Two windows in each wall gave one a view of the island and the lake in all directions, and let in plenty of natural light. There were two doors, front and back. In one corner was a sink. The lavatory was an outhouse. There didn't appear to be any electricity or gas. I assumed the water came from a well, or maybe direct from the lake through a filtration system.

Yes, indeed, a very nice cabin. Rustic. But nice. I said as much to Milana.

"It belonged to a friend of my dad."

"You come here often?"

"Only once. But after... Well, when it was just myself, I decided to make it mine."

"Pretty safe. It will be less so when the lake freezes, but should still be alright."

"I didn't think about the lake freezing."

"A problem, but not a big one."

"Bill, will you stay with me? I don't think I can make it on my own."

"Let me sleep on it."

She nodded.

"And speaking of sleep, I'm rather tired," I said, while knocking the dottle out of my pipe.

"Yeah. Long day. You can sleep over there. Just pull one of the dividers over."

I let Bob and Bobbi out, and gave them each a bowl of kibble and fresh water. When they came in, I pulled the divider over, stripped down to my long johns, and crawled into the sleeping bag.

As for Milana's request, I already knew my answer.

2 November

I was up early, mostly due to Bob and Bobbi wanting to go out. I used the chamber pot. The balmy twenty-two outside was no encouragement to use the biffy.

There was a wardrobe that Milana was using as a pantry. I looked through it, found pancake mix, powdered milk, powdered eggs, and syrup. No butter. There was a bottle of vegetable oil. On a shelf by the sink, I found a cast iron frying pan and bowls. I was all set. Pancakes for breakfast.

Milana woke up while I was flipping the fourth flapjack.

"Smells good," she said. "Are you going to stay with me?"

"Yes. I need to go back and pick up some things, which I'll do this morning. I should be back in the afternoon."

She was all smiles. You'd think she'd won the lottery. From her perspective, maybe she had.

After breakfast, leaving the dogs in the cabin, we took the boat and paddled to shore. I got the van out of the garage and transferred quite a few of my things to the boat. I kept my revolvers, shotgun, and Thompson submachine gun. Never know when a feller will need a friend.

I gave her a walkie-talkie and showed her how to use it. "I'll call you so you can pick me up."

"Okay, Bill. I'll be waiting."

THE DRIVE DOWN to Circle Pines was uneventful. I passed a pickup and two SUVs heading north. In my opinion that was the right direction: out of the city.

I parked in front of my house just after nine. The morning sky was bright blue, but clouds were building out to the west. Which meant there was a good chance we'd be getting some snow. Being November, in Minnesnowta, it's bound to come sooner or later. And once the snow arrives, we'll be pretty much housebound. Kind of difficult to drive a car through three or four feet of the white stuff. Snowshoes, skis, and snowmobiles will be our only way to get around. Which meant it was a high priority to find one or more of those items so Milana and I could continue to scavenge.

I got out of the van, and waved to Sandy and Louise. They were carrying firewood in to our fearless leader's house.

Once inside my own place, I collected tools, clothes, a couple firearms, ammunition, my handloading ammunition supplies, knives, food, paper products, pots and pans, food for the dogs, and paper, pens, and pencils.

I looked over the pile of stuff, boxed it up, and hoped it would fit in the van. Then began ferrying the boxes to the old Ford.

Halfway between the front door and the van, Sam ventured out of his house next door and wanted to know what I was doing.

"What's it look like I'm doing?"

He scratched his head. "I'd say it looks like maybe you're leaving."

"I suppose it does."

"Are you?"

"I suppose I am."

"Kenny ain't gonna like it you takin' all that stuff," he said, while walking with me up to my open front door.

"It's my stuff. Not his."

"He doesn't see it that way."

"Well, that's just too bad. It was my stuff before Kenny was born, and it's staying my stuff."

"He's not going to like it."

I continued hauling and Sam left. Knowing there'd be trouble sooner rather than later, I took a revolver from the van and slipped it into my left parka pocket. For a less lethal option, I put my slungshot in the right pocket. Sufficiently armed, I headed back to the house.

Before That Day, slungshots were illegal. Mine's made out of rope tied in a Monkey's Paw Knot around a one and one-eighth inch steel ball bearing. That's three and a third ounces of nasty.

I picked up a box, walked out the door, and there was Kenny, big as a moose, with four of his buddies, standing between me and the van.

"Sam says you're leaving. Is that true?"

"It is."

"Go on and go, but the stuff stays."

I set the box down, and put my hand in my right parka pocket. "This is my stuff, Kenny. It was mine before I met you and it's going with me."

"Not how it works, Bill. You know that. We're a group and everything belongs to the group."

"Not in my world. We're all individuals and we all contribute so we all can continue to survive as individuals. Now, I suggest you leave and take your boys with you."

"No way. This is our stuff you're stealing."

"There's still plenty in the house. You're welcome to it."

"Uh-uh. All of it. You can go wearing the clothes on your back. Even this here van is ours."

I let out a big sigh. Two of Kenny's buddies turned to the van, reaching for boxes. The Thompson was in there and if they found it, I'd be in a deep pile of dog doo. Releasing the fiercest yell I could muster, I ran in low, and, before Kenny could react, swung the slungshot into his knee.

He screamed in pain and crashed to the ground. I stood, turning at the same time, twisting to the left. The slungshot slammed into the shoulder of one of Kenny's goons. He cried out in pain and fell down. I turned to my right and faced the other three. One guy had a great big kitchen knife in his hand. I took the revolver out of pocket and put a bullet between his feet. The guy dropped the knife and took off running. The other two dropped the boxes they'd taken from the van and joined their friend.

The rest of the community had come out to watch, and now they were all slowly backing away. All except for Jenny and Hank. Kenny, of course, was still on the ground cursing and moaning. The other guy I'd whacked was nowhere to be seen.

"You have room for us, Bill?" Hank asked.

"We'd like to come with you," Jenny added.

I thought over the past few weeks. They were perhaps the

best of the lot. After a moment, I nodded and told them to get their things.

THE TRIP back to the island was uneventful. Milana, in response to my call on the walkie-talkie, was waiting for us. She was very happy I'd brought friends.

After introductions, we got in the boat and paddled back to the island.

Hank and Jenny were a few years on either side of forty. They were followers, but followers with a fair amount of common sense. They weren't especially hard workers, but they weren't slackers either. Like most people I've known.

Hank and I dropped off the ladies and paddled back to get our belongings.

"I can see why you wanted to leave the group."

"It's not what you think, Hank."

"No?"

"No. She sees me in the same way she saw her father. And I'm not going to take advantage of that."

"If you say so, Bill. But personally…"

"Yeah. Maybe if I was younger."

It took four trips, but we got the stuff to the island and the van secured in the garage. The last thing I did before the final trip was to set traps to catch the gazillion squirrels and rabbits that were about.

Some of you might think that eating those little critters sounds revolting. But I'm here to tell you, that like most things we eat, they taste like chicken. Hopefully, in a day or two, we'll have plenty of fresh meat.

For supper that night, not wanting another meal spooned out of a can, I broke into my supply of dried beef and green beans. I had Jenny and Milana pound a half-pound of each into a chunky powder, and then mix the powder with some water. While they were doing that, I had Hank bring in more firewood and I mixed up a pancake batter from buckwheat flour, powdered eggs and milk, and baking soda. To which I added the reconstituted meat and veg. Once the fire was going in the wood stove, I made a pile of hearty and nutritious flapjacks.

In between mouthfuls of pancake, Hank and Jenny kept going on about the chances of the group we'd left surviving the winter.

"Without you, Bill," Jenny began, "Kenny's going to be hurting."

Hank added, "Never did see what he had against you. At least you know what you're doing. He shoulda listened to your advice."

I shrugged. "Water under the bridge. It's the four of us now."

Milana smiled at that.

The four of us. A new beginning. The question before us was, would we survive long enough to build a larger community to insure our long-term survival?

5 November

We've quickly fallen into a routine. Jenny and Milana maintain the Homefront, while Hank and I scavenge the surrounding area.

I know, I know. Readers of this journal, should there ever be any, who lived before That Day will decry our arrangement as sexist and will label me a male chauvinist pig. What I want you to know is that the arrangement was dictated by purely practical considerations.

Hank and Jenny are completely ignorant when it comes to firearms. They couldn't hit the side of the cabin with the muzzle of the firearm mere inches away from the siding.

Consequently, it seemed to me to make the most sense to pair up the women and leave them on the home front. They'd have the cabin as a defensive position should anyone make it out to the island. In addition, Milana was not gun shy and knew which end of the rifle was the business end. And when it comes right down to it, generally speaking, women are physically weaker than men. Therefore, it makes the most sense to give them the stronger defense position.

Jenny had no problems with the arrangement, and Milana eventually saw that it made the most sense. And that left Hank and I to do the scavenging.

In our brave new world, there isn't any time for sexism. Or any other -ism for that matter. Except pragmatism.

This world that we who survived woke up to is literally dog eat dog. And if the reports I've heard are the least bit true, it's also a world of people eating people. As I noted previously, the city is no place to be — if you want to survive.

6 November

Today was a bad day. One of those days you wish you could live over and make different choices. Have different outcomes. Unfortunately, life does not have a reset button. We must live with our decisions — both the good and the bad.

Things started innocently enough. Hank, Milana, and I paddled the boat to shore. I checked the traplines, and was delighted to see two rabbits and a couple squirrels in the traps. Our future supper I turned over to Milana, and watched her paddle back to the island. After she disappeared from view, Hank and I got the van, and I turned her east for the day's scavenging.

We were far enough out in the country that houses tended to be few and far and between. I turned off the main county road and headed north on Mountain Ash Road. Nice name, although there wasn't a mountain ash in sight. Just maples with an oak or poplar here and there.

A mile up the road, we came upon a row of five houses. They'd been there a while because the trees around the houses were quite large. Perhaps fifty years old. Across from them, on the other side of the road was a large field filled with dry, brown stalks of corn. The farmer probably sold off five lots for a big pile of cash. Of course, it probably wasn't doing him much good now.

I turned the van around in case we needed to make a fast exit. The middle house I figured would be the best bet. Others, if there had been others, had probably hit the end houses.

Hank, armed with a shotgun and a revolver, and I, with three revolvers, exited the van and made our way to what would hopefully be Ali Baba's treasure room.

While Hank stood at the end of the walk facing the house and keeping an eye out for potential trouble, I walked up to the front door. I found it locked, and signaled to Hank that he was to stay put while I went around back.

The place was a two-story bungalow, as were the others. Probably built by the same builder. The windows were intact, which was a good sign. Being the destructive creatures that we are, windows are one of the first things to get broken.

I rounded the corner and mounted the three steps to the back door. At some point it had been forced, which meant that it had either been cleaned out or it was someone's home.

After a moment's deliberation, I stepped to the side and pushed open the door, while calling out, "Is anybody home?" If it was someone's home, they might have set up a trap, which is why I didn't want to be standing in front of the door.

Having gotten no answer to my first query, I called out again asking if anyone was home. After all, just because no one answered that didn't mean someone wasn't there. When silence answered my second inquiry, I walked in making sure my short-barreled revolver was in my hand. Six rounds of .357 magnum hollow points will take down pretty much anything other than an elephant, and I probably wasn't going to find one in the house.

I was standing in the kitchen. My eyes slowly took in the room. There was a layer of dust on the counters, table, and chairs. The linoleum tiled floor had a couple faint footprints. I kneeled down and touched them. There were the faintest traces of loamy earth greeting my fingertips. My guess was several weeks had passed since whoever had left the prints had visited.

I moved from the kitchen to the dining room, which was connected to the living room. Again, there was no sign of a recent visitation. I checked the bedrooms and bathroom. Nothing.

There was the upstairs and the basement, but I was feeling pretty confident no one was home, or had been for quite some time. I walked through the living room, entered the small four-season porch, opened the front door, and waved for Hank to join me.

He trotted up the walk and entered. "I assume no one's here," he said.

"I haven't checked upstairs, yet, nor the basement. Start going through things here, and I'll check upstairs."

"Sure thing."

I stood against the wall, separating the dining room from the kitchen, turned the doorknob and pulled the door open to the stairs going to the second floor. The door swung open and no booby traps went off. So far, so good. I slowly mounted the stairs. No booby traps. No one shooting at me. No one swinging a club at me. All was good.

The second floor was small. Perhaps only half of the footprint the main floor. Whoever had owned the house used the space for storage and there were lots of goodies. Enough to fill up the van. I went back downstairs to see how Hank was doing, and that's when I realized we'd walked into a trap.

There was Hank. And a man pointing a pistol at his head. From the kitchen, stepped another man holding a shotgun. He said, "Put your guns down nice and slow. After all, I don't think you want to see your buddy's brains splattered all over the walls and windows."

Hank was looking at me. "Don't take too long, Bill. I'd like to see Jenny again."

"Yeah, Bill," the guy by the kitchen said. "Don't take too long, or your friend won't be seeing his woman again in this life."

I would have loved to have slapped the grin off his face. This was the classic lose-lose situation. If I put down my gun, then the yahoos would shoot us, take our guns and ammo, and the van. If I killed the guy by the kitchen door, then Hank was probably going to die. Perhaps not. We might get lucky. Hank might throw him off balance, allowing me to dispatch the guy. Or I might get in a lucky shot. Might.

In the end, the choice was pretty simple. It was Hank and me; or it was the yahoos, and fifty-fifty about Hank.

Now you might be wondering why I excluded possibility of the yahoos letting us live. Without going into detail, all I'll say is past experience, if you survive it, it is a great teacher.

While it took me a fair amount of time to write all this out, the actual thinking process was no more than a second or two at the most.

Without saying a word, I raised my empty left hand and arm, and held my right arm and the revolver out to my side, in the general direction of the guy by the kitchen door. Slowly I squatted until I could place my left knee on the floor.

Then I fired two bullets at the guy by the door. At the same time, I heard an explosion, saw the guy let go of his shotgun, and fall back against the wall. I brought the revolver around and took aim at the other guy. Hank was falling to the floor, and the muzzle of the pistol was moving in my direction. I squeezed the trigger on my handgun, and kept squeezing, until the hammer fell on a spent cartridge.

My ears were ringing so loud I couldn't hear anything. I scrambled over to Hank. His eyes were open, blood was forming an ever larger pool, and I felt no pulse.

It was not our lucky day. Fate had clearly dealt us a bad hand.

The guy who'd killed Hank had taken a bullet right through the sternum. Another had caught his right shoulder. I got up and walked over to the other guy. He was dead. Both bullets catching him in the chest.

I reloaded and then wrapped Hank in a sheet I took off of the bed and put his body in the van.

On the way back, all I could think of was Jenny. How would she take it? Many people are fragile these days. And why not? We've all lost everything that once mattered. Every day is a struggle to survive, and then pile on more loss, and, well, some people just go over the edge. And I don't know that I fault them for that.

What I did know for sure was that I didn't want to be the one to tell Jenny the bad news.

9 November

Jenny won't talk to me and will barely bring herself to look at me. When I broke the news to her, she attacked me and damn near scratched my eyes out. A bucket of ice water dumped on her by Milana ended the hysterics, and brought on the sobbing. That went on for hours, to be replaced by her staring at the wall.

The ground is too hard to dig a proper grave, so we ended up burning his body. Jenny screaming at me that we weren't putting Hank in the "goddamn lake". That was on the seventh.

Yesterday, I went off by myself all day. Well, I wasn't completely by myself because I took Bob and Bobbi with me. I felt badly about leaving Milana with Jenny, but she was okay with it. Agreeing that it might be best if I was gone for a while.

I did some scavenging, but mostly just smoked my pipe and thought about life as it now is. And to tell the truth, I was thinking mighty hard that the dead were the lucky ones.

At one of the places I went through, I found a nice wood box that I brought back for Jenny to put Hank's cremains in. I got no thanks, but then I didn't really expect any. Perhaps someday in the future she'll be able to thank me. Maybe even forgive me. Perhaps. Maybe.

Today, Milana, the dogs, and I went out to do some scavenging. Even with our small numbers, there is still a good deal of competition for goods. So scavenging is pretty much a daily affair. And because of that competition, it isn't safe to be alone. Nor is it overly safe even if you have companions, as recent events reminded me. Granted I was alone yesterday, but I didn't want to push my luck. Tempt fate, as it were.

We found a cache of canned and packaged food, and a big supply of craft items. But other than that, the pickings were slim.

At what turned out to be the last place of the day, Milana slipped on a patch of ice and fell on some broken glass from a window. The problem wasn't the torn jeans and scraped knee, it was the shard of glass that went through her glove and impaled her left hand.

I pulled out the glass, cleaned the pebbles out of the knee scrape, sprayed on antiseptic, and bandaged her up. We also called it a day, and I drove us back to the lakeside development.

We'd hidden the boat behind a house under a pile of tarps, and after emptying the van of goods and parking it in the garage, we dragged the boat back to the lake, put in our loot, and paddled back to the island.

What we found was not pretty. And the note on the table explained it all. Jenny, having "lost everything a second time", decided she did not have the will to go on living. She killed herself using the shotgun. And that is a very messy way to go.

Milana broke down and sobbed her heart out. I had her sit behind one of the screens by the fireplace, while I cleaned up the mess and "buried" Jenny's body in the lake. She probably wouldn't have liked what I did, but smoke and fire draws attention and I didn't want another big bonfire just in case someone had noticed the Hank's pyre or our heat and cook smoke.

After the funeral chores, I made supper: canned soup and saltines. Not fancy, but I was tired.

Milana said nothing throughout our meal, and only said, "goodnight", when she went to bed.

Sometimes, in fact, fairly often, I wish I'd died in whatever it was that struck down everyone. Being a survivor is very hard work, and some days I don't think it's worth the effort.

13 November

I've stayed near the cabin playing nurse to Milana. But I don't make a good nurse because her hand is infected and doesn't look good. I'd say it even looks kind of puffy. So much for spray on antiseptic. And on top of everything, her skin feels rather clammy. She probably needs a doctor or a trip to the ER. Good luck with finding a doctor or an ER.

14 November

Not good. Things are definitely not good. Milana's pain is worse. She has a high fever. The wound hasn't healed and her hand is definitely swollen. If she has sepsis, there is nothing I can do for her. I don't have the medical knowledge, nor the necessary medicine. I'd perform a field amputation, but not having the training and only a book to go by, she'd probably bleed to death. And even then, there is no guarantee she'd live. She could still succumb to infection.

God, I hate this world.

15 November

From bad to worse. Delirium has set in. The wound is oozing pus. She is going to die. I can no longer kid myself that she's going to pull through.

So I ask myself, do I let her live until nature takes its course? Or do I become the angel of mercy and end her suffering? Can I play God? In this brave new world, am I allowed to be the arbiter of life and death?

I was brought up in a nominally Christian home, and I have extensive religious training, which is why I balk at stepping into God's shoes. After all, killing another person is murder.

On the other hand, is it truly a sin to hasten a person to the freedom that ultimately awaits us all? Especially if that end is imminent and the person is suffering?

There are those people who want just one more breath no matter what their condition is. But why? Why suffer when freedom awaits?

Isn't a death well died, even if by my own hand, or by the aid of someone else, just as important as a life well lived?

And what if Milana comes through this with organ or brain damage? She's burning up with fever and I can't get it to break. If she isn't one hundred percent, she will die anyway — and be a burden in the process. A burden in a world where burdens are a liability.

Our ancient ancestors left the sick and the old behind as they followed the herds of animals that were their source of food. Were they cruel to do so? Or did the survival of the group outweigh the survival of the individual? And aren't we in the same position today? Even our primate cousins do the same.

There is no place for the weak in a world that is dog eat dog and every day is a battle to see the next day.

I've spent the day nursing her as best as I can. I've lost valuable days of getting food and fuel. The snow is late, but it will come. This is Minnesnowta. The snow and bitter cold will settle in.

Do I have the right to take her life? Take it so she no longer suffers and I can continue to survive? And if I do have the right to take her life, can I live with myself if I do?

16 November

The boat rests where I first found it: on the sand bar. This is my last trip. I've taken everything of value from the cabin and stored it in one of the houses.

Snow is falling, and the wind is picking up. We could be in for a doozy of a snowstorm.

I take one last look at the island. The flames are clearly visible now. Milana's funeral pyre. The place she went to for safety will be one of everlasting rest.

She was a beautiful young woman, with a good head on her shoulders. The very person needed to rebuild all that we've lost. But she won't be with us, those of us who continue to survive. All because of a cut. I just hope she forgives me.

The van is loaded to overflowing. I take one last look, wipe my eyes, and set off to find a new home. The snow is really coming down. The winter won't be easy, but come spring even nature starts over.

Author - Kelly Marshall

Most writers will tell you they have a passion for words. I'm no exception. From the time I could read, my face was stuck in a book. I've always loved adventure and books were my ticket out of teen boredom into of world of adventure from the Alaska wilderness to the sweltering jungles of Vietnam, to the colorful world of the Caribbean. As an adult, I worked as a radio announcer for many years and enjoyed the heck out of that. It was a fun, exciting career, but eventually, I came home to my real love...books. I write murder mysteries and invite you to learn more about them on my website: http://www. kellymarshallbooks.com/

Blog: https://kellymarshallnews.wordpress.com/
Twitter: @kellymarshall48
Facebook: https://www.facebook.com/KellyMarshallBooks/

MOONLIGHT

SWIM

BY:

KELLY MARSHALL

7

Moonlight Swim

Kelly Marshall

Blood boiling—I'd heard that expression all my life and until I saw my lover kissing another woman, I had never truly understood how descriptive those words proved to be. As rain pelted my face and mixed with tears, my heart pounded in my rib cage like a jack-hammer. An insufferable headache exploded on the right side of my head leaving me dizzy, weak, unsteady on my feet. The persistent drum beat in my head synced in rhythm with the throbbing of my heart. I sank against my car door to keep from pitching over on the pavement.

From my vantage point across the street, I watched them through his large bay window. Jeff embraced her again. Even from this distance in the cascading rain, I could see she was thin and model-perfect with long blonde hair that framed a fair face. His hands slithered down her back then rested on her hips and pulled her against him. Full of driving passion, we had also clung together in a full body embrace and ground our hunger against each other until we ripped off our clothes and satiated our hunger in his bed, on the floor, and in one mad moment, on the dining room table. Now, he was groping this woman just as he had me so many times. How easily he surrendered our love for the craving of another.

How long had he been betraying me? He thought I was still in San Diego on a business trip. But I had resolved issues early with our parent company and I took an earlier flight home. I had been excited, hoping we could steal away on a quiet trip to the coast. The pristine beaches in San Diego made me hunger for sand and wind and lazy mornings without an alarm clock.

I eased open my car door and collapsed in the driver's seat. I shut my eyes and tried to close out the scene in the window that transfixed me, but I could not. How brazen he was to perform this tryst in front of his neighbors for all to see! I was on a first name basis with most of them. I imagined how they would look at me in pity and whisper, "I wonder if she knows." I wanted to storm across the street and through the door to confront the man that had whispered he loved me for the past three years. Sick at heart, I didn't have the energy for the fight. Across the street, the living room went dark. I started my car, pulled away from the curb, and headed to my studio apartment.

I didn't sleep. I couldn't. Images I abhorred replayed over and over in my enraged, crazed brain. At seven a.m., I called in sick via email. My boss Kevin would be cool with that. Besides, it gave him a paper trail. I feigned possible food poisoning and wrote I would spare him the ugly details. LOL.

For breakfast, I downed a bloody Mary, then another, and another. After all, it was a healthy meal, I told myself, lots of tomato juice and celery. I fell into a stupor sometime after lunch and slept until six. When I woke, there were two messages from Jeff. At first, my heart raced in anticipation, then anger rode in on a very dark horse. Hate crystallized in my heart, and I wanted my revenge. Hands clenched, I forced myself not to call him back. I refused to listen to the voice mail. The texts were harder to ignore. I caught sight of just a couple of words like missing you. Where are you? I deleted them before I could sneak a peek. Hungover and exhausted, I fell into a coma-like slumber again.

I pretended sickness for another day, took a couple of Xanax and read an excellent book by Northwest Author, Gregg Olson. The well-written novel held my interest for a while, but the meds took me down the rabbit hole again where I floated into unconsciousness. A loud pounding roused me and forced me out of bed. I knew it had to be him. I made my numb legs work and staggered to the bathroom. One-two-three, I swished around some mouthwash and spit, wiped my face with a towelette, then ripped a brush through my hair. I slow-walked to answer the traitor at my door.

I yawned as I opened the door and feigned a loving attitude. "Hello, Honey."

"Where have you been?" he demanded and pushed his way into my apartment. "I've been worried sick about you. Have you checked your phone? I've called several times. For God's sake. You look a mess."

"That's what food poisoning will do to you. I've alternated between the loo and bed for the past couple of days. I've been very miserable."

"Why didn't you call me?" he insisted. "My poor baby." He stepped forward and folded me into his arms. My body was as tight as a stretched rubber band, so I took a couple of deep breaths to force my muscles to relax. He sniffed my hair. "You could use a bath. Let me help you."

"No really, Jeff. My stomach is still doing flip-flops. I'd feel terrible if I pitched my cookies all over you. That's really quite unromantic. Let me get well, and I'll give you a call tomorrow."

He whined. "I haven't seen you in days. I've been lonely."

My spine snapped back into a locked position once again. More deep breaths.

"Honey, you sound like you're having a hard time breathing."

If you only you knew, you bastard. "You're right. I am going to turn on my humidifier and get more moisture in the room. Go home, Jeff. I need some me time to get myself together. I feel yucky. You're right. I need a long, quiet bath to soak this aching body."

"Well, I don't like leaving you in this condition."

"I don't want to make you sick. I'll just give you a little peck, here." My lips barely brushed his cheek. A lightning thought exploded in my mind like a loud firebomb on the 4th of July. I pictured sinking my teeth into his cheek and ripping it open.

"Ok, Babe. Take another day, but I want to see you soon. We've got some catching up to do." He pulled me close to him and pressed his excitement against me. "See what I mean? You've been gone too long."

I teased him. "I just can't wait. We need to have a very special reunion. Something unique that neither one of us will ever forget."

He paused at the door, looked deep into my eyes, then leaned down and kissed me full on the lips.

"I could make you sick."

"The last I heard food poisoning wasn't contagious."

Of course, it isn't. What was I thinking?

He instructed, "Call me as soon as you are feeling better."

I closed the door behind him. Hmm. Yes, we do need a special reunion. I sat down on my couch, opened my computer, and looked for a remote spot where we could be totally alone.

I called Jeff on Thursday. "I know the perfect place for us to share a romantic weekend. I located a cabin rental on Lake Crescent. A wonderful little place, quiet, cozy, and remote where we could be alone, relax, rejuvenate."

"Isn't that the place where they found an old car in the water a while back?"

I'll admit I was surprised by Jeff's long-term memory. A number of years ago, a submerged car was found below Lake

Crescent in Clallam County. It was a decades old mystery that was finally solved when volunteer divers and a National Park Service search team spotted a submerged car one-hundred-sixty feet below the surface. The car proved to be the 1927 Chevrolet driven by Russell and Blanch Warren who disappeared July 3, 1929. Searchers surmise the couple missed the narrow curve that hugged the lake shoreline and their car hurtled into the water and sank.

Lake Crescent—dark and deep. The official depth is measured at 624 feet, making it the second deepest lake in Washington. Measurements of more than 1,000 feet have been rumored by the locals for years. Six-hundred-twenty-four feet or a thousand feet…it would be deep enough.

"Yup, that's the one," I answered.

"That's a long way to go for just a getaway."

"Just a couple of hours. Come on. Don't be a sourpuss." I lowered my voice and gave it my best sexy timbre. "We can go skinny dipping."

"Are you freaking kidding me? Nothing like cold lake water to dampen a man's sex drive."

"You're selling me short, Jeff. You know I can warm things up for you."

He laughed. "Yes, my love, you certainly can do that. Book it. I'll go."

"Perfect."

I hung up and dialed the number for Lake Crescent Cabins. The ad promised a rustic setting with seclusion a guarantee. The rental included a one-bedroom cabin, canoe, rowboat, and basic fishing gear, along with linen and a full kitchen.

I scheduled for the entire week, and told the proprietor it would be a single occupancy. "I am a writer and need complete quiet to finish my novel."

I imagined him a grizzled old cuss because he just grunted a response and asked for my credit card information.

"There's a seventy-five-dollar cleaning fee too."

"No problem," I assured him.

"I have a lock box next to the door with the key inside. The security code is 7545. When you leave, put the key in it and re-enter the code. It will lock."

After hanging up, I thought I needed a celebratory drink, so I fixed a vodka martini. One became two and I climbed between the sheets to delve into another Gregg Olsen book. His mysteries were to die for.

I sneaked away to Lake Crescent a day ahead of time to get things in order. I had done my homework and brought with me arsenic, compliments of my local hardware store. I told them I needed to get rid of some rats…well at least one big one. The cabin had two boats, one a regular small rowboat for fishing and the other, a charming turquoise canoe. Just right for two lovers to take on a moonlight swim. I was sure, plied with enough alcohol incentive, I could convince Jeff to shed his clothes. I made the long drive back to Seattle so that Jeff and I could make the drive together on our romantic get-a-way.

Jeff arrived at my place with wine and flowers. I give him credit for that. It almost gave me pause about my plan to get the ultimate revenge, but then I thought about the blonde in the bay window, and decided, nope, he needed to pay.

Jeff complained as I steered my car onto the unpaved road into the property. "We're definitely in the boondocks. Some-body could get lost out here." We bounced along the rutted road, our bodies swaying back and forth as I struggled to steer clear of huge potholes dug out by relentless winter rains in Washington.

"There's only one way in and one way out, Jeff. Unless we head out hiking without a compass, I doubt we're going to get lost."

"How do you know this is the only road?"

Well, crap. He was actually paying attention to what I was

saying. "The owner commented on it when I contacted him for the rental."

He nodded in approval as we pulled in front of the basic wood cabin.

"Rustic and remote the brochure promised."

"I'd rather be at Snoqualmie Falls, Babe, sitting in a hot tub with a bar fridge in my room, but hey, if this floats your boat, I'm game."

"We're going to have an experience of a lifetime. I promise."

We dumped our luggage in the bedroom and transferred our food from the cooler to the refrigerator.

Like serving a prisoner on death row, I fixed Jeff his last dinner and went all out—fillet mignon, roasted red potatoes, salad, asparagus dipped in olive oil, sprinkled with parmesan cheese and garlic and baked for fifteen minutes. Perfection! The meal was complete with lit candles, Cabernet Sauvignon for dinner and a "special" lavender margarita concoction for our ride in the turquoise canoe.

Jeff's eyes opened wide as I sat down in barely-there lingerie for our feast. "Well, maybe I should have packed my little blue pills."

I gave him my best husky-throated answer. "I'm the only medication you'll need, dear. I promise."

Dinner was memorable with lots of toe play under the table and light butterfly touches to his neck whenever I got up from the table to fetch forgotten items like butter and Heinz 57. Yeah, I know. Steak shouldn't need it, but Jeff was a midwestern boy and poured the sauce on like ketchup on fries. He glanced at me often. "I'm so damned glad I have you. After three years, you're still as hot as the moment I laid eyes on you."

I played coy. "You never desired another? Not even once."

"Not even once."

LIAR!

My lips parted in a smile that I hoped was seductive because my damn jaw was balled so tight, it was close to popping out of joint. "Well, aren't I blessed with that rare faithful lover."

"Yes, Ma'am." He popped another piece of steak in his mouth and masticated it like cow chewing her cud. Steak juice rolled down his chin.

"Here, let me get that for you." I dabbed the dribble before it dripped.

Jeff gave me a goofy grin. "I say we try that bear skin rug before we go for a dip. I'll light the fire."

My Boy Scout did it right with paper, wood chips and teepeed split logs. Soon he had a roaring fire. "I wish I had music, Babe, but here goes." He did his best Chippendale impression and tossed each article of clothing across the room as he peeled out of his jeans, Scotch plaid shirt, and Hanes underwear. He added a flourish at the end by taking one of his socks and rubbing it back and forth across his butt like he was drying his backside with a towel. He spread his legs wide in a cowboy stance, put his hands on his hips, and said, "Your turn."

I did my best Demi Moore strip tease, and it was clear from his response that he appreciated my efforts. Whoever touted bearskin rugs as a sexy place to make love must have been a man in the traditional missionary position. My skin did not appreciate the bear's rough hide on my backside one bit. I got through our coupling by moaning periodically, running my acrylics down his back and leaving scratches, and by staring at the massive buck head mounted on the wall. I imagined my lover's head there, but, well, that would be just too messy.

He wanted to shower afterward, but I insisted. "No, Jeff. We're going on a moonlight swim and make this our most memorable date ever. I've got everything ready. Put on that robe, and look, there are slippers on the floor for you." Part of my preplanning had been to pack a very large picnic basket with my homemade bottle of lavender margaritas, plastic flutes, soap, and towels. I laid the Cabernet Sauvignon on top of the towels, then slipped into my robe and slippers and asked Jeff to grab the basket and follow me. My love-whipped boy did as I asked, and we trooped out into the dark with me holding a battery-powered lantern.

We worked well as a team and soon had the canoe and oars off the rack and on the ground. We packed our provisions, and I told him, "Let's pull it to the water, I'll climb in, then you push it out just aways, and you scramble in. It might be better if you took your slippers off and put them in the boat first." Like Mommy's compliant child, he did as I asked, and in moments we were drifting over Lake Crescent under a raging super moon that reflected in the black water. We floated in silence, taking in the sheer magic of the night.

"You're right, honey, this is our best date ever. Thank you for making tonight so great."

"I think we need a nightcap. Let's open up the lavender margaritas."

"That sounds weird. I've never heard of those."

"I think you'll like them. A good friend showed me how to make them when I went on a girl weekend to the coast. They're yummy."

Jeff opened the basket, found the plastic glasses, and opened the twist top bottle of margaritas. He poured a glass and handed it to me.

I shook my head. "No, love, I've got a taste for more Cabernet. Take a big swig of the drink then hand me the wine."

He rocked the boat as he juggled his glass and the bottle of wine. "Here." He handed me the Napa Valley Red. "Let's toast." I raised the bottle in salud as he did with his glass. Then he brought the glass to his lips, sniffed it first, shouted, "Down the hatch," and gulped the entire flute.

"Have another," I encouraged him. "They're small glasses. You won't get a good buzz on unless you have three or four."

"It has a weird taste, babe, a little sour."

"Trust me. I had a whole wild weekend on that stuff. It's got a kick on the tail end of it."

He did as I asked and downed four.

The wind chilled me with goosebumps so I pulled my robe closer and yanked the belt tighter.

An owl hooted his presence high in a tree, then I saw his dark shadow swoop out over the water like a predator going for the kill.

I waited for Jeff to say something. Water lapped at the canoe. Finally, he said, "Honey, this stuff is not settling well on my stomach. I feel like I'm gonna puke my dinner up."

"If you do, lean over the side. I don't want to have to clean barf out of the bottom of the boat. The owner is charging me a cleaning fee. I don't want him adding more to it."

Even with the brilliant moon, it was hard to see Jeff's face, but I heard his sudden rolfing and the volcanic vomit hit the water. The canoe tipped precariously as he leaned over the side.

"Carefully, honey. Don't capsize the boat."

He vomited again and again, gagging on his emesis. He gasped for breath, tried to say something, and reached out a hand to me.

"Sweetheart, you sound so miserable. What can I do to help?" I extended my hand to him, but my fingers never quite touched his.

I smelled shit. Wow. Arsenic worked quickly.

I saw him grasp his throat and heard him vomit again, then strangle. His head cracked against the bow of the boat as he collapsed backwards. Silence.

"Jeff?" I whispered. "Honey, are you all right?" Water lapped at the side of the canoe.

I fetched a plastic kitchen bag from the basket and felt along the bottom of the boat for his plastic glass. I found it mired in his shit. I gagged and tossed my own cookies over the side of the boat. I breathed deep and sucked in the frosty air to calm my gastric cramping. After the pitching and rolling of my stomach went away, I cleaned the bottles of wine and margaritas with Clorox wipes and put them in the plastic bag. I swished his plastic glass in the frigid water, then tossed it in with the bottles and tied the bag shut.

Slipping out of my robe, and without pausing to think, I rolled over the side of the canoe, and slithered into the arctic water. The cold slammed my body, and for a moment I struggled to breathe. Seizing the side of the boat I pushed it down, and the canoe flipped over. Jeff rolled into the water with a splash. The ghostly shape of his white robe faded as he drifted deeper into the lake's depths.

I managed to roll the canoe upright, but water lined the bottom, and I worried it would join Jeff on Lake Crescent's inky bottom. As the wicker basket bobbed in the lake, I clasped the handle and after several tries was able to throw it into the boat. Though weighted down by heavy glass bottles, the plastic bag hadn't sunk yet, so I pitched it also into the canoe. One of the oars floated by and I grabbed it and tossed it in as well. Now, to get back in the damn boat before hypothermia did me in. My teeth chattered so violently, they sounded like a pair of clacking teeth popular in Halloween stores. I hadn't planned this caper as thoroughly as I should have. Time after time, I thrust my leg over the side of the canoe to no avail. I floated toward the center of the canoe and pulled it down as if I were going to overturn it again. But this time, I clenched the boat's center seat and flung my now bleeding leg over the side. With one giant effort, I pitched myself into the boat. I landed on the wicker basket and pain exploded in my head. It felt like every part of my body was either bleeding, scraped, or torn. I drifted for a few minutes to let the pain subside. Eventually, I sat in the bottom of the boat, and, taking oar in hand, I inched towards the cabin.

I shook violently as I pushed the paddle through the water, but stroke by stroke, I finally made it back to shore. I don't know where the strength came from—every breath was tortuous, every pull on my arm felt like it was being ripped from the socket. Despite the agony, I hauled the canoe ashore and stumbled to the cabin. Oh, dear God, the fire still had some fading embers under the grate. I added more paper, more wood chips, and more split logs. I wrapped myself in a blanket from the bed and collapsed before the fire. The searing heat finally stopped my body's shaking. When my skin warmed and took on a rosy hue, I tossed Jeff's clothes into the fire and watched while the flames enveloped them. For one brief moment, my heart clenched as his pants collapsed beneath the grate into a pile of ashes. Jeff was finally and forever gone. Light from the fireplace emitted a soft glow, but dark shadows clung to the corners of the room and in my soul. I had exacted my pound of flesh, my revenge. Prayers died on my lips and the shadows seemed to draw closer. What do I do now?

I passed into an exhausted sleep, and when I awakened, the ennui had passed. I got busy and burned the rest of Jeff's belongings. I shoveled the ashes into two ten-gallon paint cans and carried them to the shore. I had hoped to row the cans out into the center of the lake in the skiff and dump them there. Then my plan would be fait accompli. Behind me, I heard the drone of a car engine.

An old red Chevy 350 chugged onto the property and stopped in front of the cabin. Who could be here? A grizzled, white-haired man dressed in black coveralls emerged from the truck. He put his hand over his brow perhaps to shade his eyes from the brilliant morning sun and peered in my direction. He waved and shouted, "Miss Russell? Is that you?"

Well, hell. It must be the old coot that owned the property. He had promised me seclusion. What the hell! The last thing I needed was that old codger questioning why I was dumping gallons of ash into his pristine lake.

I stashed the buckets behind a tree and rushed towards him before he could make his way to the edge of the lake.

"Yeah, that's me. And you are?"

"Arnold Gaspar, owner of this here property."

I looked into his unfriendly eyes. "Something wrong?"

His rough voice sounded like he gargled marbles for breakfast. "Couple of things. It's pretty quiet here at night and some neighbors thought you might have had some trouble last night."

"What kind of trouble?"

"They thought someone may have been out on the water after dark. They heard a bunch of splashing around. Stuff like that. They were going to call the sheriff. They were worried someone might be in trouble."

Crap. I need to clamp this down right now.

"Well, as a matter of fact, Mr. Gaspar, I did take the canoe out for a bit. It was such a beautiful moonlit night. I wanted to enjoy the sheer beauty of it. It was quite soul cleansing, actually."

"Were you out there alone?"

"Yes, remember I told you, this was a writing week for me. Perhaps, the splashing they heard was me trying to catch one of the oars. It toppled overside when I was putting my cooler in the canoe." I gave him my best lost little girl look. "I'm so sorry, I was clumsy. At one point, I thought I had it and was fishing for it with the other oar, but I had to give it up because I was worried I would lose the other one and then I'd be up the creek without a —well you know the rest."

Gaspar cleared his throat. "Ma'am, that was a foolish thing to do last night. Going out alone. Didn't anyone ever tell you about water safety rules? Now, I'll have to charge you for that oar."

"Absolutely, sir. I can pay you now, if you'd like."

"I've got your card on file. I'll charge it when I get back to the office."

I breathed easier. The lost little girl look worked every time. "You said there were two things."

"Yeah. We get bad cell coverage way out here, so I didn't figure you'd heard. It's nice and sunny now, but there's a real bad weather front rolling down from Canada. Electricity most likely will go out so you should be prepared. There's battery-operated lanterns in the kitchen cupboards, and plenty of wood for a fire, but you might have to rough it through a cold night."

"When is the front expected to be over us?"

"KOMO Radio says by nightfall."

"Hmm. You've given me food for thought, Mr. Gaspar. I just might get my things together and head home. That's not a problem for you, is it?"

He looked down at the ground. "Well, I reckon I can give you a credit. For a few nights."

"Tell you what, don't bother with that. I enjoyed my time here, and I don't want you to pay for the whims of Mother Nature. Let's call it even, and I'll come back some other time and spend a few days."

His eyes softened and his lips drew back into a brown-stained toothy grin. "That's mighty nice of you. It's been a tough year. I'll take you up on that. Next time you come, I'll give you the credit. How about that?"

"Deal."

"Well, I'll leave you to get your stuff packed, Miss Russell. Have a safe trip back to Seattle."

"Thank you, Mr. Gaspar."

The old Chevy belched out black smoke as he turned the truck around and rumbled back down the road.

I expelled a huge sigh.

I hurried to the boat rack and dragged the small skiff to the shore and placed the two large cans of ashes in the rear of the boat. Despite Gaspar's weather warnings, I had to get rid of these ashes; otherwise, they'd just clump up along the edge of the lake

146

and leave more questions for the nosey neighbors. It was a cumbersome job and I soaked myself up to my knees getting the cans loaded and the skiff pushed out enough into the water for me to climb in and get a good pull on the oars.

I rowed to a more remote part of the lake and slipped into a cove out of sight of any cabins. After removing the lids, I slowly poured small portions of ashes into the water, then rowed further and released more. It was an arduous and dirty job, but I finally completed the task. I rinsed out the cans, capped them, then rowed back to shore.

I gathered my luggage, food, and garbage, including the empty paint cans, and dumped it all into the trunk of my car. I did one final search through the cabin to make sure there was no trace of me or Jeff.

As I drove away, tension ebbed from my body. I could breathe again; the tremor in my muscles eased, and the four-hundred-pound gorilla sitting on my chest for the past week got up and loped away. I stopped in a back alley in Port Angeles and dropped the paint buckets and garbage in a dumpster. When I got home, I shredded all pictures of Jeff. Finit. Done. Or so I thought.

Six months of chastity is a long time in the life of a thirty-year-old woman. I joined an online dating site and picked a blue-eyed babe with muscles down to there. (And yes, there too.) Younger than me, of course; you can count on their virility at that age. We sent pictures of hearts and flowers to indicate our interest. Kevin and I clicked in all ways. On our first date he broke my period of abstinence. After that, what followed was months of dates at least three times a week, two of which ended up at his place or mine. One night after a particularly lovely evening, I got up to refresh myself in the bathroom. While washing my face, I heard the familiar ringtone of his cell. I looked down on the floor where he had left his clothes before showering. His iPhone lay half out of his pants pocket. The ringing stopped for a minute, then rang again. Should I?

I couldn't stop myself. I picked up the phone and thumbed in his access code. Kevin was very trusting with me. He was such a boy. I slid the bar across and a woman's picture flooded the screen. Hot, blonde, and only in her underwear. Her voice demanded to know, "Kevin, where the hell are you?"

I hung up, then placed his phone on the floor next to his trousers. I went back to the sink and finished my toilette. When I walked back into the bedroom, Kevin sat up in bed, his eyes disoriented from sleep, his hair like an eggbeater had twirled it into a bird's nest. "I'm ready for a repeat."

I glided over to the bed, laid down, and cuddled close to him. "You know, darling, I was thinking. I know the perfect place for a weekend get-a-way. It's this cozy, secluded cabin on the shores of Lake Crescent. I'd love for us to go on a moonlight swim."

Author - Caleb Pirtle III

Caleb Pirtle III lives in the present but prefers the past. He is the author of more than eighty-five books, including the Ambrose Lincoln noir-thriller series: *Secrets of the Dead, Conspiracy of Lies, Night Side of Dark,* and *Place of Skulls,* all set against the backdrop of World War II. His *Lonely Night to Die* features three noir thrillers following the exploits of a rogue agent who has fled the CIA, takes the missions no one else wants, and knows he is expendable.

His award-winning Boom Town Saga includes *Back Side of a Blue Moon, Bad Side of a Wicked Moon, and Lost Side of An Orphan's Moon.* The stories involve a con man who comes to a dying East Texas town during the Great Depression and drills for oil. Greed, money, and murder always follow the riches of oil.

He has published three acclaimed narrative nonfiction works, *Gamble in the Devil's Chalk* about the controversial Giddings oilfield, Never Afraid, Never A Doubt: The Legacy of a Hall of Fame Basketball Coach, and a coffee-table art book on The American Cowboy.

Pirtle has written two teleplays: "Gambler V: Playing for

Keeps," a mini-series for CBS television, and "The Texas Rangers," a TV movie for John Milius and TNT television.

He was a police reporter for *The Fort Worth Star-Telegram* and served as the first travel editor for *Southern Living Magazine*. He was editorial director for Dockery House, a custom Dallas publisher.

Links:
Website: https://www.calebandlindapirtle.com
Facebook: https://www.facebook.com
MeWe: https://mewe.com/i/calebpirtle1
Twitter: @CalebPirtle

Hemingway's
Boat

By:
Caleb Pirtle III

8

Hemingway's Boat
Caleb Pirtle III

Part 1

ADAM GRAY SAW the small wooden rowboat bobbing in the distant waves like a cork in a crystal bowl of dark rum, or maybe it was bathtub gin.

Probably spilled by some drunk.

Wandered in late.

Didn't belong.

Who'll stop him?

Why stop him?

He brought the rum.

The waves were streaked with splashes of red and yellow by a late afternoon sunset. The tides pulled at his bare feet as if they had fingers. The surf turned the color turquoise awash with foam as it came rolling madly out of the Atlantic.

Reminded Gray of a woman he once knew.

Tanned.

Sultry.

Tempestuous.

Carried a hammerless Colt pocket pistol.

Didn't know she had it until she shot him.

Could have killed him.

Didn't want to kill him.

Wanted to make a point.

Did.

Gray stopped going to the Speakeasy where she danced.

A week later, she found him sitting on the backseat of a trolley car in Brooklyn, reading a newspaper, reading his column, and shot him again.

"Why?" he asked as he slipped to the floor.

"You don't come see me no more," she said.

"You killed me for sure this time," he said.

"Tried to," she said. "Aimed a little too high."

She shrugged and stepped down into the night.

Gray was a damn good reporter.

He was lousy at medical diagnoses.

He bled.

Like a stuck pig.

He didn't die.

Doctor gave him the bullet for good luck.

He lost it in a poker game.

Dealer thought it was a half dollar.

He was drunk.

He brought the rum.

And that, Gray knew, was pretty much the reason why he had wandered out of the surf and was standing on a long wooden pier as night crept in to erase the last vestiges of daylight. His white shirt had faded to the muted color of seashells scattered on the beach like chips at an all-night poker game. His khaki trousers looked as if they had been slept in for a week. Probably had been. His shirt sleeves were rolled up to his elbows. The hems of his pants were sopping wet with saltwater.

Washed, perhaps.

Never ironed.

Why bother?

He saw different people every day and not one of them had ever complained about the wrinkles.

That's why he liked writing about the dead.

Get the name wrong.

Get the age wrong.

Get the motive wrong.

They never complained about anything.

His eyes remained steadfast on the small rowboat fighting the tide and the surf as it was tossed from port to stern back toward the sands of Ormond Beach.

Solitary man.

Solitary boat.

Solitary moment in time when the waves caught their last breath on the shadows of the waterfront before slipping back to give up the ghost where the edge of night touched the strands of turquoise.

No reason to be on the pier.

He could be anywhere.

Adam Gray had made the journey to Ormond Beach because his newspaper editor thought he needed a change in the sordid realities of his unsavory life.

He covered the big stories.

The front page stories.

Where men died.

And women cried.

And juries condemned the guilty.

Sometimes the innocent suffered the same fate.

All it took was twelve votes.

A life taken.

A life spared.

Let's see a show of hands.

Twelve?

That's good.

We agree.

Let's go home.

Adam Gray was slightly built, sometimes six-feet tall, some-times less depending on the shoes he wore. He had the face of a boy, the eyes of an old man. The curls in his unruly brown hair caught the fancy of any wind blowing his way.

His job kept him on the bad side of town, and every town had one where the only thing cheaper than a man's life was the promise of love, and love could be bought by the hour or by the bottle. The price tag varied depending on the time of night.

Whiskey was against the law.

But then, so was murder.

The consorts of high society worried about murder.

They drank the whiskey.

My wife.

Your wife.

Somebody's wife.

Didn't matter.

The consorts never went home alone.

Sometimes they didn't wake up.

Front-page news.

Page-one byline.

Lord, how Adam Gray loved page-one bylines.

But the deaths added up.

So did the gunshots.

Winos.

Deadbeats.

Society dames.

All the same.

Death was the great equalizer.

The gunshots that broke his heart didn't help matters. They

left splinters of lead just below his ribs and above his left knee. He limped when it rained.

"Go someplace and heal," his editor said.

"I'd rather write."

"Then write."

"What about?"

"War's been over a while," the editor said. He sat back in his chair and propped his feet on the desk. He was a little pudgy, a little short, a pencil black mustache, and he wore a gray-striped suit that had as many wrinkles as stripes. "Good times are here again. Cars are selling. Roads are crossing one state before they dead end in another. Trains are headed from here to yonder and sometimes even farther. People are on the move. Lost as wild geese in a thunderstorm, but they want to see what's out there in this land of ours. They know a few names on the map but little else. Why don't you spend some time on the road?"

"Doing what?"

"Go to places where people want to go," the editor said. "Big towns, fancy towns, little towns, towns with funny names, and see what makes them different. Find out what makes the people tick. Folks in New York aren't like folks in Tallahassee, Tishomingo, or Timbuktu. Wire me stories about those places, and I'll run your travel column on page one."

"Can't."

"Why not?"

"I'm a police reporter."

"Not anymore."

"Then what am I?"

His editor grinned and rubbed a beefy hand across his bald head. It glistened with sweat in the overhead lights. "We'll call you a Travelist."

"I write about crime."

"Not really."

"Then what do you think I do?"

"You take words and play with people's lives," the editor said. "Nothing's changed. You'll just be writing about a different cast of characters. I'm tired of wasting ink on all the dead ones. See what the lively ones do for a good time. These are the Roaring Twenties, for God's sake."

The editor handed him a ticket for the New York Southern Railroad.

"When do I leave?"

"Train leaves tomorrow morning at seven."

"Where's it going?"

"Doesn't matter."

"Why not?"

"You can get off any time you want." The editor turned his chair around and began to scan the layout of the bulldog edition. "Wire us when you need money."

"How much."

The editor winked. "We'll send you half of everything you ask for."

One night.

A short night.

New York vanished behind him.

The rails rolled on forever.

Two days later, Gray found himself standing on the sidewalks of Ormond Beach, Florida.

Didn't know why he stepped off the train.

But it seemed like the right thing to do.

Adam Gray felt the same way he always did when someone was ready to die.

PART 2

ADAM GRAY WALKED down to the edge of the Atlantic

as the wooden rowboat was picked up by the waves and thrown rather rudely back onto shore.

An old man was sitting in the stern, a weathered paddle in his hands.

Hair white.

Face gaunt.

A three-day growth of gray whiskers on his face.

His eyes the color of slate.

Gray saw the barrels.

About a half dozen of them.

Three-feet high.

Wedged into the back of the boat.

The old man stood and looked as if he hadn't had a meal for days. His stained purple shirt and dark brown khaki trousers hung loosely on his skeletal frame. Tobacco juice had dried on his chin.

His smile was soft and genuine.

"You thirsty?" he asked.

"Could be." Curiosity clouded Gray's face.

"I'd offer you a drink," the old man said, "but I don't have a crowbar in my britches, and those barrels are hammered down tight, and even if I could get the lid off, I don't have any glasses, and you don't look like a man who could pay for a jigger of Irish whiskey even if I poured you one."

"Don't drink Irish Whiskey."

"Don't have any."

"I'm a Dewers man."

"You're an expensive drunk."

"Have been." Gray grinned. "Might be again someday."

The old man rubbed the palms of his hands against his khaki pants to dry them. "You can get your Dewers down at Delaney's."

"Thought it was illegal."

"Everything's legal at Delaney's." The old man winked. "I know. I keep him supplied with rum."

"You a smuggler?" Gray asked.

"I'm the man in the middle," the old man said. "Big boat brings the barrels to the island. The little boat brings them ashore."

"What if the prohibitionist boys catch you?"

"I have a choice." The old man laughed out loud and wiped his mouth with the back of his hand. "I can give them a barrel, or they can give me ninety days."

"Doesn't sound like they care much about the law."

The old man reached down and struggled to lift a barrel out on the sand. "Ormond Beach doesn't have any law pertaining to liquor," he said. "Got a few old women who march in the streets and carry signs that say the likes of me and you are going to hell because we partake of the devil's evil elixir of life. But the sheriff, he runs the town from a back table at Delaney's."

"Delaney pay him off?"

"His name's Delaney."

Gray reached down and lifted a barrel out of the boat. "You scared of hell?" he asked.

"Can't say as I am."

"Why not?"

"I been to Florida in August." The old man shrugged. "I go to hell to cool off."

"What about the devil?"

"He tends bar at Delaney's."

Gray removed the last barrel from the boat. A gentle breeze dried the layer of sweat on his face. "You got a name?" he asked the old man."

"Hemingway."

"Like the writer?"

The old man shook his head. "Don't know the writer," he

said. "My name is Maxwell. Everybody calls me Max. Mad Dog Max." He chuckled.

"Why Mad Dog?"

"Killed a man once with my bare hands."

"Why?"

"Didn't have a gun."

"What'd he do?"

"Just lay there in the surf with his eyes wide open, staring at the moon and looking like he'd seen something that the rest of us haven't seen yet, and maybe he did, and maybe he didn't. He was a lying sonuvabitch anyway."

"He must have upset you pretty bad," Gray said. He took a notepad and pencil from his shirt pocket and began to scribble.

"Same old story," Hemingway said.

"Tell me the story."

"Two men. One woman. Same town. Same hotel." The old man shrugged. "Never works out to everybody's satisfaction. He worked nights. I worked days. He came home early one night."

"You in love?"

"I was."

"How about the woman?"

"Said she'd wait for me."

"Did she?"

"Waited 'til the trial was over."

"Then she left you?"

He laughed.

"Nobody knows for sure," he said.

The old man who called himself Hemingway crawled back into the boat and used his splintered paddle to push himself back into the sea.

The tides were leaving Ormond Beach.

He would be at their mercy.

It was his lot in life.

"Where you going?" Gray called after him.

"Home." A southerly wind swept gingerly across the sand.

"What about the barrels?"

"Delaney will send somebody down to pick them up when it's good and dark."

"What if somebody steals them?"

"Nobody will."

"Why not?"

"Everybody in town knows Taffy McVeigh."

"He work for Delaney?"

"Never lost a fight."

"He that tough?"

"He tends bar at Delaney's."

"What about strangers?"

"Ormond Beach don't have any strangers."

Gray laughed. "What about me?" he asked.

"You won't be a stranger come morning."

Adam Gray watched the boat bobbing in the waves, moving west, easing from sundown to dark, caught in a slender shaft of light spilling from the tip of a pale moon.

Didn't know how long he waited.

Didn't carry a watch.

But he was walking down the beach toward the hotel long before Hemingway was out of sight.

PART 3

ADAM GRAY ATE two slices of French toast and drank a glass of freshly squeezed orange juice, then wrote the opening lines to his travel story about the Florida Beach, seated at a Barley Twist Oak writing desk in his room on the third floor of the Hotel Ormond.

I have stayed in a lot of sleeping rooms in my time. Mostly, they were cheap walkup hotels down where the railroad tracks separated the good side of town from the bad, and they smelled of hog lard, body sweat, and urine. They were the kinds of places where desperate people went to live the final years of their lives regardless of how old they were.

No more. I'm through with those. For the last two nights, I have been a patron of the Hotel Ormond down on the sands that overlook the Florida shoreline of the Atlantic. It is a mesmerizing place, a palace that sits on eighty acres and features four hundred rooms, as well as eleven miles of corridors and breezeways. It is the largest wooden structure in the United States, and Henry Flagler is responsible for turning the Ormond into the best known hotel in the world.

Want to escape New York when it's cold? Thaw out at Ormond Beach, a resort city that has miles of compact white sand that wander past sugar plantations along the Atlantic coast to Ponce de Leon Inlet. From what I've been told, Old Ponce was only looking for the Fountain of Youth. I may have found it.

He read the story once, then again.

It wasn't particularly good.

He would be the first to admit it.

But the story was readable, and it just might be exactly what his editor wanted when he sent Gray on a journey into the untraveled America nobody knew. He sat back and looked at the elegant furnishings surrounding him. Gray smiled, picked up the decanter from a lace tablecloth, and poured himself another glass of orange juice, this one laced with a touch of vodka.

He felt exhilarated.

He felt guilty.

This might not be such a bad assignment after all. He had seen the clientele who flocked to the Hotel Ormond.

Aging gentlemen wearing black ties.

Ladies adorned in long French gowns.

Strong aroma perfumes he could neither spell nor pronounce.

Scions of society, all walking with class and dignity through those eleven miles of corridors and breezeways. They were, he figured, the sort who would have considered it vulgar to even think about someone dying.

Only the poor died on the streets.

The rich went straight to mausoleums.

GRAY SAUNTERED INTO the lounge while the overhead fans were working hard and failing miserably to beat back the sweltering heat of a sultry afternoon.

Cool.

Not dark.

But dimly lit by electric candles.

It smelled distinctly of fine wine and a smuggler's imported scotch.

He sat down at a table beside a window that overlooked the bay. He placed his leatherbound notebook on the white lace tablecloth and saw suspicious eyes all begin turning toward him. The beautiful people didn't have to speak. He could read their faces.

Who's he?

What's he doing here?

Doesn't belong.

Shows no respect.

The man without a tie.

The man with the pencil.

What's he writing?

What does he know that we don't know?

Yet.

Gray smiled faintly. In war, they would say he had been dropped behind enemy lines. The beautiful people were too old to be beautiful anymore, so they had no doubt outlawed mirrors and anything else that suffered them the indignities of a reflection.

The enemy sitting at the bar had never looked so lovely.

She didn't shy away from mirrors.

Mirrors were made for her.

She sat alone.

Tall.

Slender.

Dark hair draped around her shoulders.

Black eyes.

They shone like moonlight on obsidian.

A beauty mark on her left cheek.

Might have been a mole.

Didn't bother him.

She was dressed in a long silk gown the color of sunrise, and she was sipping on a frosted glass of some exotic drink that looked as if it might have been concocted from rum or perhaps even lemonade. A slice of pineapple floated on top.

Gray had lived thirty-six years and had never seen anyone quite like her. Then again, he had never darkened the doorway to Ormond Beach until today. He spent his time on the mean streets and back alleys of a deadly town her six-inch heels would never touch.

He had been around a lot of interesting women.

Most were in the backs of squad cars.

Or lying with bullet holes tucked away in the most unlikeliest of places.

Men die.

Women only cease to exist.

God bless them everyone.

She smiled.

Couldn't be smiling at him.

He turned around.

Nothing behind him but the window.

She slid off the stool and walked toward his table. He had seen willow trees sway the way she did, but only if the wind was blowing the right way. She sat down, crossed her legs, and asked, "Mind if I smoke?"

He didn't.

She produced a package of Old Gold cigarettes.

Gray had no idea where she had been hiding them.

He lit the tip of one with a candle burning at the table and watched her inhale deeply before a circle of smoke curled toward the chandelier above them.

"You smoke?" she asked.

"Never when I'm drinking."

She frowned. "You're not drinking," she said.

"I will be."

She snapped her fingers.

A waiter appeared. Even he wore a black tie and white jacket.

No stains.

No wrinkles.

"Scotch," Gray said.

"Glen Scotia be all right?"

"Glen Scotia's fine."

The waiter turned, and the dark-haired girl asked, "You always drink Glen Scotia?"

"Never heard of it."

"Then why order it?"

"Why not? After the first sip, all scotch tastes the same." Gray sat back and watched the frown cross her face.

"You're a stranger here," she said.

"I'm a stranger everywhere I go."

"Where's home?"

"Right now, it's on a train."

"Where's the train headed?"

"I get on. I get off." Gray shrugged. "I have no idea where it goes when it leaves me."

"Do you have a name?" she asked.

He told her.

"I'm Vera," she said.

"Vera Summers," he said.

"How did you know?"

"I read the brochure." Gray picked up a crystal glass the waiter placed before him and took a sip. "You are, I believe the fine print says, the lovely songbird from Chattanooga who has come to Ormond Beach from the concert halls in New York."

She smiled and took a bite from the pineapple in her drink.

"I'm from New York," Gray said.

"Never been there," Vera said.

"The smart songbirds never do." He lit a second cigarette for her.

Vera laughed.

"So you're from Chattanooga," he said.

"Never been there either." Her eyes turned sad. "I'm from Indiana. Farm girl. Sang at church. Sang in the school choir. Wanted to make the big time." She looked around her and tapped the cigarette's ashes in a porcelain tray beside her. "I guess this is as close to the big time as I'll ever be."

"What do you sing?"

"The blues."

"Why?"

Vera sighed. "That's what I live," she said. "I live the blues."

"But I've read where the Ormond may be the finest hotel in the country," Gray said. "This is where the rich, the politicians, the tycoons, the famous, the beautiful people come to get away from it all."

"You can't believe what you read," she said. She blew a perfect circle of smoke, then asked, "Do you always believe what you read?"

"Never."

"Why not?"

"Mostly I write it."

"Really?"

Gray nodded.

"What do you do?"

"I'm a Travelist," Gray said.

"What's that?"

"Still trying to figure it out."

Vera Summers looked up, and the laughter died in her throat.

Gray glanced up and watched a man dressed like the rest walking heavily across an empty dance floor.

Black tie.

White jacket.

Black hair.

Slick with grease.

Black mustache.

Scar on his neck.

Eyes has hard as flint.

Might be Cuban.

Hard to tell.

The only Cubans Gray had seen were lying on a slab.

Vera quickly rose to her feet. "I have to go," she said.

Flint Face grabbed her wrist.

She stifled a whimper.

Gray stood. "You all right?" he asked her.

She nodded. A cloud worked its way across the splinters of sun in her eyes. "George is my manager. Doesn't like it when I drink in the afternoon. Says liquor ruins my voice."

George slapped her.

Gray clenched his fists.

"Forget it," Vera said.

He watched her until she vanished behind a velvet curtain draped across the stage.

"Miss Vera's right," the waiter said. He placed another glass of Glen Scotia on the table.

"About what?"

"You should forget it."

"He can't treat her like that," Gray said. "I don't care if he is her manager."

"You don't understand the business," the waiter said. "He owns her. You think she is a beautiful woman. I think she is a beautiful singer. He thinks she is a piece of merchandise. She will sing until she is too old to sing anymore, then he will dump her."

"Where?"

The waiter smiled.

He knew something.

Wasn't saying.

Gray started to speak.

The waiter was gone.

PART 4

ADAM GRAY WORE a tie for dinner.

Wasn't black.

He wore a jacket.

Tweed.

Not white.

He wasn't hungry.

But he did want to hear the lovely Vera Summers sing.

The waiter seated him at the same table for two.

Out of the way.

Through the window, he saw the turquoise sea turn the color of ink.

"Glen Scotia?"

"That'll do fine," Gray said. "What time does Vera sing?"

"First show is nine o'clock."

Gray glanced at the clock on the wall behind the bar.

Nine o'clock was still sixteen minutes away, and the candles were doing their best to shove the darkness back outside.

It was a good night for fine wine.

Prime rib.

And the blues.

He watched the piano player shuffle through a packet of music. The trumpet player was drinking beer. The clarinetist stumbled on the cord running to the microphone. Then again, it may have been the strong liquor. The drummer was blind.

The music men wore black ties.

And jackets.

White.

The drummer was whistling.

Gray waited. He had stepped off the train to write about the sea, sand, and surf of Ormond Beach. Vera Summers had a better story.

Didn't know what it was.

But one thing was for certain.

Her story was better than the one spun by the brochures of Ormond Beach.

The hands on the clock reached nine.

The stage lights dimmed.

The piano player began pounding out his own version of Bessie Smith's "I Ain't Got Nobody."

Gray had heard it before.

He waited.

The clock kept ticking.

It stopped for no one.

Not even for the lovely Vera Summers.

The crowd of beautiful people was growing restless.

So was Adam Gray.

A tall, thin-faced man he had never seen before walked

slowly onto the stage. His shoulders slumped. His face was the color of spent ashes. His eyes swept across the crowd, and he said in a soft, grief-stricken voice, "I regret to inform each and every one of you that tonight's musical interlude by the lovely Vera Summers has been cancelled."

He turned hastily and disappeared behind the velvet curtain.

Gray caught up with him by the time he reached the back-door. He grabbed the man's shoulder and spun him around. "What's wrong?" he asked.

"It's Vera," the man said.

"What about her?"

"She's dead."

"What happened?"

"Somebody jammed the barrel of a gun against the soft spot in her throat and pulled the trigger."

"Who?"

The man began to cry softly. "We'll probably never know," he said, his words a hoarse whisper.

———

DELANEY'S WAS FILLED beyond capacity when Adam Gray hurried into Ormond Beach's own self-styled, self-anointed den of iniquity. Men cursed at a poker table. Women squealed with laughter coaxed from their innards by cheap whiskey. A Wurlitzer music machine in the corner spit out "Waiting for a Train" by Jimmy Rodgers.

He rushed to the bartender. "I understand the sheriff spends his time here," he asked.

"Who wants to know?" The barkeep wore Levi britches and a threadbare flannel shirt, both stained by blood and beer. A two-days growth of whiskers clung to his face.

"A woman's dead."

"Won't be the last one."

"She was murdered."

The bartender nodded toward the poker table. "Delaney's the second man on the left-hand side of the dealer."

Gray hurried across the room. Delaney had his badge hanging on his coat, just below his left nipple. He had grown wider as he grew older. He was wearing a black suit over a white shirt yellowed by age. A pencil-thin tie hung from his neck. His hair was beginning to leave his head.

"Sheriff Delaney," Gray said as soon as he reached the table.

"You've found him." The sheriff didn't bother to look up. He sounded as if someone with muddy shoes had been walking across his windpipe.

"A woman's dead," Gray said again.

"You mean the singing girl over at the hotel?"

"Vera Summers."

"It's a shame, ain't it?"

"You planning to do something about it?"

"Not tonight."

"Why not?" Gray felt his anger rising, or maybe it was frustration.

"It's dark. The killer's hiding. Can't find him in the dark." The sheriff chuckled. "No use to look for him in the dark."

"Tomorrow could be too late."

The sheriff glanced up as he folded his cards. "Tomorrow's never too late," he said.

"Might let the killer get away between now and then."

"Might not even be a killer." Delaney stood up. He was a mountain of a man, well over six-feet with a barrel chest, squinty little eyes, and large beefy hands. "Son," he said, "we got two laws down here that'll send you to prison quicker than a gnat dodging a flyswatter. One is leaving the bar without paying your tab, and the other one is telling me how to do my job."

Gray quietly swallowed his thoughts and headed for the door.

Remember these things, the sheriff said.

Vera Summers wasn't one of us.

She was an outsider.

Outsiders come.

And they go.

I don't stop them from coming.

I don't stop them from going.

Vera came.

She went.

What happens in between is none of our business.

The patrons of Delaney's was roaring with laughter as Gray walked out the door.

Chapter 5

HEMINGWAY WAS WAITING for him as Gray turned toward the beach. The old man stepped out of the shadows.

Same clothes.

Same tobacco stains.

Same haggard look.

Still barefooted.

His wide grin showed his teeth.

Count to six.

You had them all.

Hemingway walked alongside him until they could see the top of the hotel rising out of the fog.

Neither had spoken.

Finally Hemingway did. "You're upset about the girl, aren't you?"

"I met her this afternoon."

"Fall in love with her?"

"Infatuated is a better word."

"Most men fall in love with her." Hemingway's laugh was a cackle.

"What does it get them?"

"Usually a broken heart."

They walked on in silence.

The sea gulls were complaining down beside the beach.

Looking for fish.

The beautiful people didn't fish much.

They ate.

They drank.

They danced.

Occasionally, one of them died.

Occasionally, one of them killed.

No need to feel guilty.

No need to worry about an alibi.

For a fistful of dollars, Delaney would acquit you on the spot.

"You think you know who killed her, don't you?" Hemingway waited for an answer.

Finally, Gray gave him an answer. "Probably her manager?"

"The tough guy?"

"He acted tough."

"He wouldn't kill Vera."

"Why not?"

"She was his meal ticket."

"There are other girl singers."

"None like Vera."

Gray stopped at the corner and turned to face Hemingway. "She hated Ormond Beach."

"Maybe." The old man cackled again. "But Ormond Beach sure loved her."

Gray studied Hemingway for a moment, then asked, "Do you know who killed her?"

"I know where he hid his gun."

"The murder weapon?"

"A Colt M 1900 semi-automatic."

"Pretty potent."

"Leaves a big hole."

"Where is it?" Gray asked.

Hemingway motioned for Gray to follow him, and both men turned toward the beach. Only a pale half-moon lit the way. The sands were packed, and seashells, gifted by the tides, glittered like silver dollars down where the foam of the surf came rushing on shore.

THE SEA WAS as calm as a dead girl's eyes. Gray knew. He had written about so many of them. He had always used words like *brutal* or *vicious* or *ruthless* in his stories. Not once had the word *calm* ever crossed his mind.

Curiosity had fled their eyes.

Terror had vanished.

Anxiety had disappeared.

He thought it odd now.

Everyone feared dying.

Yet, they were so peaceful when the last breath crossed from here to there, and only they knew where they had gone.

Maybe dying wasn't so bad after all.

Gray shuddered.

He had no interest in finding out.

Hemingway rowed to a narrow inlet on an island that clung to the western side of Ormond Beach. He waded through the surf and pulled the boat into the seagrass.

He took off without a word, and Gray trailed along behind him.

"Who hid the gun?" Gray yelled after him.

"A man with a broken heart."

"What happened?"

"Same old story," he said. "Two men. One woman. One town. One hotel. Never works out to everybody's satisfaction."

"Who pulled the trigger?"

"A rich man. Comes every year."

"He here alone?"

"He is now."

"Who's the other man in love with Vera Summer?"

"Besides you?"

Gray grinned.

"Does it matter?"

Hemingway knelt beside a pile of driftwood. He removed two logs off the stack. A pistol wrapped in oilskin lay on the sand, a Colt M1900 semi-automatic. The metal barrel glittered in a broken splinter of moonlight.

Gray sadly shook his head. *Anything that deadly shouldn't sparkle in any light.*

"You touch it?" Gray asked.

"Left it like you see it." Hemingway laughed out loud. "Only has one man's fingerprints on it, the man who fired it."

"He's a walking dead man."

Hemingway laughed again. "Not in Ormond Beach, he isn't."

GRAY DIDN'T SLEEP all night. He sat beside his dark window on the third floor of the hotel watching the clouds gather darkly above the beach, watching until daylight came to scatter the seagulls and send the terns running stiff-legged upon the sand.

He splashed cold water on his face, wrapped the Colt pistol in his jacket, tucked it under his arm, and walked downstairs. He stopped in the lounge one last time and looked at an empty stage, remembering a girl he would never hear sing the blues. He slowly shifted his gaze toward the bar stool. It was empty. As far as he was concerned, it would always be empty.

Gray stepped out into the cool morning and headed toward Delaney's. He was sitting at the bar, nursing a scotch mist, when the sheriff walked in.

Only three men were standing inside the speakeasy.

Gray.

Delaney.

And the bartender.

The bartender didn't count.

Gray dropped his jacket on the table between them and unwrapped it.

The sheriff looked down at the pistol. He raised an eyebrow. "What's that?" he wanted to know.

"The gun that killed Vera Summers."

"Don't know anything about Vera dying."

"You knew last night."

"I've slept since then."

Gray defiantly folded his arms across his chest and cocked his head to one side. "This is not difficult," he said. "You have a murder to solve. I've solved it. Just do your job. You'll find the killer's fingerprints all over the gun. Won't be hard for you to track him down."

"Can't help you," the sheriff said. He reached over the bar, pulled out a bottle, and poured himself a glass of rye whiskey. Straight.

"Why not?"

"We don't have a Vera Summers in Ormond Beach."

"You did."

"She's gone."

"Check the funeral home."

Delaney shrugged. "Haven't had a new grave in thirteen years," he said. He reached down and picked up the gun. "How did you find this pistol?"

"Hemingway carried me over to the island last night." Gray's voice turned cold. "He watched the killer hide it. He knows who did it."

Delaney laughed. "You mean old Mad Dog Max?" he asked. "That's the one."

Delaney's laughter faded. "Impossible," he said.

"What makes you say that."

Delaney was dead solid serious. "Max Hemingway died fifteen years ago," Delaney said. "Man beat him to death with his bare hands over some woman."

"What about his boat?"

"Left it," Delaney said. "Nobody wanted it."

Gray slumped down into the chair. He counted his breaths. He waited for them to slow down. "So no one cares that Vera Summers died," he said.

"Did you see Vera?" Delaney asked.

"When?"

"After she was shot."

Gray shook his head.

Delaney stuck the Colt M1900 semi-automatic in his belt and walked to the bar. "Waiter over at the hotel said he saw her."

"Where?" Gray was on his feet.

"Catching the train sometime around midnight."

"Where was she going?"

Delaney grinned, but the humor did not quite reach his eyes. "North," he said.

By the time he turned around, Gray was out the door and walking down to the beach, down toward Hemingway's boat.

Ormond Beach, he thought.

The city where nobody dies.

Nobody's buried.

Nobody's tried.

Nobody's convicted.

Nobody's guilty.

No attorneys.

None needed.

Just write a check.
Delaney cashes them all down at his seaside bar.
Great story.
But he couldn't write it.
No.
Not now.
His editor didn't want it.
Adam Gray silently cursed himself.
He was a damn Travelist.

Author - Linda Pirtle

Linda Pirtle is a retired educator who taught the art of writing and understanding literature for years as an English teacher at St. John High School, Lancaster High School, and Ennis High School as well as Business Communications at Navarro College in Waxahachie, Texas. She also served as principal of Ennis High School and Program Director/Grant Writer for Ennis Independent School District.

Linda is a member of several professional writing associations – East Texas Writers' Guild; Silver Leos (Texas A&M, Commerce); Holly Lake Book Club; and Keller Writers' Association. As a public speaker, Linda talks about writing techniques and works with beginning authors. She served as President of the East Texas Writer's Guild. Linda is a beta reader for her author friends whose works include a variety of genres – historical fiction, nonfiction, fantasy, mystery, romance – all of which are presently in the marketplace.

She and her husband Caleb Pirtle III are devoted to connecting readers with today's growing population of authors throughout the world. They post blogs and promote Indie authors in their monthly newsletter and on their website calebandlindapirtle.com.

Social Media Information:
   Calebandlindapirtle.com
   Lsgp2019@yahoo.com
   Twitter@LindaPirtle1
   Linda.pirtle.10@facebook.com
   https://www.amazon.com/s?k=Linda+Pirtle%2C+ Author&ref=nb_sb_noss

The Girl in the Turquoise Bikini

By:
Linda Pirtle

9

The Girl in the Turquoise Bikini
Linda Pirtle

Jeb McGrierson considered himself a lucky man. Not everyone could afford the luxury of owning a house overlooking the Quansea Bay. He took great pride in his white stucco two-storied mansion with its wrap around walkway. Jeb, an international award-winning mystery/suspense author wrote under a pseudonym. Not once had he made a public appearance promoting any of his thirteen books, choosing instead to pay his publicist a hefty salary to market his mysteries. Only two of his titles failed to make the New York Times Best Seller List.

All morning Jeb had sat in front of his computer. He had created a new Microsoft Word document, formatted the paragraph indentions and margins as well as the line spacing. He had typed the title: *The Case of the . . .*

The case of what?

Jeb deleted the title.

Nothing came to mind.

No dastardly deed.

No murder.

No breaking and entering.

A big fat nothing came to mind.

Jeb hit the return key and typed: *Darkness surrounded Greg Watts as he entered. . . .*

No, that won't do. Greg's last escapade in Italy began with those words. Jeb pushed the delete key and watched it scamper backwards across the page.

Then he typed: *Greg heard a scream. It sounded like. . .*

That's too cliché, he thought. He watched the letters disappear one by one as the delete key made another U-turn on the page.

Try as he might, Jeb could not conjure up another mystery for his protagonist Greg Watts to solve. Though he knew about writer's block, Jeb McGrierson had never personally experienced the curse. "What the hell," he said and pushed his chair away from his desk. "Guess I'll try again tomorrow." He chided himself, "Don't sound like Scarlett O'Hara from *Gone with the Wind.*" Then he smiled and spoke with a southern drawl. *"After all, tomorrow is another* day *at Quansea Bay."*

Each afternoon after a day of writing another chapter or two of his next great American novel, Jeb would walk from his study to the den of his house where folding patio doors remained open twenty-four/seven. Keeping his regime and despite the fact he had accomplished zero words, Jeb stopped at the bar along one side of the dining room to mix his favorite martini.

"Shaken, not stirred," he always mimicked his favorite spy James Bond. Jeb glanced at his image in the mirror behind the bar and brushed a lock of his dark brown hair off of his forehead. "I say, old man, you do need a shave and a haircut." Jeb made a mental note to take care of his personal hygiene before calling his agent the next morning.

"Hmm," he said to the image in the mirror. "Your deadline is approaching, old man. Just what excuse will you give the old buzzard this time?" Jeb had negotiated an extension of three months for the next novel, the first page on which he had written and deleted every single word. The extra timeline had expired.

He considered telling Teresa Bryant that he had been diagnosed with Covid-19 but decided not to play with fire, primarily because he feared she would hop on the next airplane out of LaGuardia and come to his rescue. "No," he muttered to himself, "that won't do. Surely, a best-selling author can think of a better lie."

No inspiration came to him, so he shook his head and walked through the den to the outdoors. He leaned his body forward, propping his elbows on the waist high stucco wall that prevented an accidental fall from the wrap around walkway. Jeb loved the view of the inlet and the mountains in the background. He spent his evenings on the patio and watched the sun make its last gasp, creating a pink/purple haze, before suddenly dropping behind the flat-topped mountain on the far side of the inlet.

Jeb raised his martini in a toast to nature's beauty before taking that first tingling, cool sip. That's when he saw something strange and unusual. No tourist had ever ventured onto his private beach, but there she was, bold as anyone could be. How dare she invade his privacy?

"Hey, you," he yelled. She didn't hear him or chose to ignore him. She didn't look his way. The girl dragged her gaudy turquoise boat onto the edge of the sand bar. "Who would want that ugly piece of junk?" Jeb asked himself and then answered. "That was a rhetorical question, old man." He pointed his thumb toward the beach. "She does."

He watched as she donned her snorkeling equipment and walked toward the warm water.

Jeb retrieved his cell phone from his pocket and snapped a photo of the trespasser. One couldn't know for sure, but he might need to show it to the police – useless as they are on the island where anything goes – to prove she had trespassed onto private property. His property. His kingdom. Didn't he have a sign that warned people not to invade his space? No one reads anymore, Jeb thought. Maybe that's why I couldn't write today. Didn't the old buzzard criticize my last manuscript? Said Greg was getting too old to seduce the young, beautiful auburn-haired model who was really a Soviet spy.

He returned his thoughts to the activity on the sand bar. "Not a bad view," he muttered. The interloper wore a bikini the same color as her boat. It fit her nicely, revealing a shapely body: long slender legs, tiny waist, flat tummy. Her long, blonde hair blew in the breeze. She bent down, revealing an ample bosom, and picked up a bag from the boat. Standing and turning her back to the shore, she ran her fingers through her waist-length golden locks and pulled it back and up into a ponytail.

"Hey, you," he yelled again. "The sun is setting. The tide. It's too dangerous now for you to be in the water."

She didn't respond to his cautionary warning.

"Well, I'll be a wonkey-jawed donkey," Jeb muttered and then asked, "What would Greg Watts do?" That was another rhetorical question, old man, he thought. "Guess I'd better walk down there and keep an eye on that foolish woman. May have to dive in and save her. That's what Greg would do." He set his drink on the ledge of the wall and hurried to his bedroom to change into a swimsuit. Jeb had seen only her shapely attributes. He wondered if her face matched her beautiful body.

It took Jeb a good twenty minutes to change. After all, he thought, I want to make a good impression on the misguided damsel in distress. Can't have her seeing me with a scruffy face. He shaved and splashed on some cologne. He raised his arms, making a ninety-degree intersection at his elbow. He made a fist and tightened his biceps, turning first one way and another. Jeb smiled at his reflection, admiring his physique in the mirror. Ready and prepared to be a hero, Jeb sauntered down the stairs and out the front door.

There was a slight berm between his front yard and the beach, blocking his view of the sand bar. Jeb climbed the steps to the wooden bridge which led from his home to the beach.

"Damn," he muttered to himself when he caught sight of the sand bar. "I went to all that trouble to clean up, and that woman has already gone." He turned around, searching for any sign of her and her boat.

Jeb shielded his eyes from the glare of the water created by the eye-level status of the setting sun. He caught sight of the turquoise boat riding the waves out to sea. No one was in it. "Now, what would Greg do?" Greg Watts wouldn't panic. He would assume the girl pushed her boat into the water before she began snorkeling. "She could have done that while I was freshening up," Jeb said. "Just goes to show, doesn't it, that she knows nothing about the tide. No telling where the tide will ditch her boat. Not my problem."

He shrugged and turned back toward home. Jeb, fresh martini in hand, reclined in a black wrought iron chaise lounge on the walkway outside his living room. He plumped up the red and white paisley pillow behind his back. "Ah," he thought, "peace and solitude. Can't beat it."

Jeb downed the last of his drink and stood up. Darkness had descended on Quansea Bay once more. Before closing the folding patio doors, Jeb stared into the blackness. "Hope you're okay, young lady," he said.

Greg Watts, detective extraordinaire, always slept in red flannel pajamas with white hearts sprinkled throughout the fabric. So did the cold-natured author who created him. Jeb had just slipped into his own red with white hearts pajamas when he heard a loud knocking on his front door.

"Drat it," he said. "Can't a man get some sleep around here?" he asked. Grabbing a robe, he threw it on as he descended from the second floor of his Mediterranean-style mansion. Jeb opened the door and was shocked to see a local police officer whom he recognized. "What can I do for you, Pierre?" he asked.

Six feet two inches, black-haired, piercing blue-eyed Pierre Corbin, a native of the island and a member of the local police force, said, "Hate to intrude, Jeb. I know how you value your solitude, but we are canvassing all of the residents in this area. It seems that a young woman, a marine biologist, left for work this morning but didn't make it to the laboratory."

"Why ask me about anyone? You know I'm a recluse. I don't allow visitors, female or otherwise." Jeb started to close the door but hesitated. Pierre's next statement intrigued him.

"I understand. But one of your neighbors, Mr. Robertson, said he saw a small fishing boat on the sandbar adjacent to your beach." Pierre opened the small note pad on which he took notes about a case. Reading the information from Mr. Robertson, Pierre stated, "It says here that he saw a boat about twenty to thirty minutes before sundown." The policeman made direct eye contact with Jeb. "He also stated that he heard someone scream."

Jeb swallowed. "That would have been me."

"Do you care to explain?"

Jeb stepped back and opened his door. "Come inside." He led Pierre into the living room and motioned to a white leather sectional sofa that faced two barrel-backed seafoam green chairs. "Have a seat." Jeb sat in one of the chairs. *This sounds serious. How would Greg Watts handle this?* Jeb clasped and unclasped his hands in an effort to calm his nerves before he spoke.

"As you know, Pierre, I don't like to be interrupted by a nosey tourist when I'm writing."

Pierre nodded. "Yes, sir."

"Well, after writing all day on my next Greg Watts sequel, I took a break." *Pierre doesn't need to know that words eluded me.* "Mixed my usual martini for the evening and walked out on my deck." Jeb took a deep breath. "From there I can see Quansea Bay quite clearly."

Jeb paused as if to recollect whether or not he wanted to back up Robertson's statements. Deciding to come clean, he continued. "I guess Robertson and I saw the same girl. In fact, I yelled at her – not a scream, mind you – to tell her it was too late to go snorkeling."

"How did you know that she planned on snorkeling?"

"Hello," Jeb said sarcastically. "Wouldn't you come to the same conclusion if you had seen her put on her mask and oxygen tank and flippers?"

"Didn't mean to insult you. Just asking for clarification."

"Sorry I snapped at you," Jeb said.

Both men were silent for a moment. Then Pierre broke the silence with his next question. "Do you think she heard your warning?"

Jeb shook his head. "Must not have because she walked right into the water and left her boat on the sandbar."

"Left her boat?"

"Sure did." Jeb scrunched his shoulders and tilted his head back. "I feared she might need my help, so I threw on my swimsuit, grabbed my Powertac flashlight, and raced downstairs."

"I see," said Pierre. "Did you get a good look at her?"

Jeb grinned. "I did better than get a good look. I took a picture of her. It's on my phone." He stood and walked to the bar. He usually plugged the cell into the outlet at the end of the counter so that his phone would be fully charged for the next day.

It wasn't there.

Jeb frowned and glanced around the room.

No iPhone in sight.

Then he remembered. "Oh, I must have left it outside." He walked to the patio doors and peered through them. "Yep, there it is." Jeb had left it on the table beside his chaise lounge. He opened the doors and stepped out.

Pierre followed him and stared into the darkness. "I'd like to see the bay from here. I bet it's breathtaking."

Jeb nodded. "You're welcome anytime, Pierre. Let's go inside. I'll pull up the photo I took." Jeb searched through the phone's photo gallery until he found the one of the woman. "Here it is." He held out the phone so Pierre could see it.

"May I text it to myself?" he asked and proceeded to do so before Jeb could respond. Handing the phone to Jeb, Pierre said, "This the only one?"

Jeb nodded.

"Wish I could see her face."

"Me, too." Jeb asked. "Does the picture of the boat jive with Robertson's description?"

Pierre didn't answer. He extended his hand. Jeb shook it. "Thanks for your time, Jeb."

He let himself out of the mansion.

Jeb stood in the middle of the room and watched him go. Grinning, the award-winning author, did a silent happy dance. "Now, I have a story." He raced to his study.

Chuckling as his computer woke up, Jeb signed in and opened a blank word document. Jeb assumed Greg Watts's persona. His fingers flew over the keyboard. In the center of the blank page, Jeb wrote:

THE CASE of the Girl in the Turquoise Bikini

JEB BEGAN his story with a reference to his previous Greg Watt mystery.

Chapter 1

VACATION. **Finally.** *Seagrove Beach, Florida. Greg Watts, private investigator, was tired. He had just solved the most emotionally exhausting case of his life. The kidnapping of a* *sixteen-year-old girl, Alisha Cateri, the only child of Antonio Cateri, CEO of the most successful social media company in the world. Returning Alisha physically unharmed to her father and apprehending the two men who had demanded twenty million dollars for her release had been a tough job, one that resulted in a gunshot wound for Greg. Fully recovered from his injury, Greg was now ready for a long break from investigations of any type. Besides, he could easily afford it. Antonio had paid him well. And Greg's financial adviser had made some good suggestions as to how Greg could invest the money. In fact, had Greg wanted to do so, he could live on the interest earned and never have to consider taking another dangerous job. Perhaps, Greg thought, it's time for me to permanently retire, settle down, and start a family.*

SATISFIED WITH THE BEGINNING, Jeb sighed and leaned back in his desk chair, thinking about how to write the perfect next paragraph of the new Greg Watts mystery. He tried several sentences and deleted them. He opened a desk drawer and retrieved a lined legal pad and began to jot down his thoughts. Several hours passed. It didn't matter. Jeb was in his creative mode. Time meant nothing.

Finally, Jeb decided to just write. "I can always edit and re-write it. Of course, I know Teresa will have a few good suggestions. She always does." Jeb glanced at the top right-hand corner of his computer screen. "Five-thirty. Can't believe it took me all night to plot the story."

Jeb glanced at the legal-size yellow notepad beside his laptop. "Yep, I did outline several scenes about the story." Scanning his notes, Jeb continued writing.

GREG SIGHED AND LEANED BACK, resting his head on the white towel draped over the back of the beach chair. He wiggled his toes in the white sand of Seagrove beach and let the warm sun soothe the tension from his muscles.

"Did you put on sunscreen?" a woman's brisk voice asked, interrupting his solitude.

The bossy voice belonged to Maddie Winthrop, Greg's long-time female companion. Without opening his eyes, Greg smiled and nodded. He felt the sand shift beneath his low beach chaise. He opened his cordovan eyes and saw two cold crystals gazing back at him. Why hadn't he noticed her eyes before?

Strange. Greg had always taken great pride in his ability to notice the smallest detail about a person's appearance. The old adage that love is blind certainly could not be applied in this case. Maddie was a friend, nothing more. Love was not part of their relationship.

"Do you know anything about pirates and shipwrecks in the Gulf of Mexico?" Maddie asked.

"Not much," Greg said and waved an arm toward the shore. "But I'm sure treasure hunters have searched these waters and could have found some sunken boats." Suspicious as always and wanting to know why she posed the question, Greg couldn't resist asking, "Did you pick up some brochures about sunken treasure in the hotel lobby?"

Maddie nodded. "Yes, I did."

Greg chuckled. Maddie's enthusiastic approach to anything new always amused him. "I bet you can find some interesting books about pirates and lost treasure in the resort's gift shop."

"I have a better idea," she said.

"And that would be?" he asked.

"I picked up a brochure about treasure hunting."

"And?"

"It offers experienced divers an opportunity to charter a boat for a day to go diving for lost treasure."

Greg looked around as if searching for something. *"I don't see any experienced divers."*

"Guess what?"

"What?" he asked, dreading her response.

Maddie pushed a stray lock her blonde hair off of her forehead and confessed, *"I lied. Said I had been diving before."*

"Are you crazy?" Greg asked. *"I hope they didn't believe you."*

"I've reserved a boat for today." Maddie stood and grabbed his hand, trying to pull him up. *"Forget about sunbathing for a while and come with me. It'll be a fun experience even if we don't find anything valuable."*

"No ma'am. I'm not letting you put both our lives in danger." Greg sat upright and twisted sideways on his chaise. *"I have no interest in diving. I came on this trip to sit on the beach, work on my tan, relax, and read."* He patted the mystery thriller that lay unopened on the sand beside his chair. *"Besides, I know nothing about handling a boat,"* he grumbled.

"I know, but guess what?" Maddie laughed.

Refusing to play her game anymore, he said, *"Not interested in any touristy rip-off."*

Maddie ignored his response. *"The boat comes with a captain and a sailor who will dive with us to make sure we'll be safe."*

"A real sailor cum diver? Whoopee," Greg exclaimed. *"Then you don't need me."* He watched the disappointment wash over her face. Feeling a smidgeon of guilt but not enough to go along with her idea, Greg used a conciliatory voice. *"Maddie,"* he said, *"I need a day or two to relax. Do you think you could wait until later in the week? Then, I'd be ready for an adventure."*

Maddie shook her head. *"I could charter the boat only for today. It's already reserved for the rest of the week. Would you mind if I go without you?"*

"No, dear." Greg leaned over and kissed her forehead. "Go have fun."

Maddie jumped up and ran down the beach. Greg watched her go. He held his breath. Maddie was beautiful. He saw several men turn and stare as the woman wearing a skimpy turquoise bikini ran past them. Greg realized he was a lucky man to have Maddie as a friend.

Chapter 2

GREG CHECKED HIS WATCH. *Only ten minutes had elapsed since he last glanced at it. Once more, he looked at the digital clock on the nightstand next to his bed. Both agreed on the time: 7:45 p.m. He had not heard from Maddie. He couldn't believe she would have forgotten all about their date. Punctuality was one of her attributes he most admired. Unlike a lot of women, Maddie had never kept him waiting.*

They had a reservation for eight o'clock on The Winslow, famous for its lobster and steak dinner, not to mention the ship's entertainment. Tonight's show consisted of an Elvis imperson- ator. Maddie had been excited about the evening.

"Where could she be?" he asked the empty room.

Ten minutes went by. Worried, he picked up the phone and dialed the concierge who answered after the first ring. "Yes, Mr. Watts. What can I do for you?"

"I'm worried about my companion, Maddie Winthrop. She hasn't returned to her room, and we have a dinner reservation – one that she wouldn't want to miss."

"Perhaps, she lost track of the time. You know how women love to shop."

Greg took a deep breath. "I didn't say anything about a shopping spree."

"Please forgive my assumption about her. Did she tell you where she would have gone?" asked the concierge.

"Yes. She had reservations for a charter boat. Said it specialized in treasure seeking. Said it catered to experienced divers – which, of course, she isn't."

"Do you know the name of the company, Sir?"

"No. She said she saw a brochure about it in the lobby. Could you look through the cabinet next to your stand and give me the name of the charter? I'll call them."

"Yes, sir. Please hold."

Greg grew even more anxious, waiting for a response. He could hear the rustling of papers. "Are you still on the line?"

"Yes. I'm looking through the brochure case." Pause. "I'm sorry, sir, but there's nothing – no brochure, no flier, nothing – advertising a charter boat for treasure seekers."

Greg ran his hand through his hair. "I'm coming down. There has to be something there. Where else would she have obtained the information?"

"I'll check with the manager who might know more about charters than I do," said the concierge. "If I'm not at my post, please wait for me."

"Thanks." Greg put the telephone receiver back in its cradle.

———

RING. The doorbell. Jeb ignored it.

Loud banging on his front door stopped Jeb's flow of words. "Damn, now I've lost my train of thought." He stood and stomped out of his study. Jerking the door open, Jeb groaned. "Pierre."

"You did say I could come any time to enjoy a good view of the bay, didn't you?" the policeman said.

Jeb nodded. "I did, indeed. What time is it?"

"Six-thirty. According to the weather report, sunrise is at seven."

Jeb sighed and waved his arm, invitingly. "Come on in." He closed the door and asked, "Would you like a cup of coffee?"

Pierre smiled and nodded. "Don't mind if I do. Thanks."

Jeb motioned toward the opened doors to the walkway and glanced across the bay. "Help yourself to the view. I'll be right back. We can both enjoy the morning with a cup of java and the beauty of Quansea Bay." He went to the kitchen and checked the water level in the Keurig prior to brewing two cups of coffee.

Pierre stood leaning over the waist-high wall, admiring the eastern sky. "Just as I thought it would appear," he said taking the steaming drink from Jeb. "Gorgeous."

Jeb took a sip of his drink. He glanced at the horizon. Turning his attention back to Pierre, he asked, "Any news about our missing girl?"

Pierre nodded. "Both you and your neighbor gave me the same description of her boat."

"Ghastly color," Jeb said.

"Ugly or not, your descriptions matched the style and color of the Quansea Laboratory boats. After our conversation last night, I called the director of the lab."

"And?"

"And I learned that one of his marine biologists was working in this area yesterday, so before heading this way, I went by the lab to learn whether or not her boss had heard from her. As of late last night, he hadn't. But. . ."

"But?" Jeb interrupted, wanting a quick answer. He was eager to return to his manuscript.

"Her boss said she called him this morning to say she might be running a little late. Pierre chuckled, took a gulp of the hot brew, and winced."

"Too hot?" Jeb asked.

Pierre shook his head and smiled. "Not as hot as she is according to her boss."

"Yeah. She looked pretty good to me, too."

Pierre's grin morphed into a frown.

"What's wrong? Is she okay?"

"Hmm," said the policeman, "I'd say so, but. . ."

"There is something on your mind. Out with it," ordered Jeb.

"Remember that photo you took of her?" Pierre asked.

"Of course. I let you send it to your phone," Jeb said.

"She's mad about it," Pierre said.

"Why?"

"Guess she thought you didn't get her good side." Pierre grinned at his lame joke.

Jeb shook his head. "Silly girl."

Both men laughed.

Pierre sobered first and said with a straight face. "There's more, which is the real reason for my early morning visit."

"Oh?"

"Her boss said that her boat's missing. She thinks you did something with it."

"Me? She's upset with me? How does she even know I'm the one who took her photo?"

"Evidently, she went by the police station which explains the reason for her call to let boss man know she would be late for work. One of the guys mentioned your name."

"Oh good grief," Jeb said. The doorbell rang. "Excuse me," Jeb said and walked through the living room. He opened the door to greet his visitor. His jaw dropped. Both door and mouth gaped at the apparition standing before them.

There she was. The girl in the turquoise bikini only now she wore a pair of black dress slacks. There she stood. Beautiful. Steaming hot. Jeb took a step back. Her glare could have started a forest fire. Before Jeb could regain his voice, she pushed her way passed him.

She took three steps into the room, turned, pointed her index finger at him, and shouted, "How dare you take a picture of me without my permission and hand it out like candy?"

Stunned, Jeb stammered what he thought was an apology. "I tried to get your attention. Didn't you hear me yelling at you? I tried to warn you about the tide. It isn't wise to snorkel late in the day in Quansea Bay. Too dangerous in my opinion. Thought the police would need it in case. . ."

"Who do you think you are anyway? I am a marine biologist. I can assure you that the police would have no need of my picture. And, FYI, I don't have to ask you for an opinion or permission to do my underwater experiments."

Jeb was silent for a moment and then calmly said, "Ma'am, I didn't know . . ." He looked into her cold, gray eyes and realized she hated him. Feeling a bit agitated, he raised his voice. "Nor do I care to know anything about you or your profession. And I'm sure you don't care to learn about me or my work."

"You're right. I don't. But my attorney does." She lifted her chin. "I plan to sue you for stealing my boat and taking my photo and giving it to the police. Would you like to know what they did with it?"

Jeb grinned mischievously. "I'll let Officer Pierre Corbin answer that question." He motioned his head, directing her attention to the policeman.

Pierre stood just inside the opened patio door. "Ma'am, as an officer of the law, my job is to protect the citizens of this island. I circulated the photo not so much to show your attri. . ." – Pierre paused, searching for the right word – "features. Mostly, we wanted folks up and down the island to see your boat. We thought that if we found your boat, we'd find you nearby."

"Oh," she responded. "I see. Thank you, officer." She turned back to Jeb. "So?"

"So what?" he asked.

"What did you do with my boat? Where is it?" she demanded.

"You don't need to be accusing me of stealing that disgusting turquoise boat. I didn't do anything with it. You should not have left it on my sand bar."

"Your sandbar? I'll have you know that's a public. . ."

Growing weary of her bossy, accusatory attitude, Jeb answered sternly, "Oh, but that's where you're wrong, Miss whatever your name is. You see, you left your boat on my property. Private property. That sandbar is mine."

"I don't believe you."

Jeb grinned. "Follow me." He led her out onto the wrap-around walkway. Pointing to a large sign sticking out of the sand, he read, "Private Property. No Trespassing. Violators will be Prosecuted." He squared his shoulders. "You should have read the sign before you parked your boat. Officer Corbin, will you read this trespasser her rights?"

Pierre took the woman's arm. "Come on, ma'am. Let's leave monsieur alone." As he followed her out the front door, Pierre looked over his shoulder and winked at Jeb.

"Ah," Jeb said. "Now I can write in peace and quiet."

Jeb sat at his computer and read the last paragraph he had written before Pierre's arrival. With fingers poised, Jeb typed the next line.

———

GREG WAS BESIDE HIMSELF. *Something bad must have happened to Maddie. The resort's manager confirmed the concierge's opinion. Yes, tourists could charter a boat to go porpoise watching. No, there were not any charter companies for tourists to treasure hunt.*

It was time to call the local law officials.

JEB LIFTED his fingers from the keyboard. He scrolled back up to his description of Maddie. Ironically, Maddie's description matched the woman in the turquoise bikini. Jeb let out a sinister laugh.

The woman who had stormed into his condo and the Maddie in Greg Watts next adventure must suffer the same fate. After all, the tide comes. It goes. Nothing is ever the same.

Jeb could feel another best seller in his fingertips.

Author - C.J. Peterson

C.J. Peterson is a five-time award-winning author. She has been published since 2012, and knows how to relate well to folks of all ages. Her bright spirit and personality shine through as she shares her various passions and heart as an author, blogger, and podcaster. C.J. brings to life not only her world of writing and being a former youth leader for eighteen years, but also shares her abuse-survival past, and how that has shaped her in order to help others. She and her sister run *Texas Sisters Press, LLC.* They created the company for not only themselves, but also to help others achieve their dream of publishing a quality book people want to pick up and read.

You can find her online at:
https://cjpetersonwrites.com
"While the stories are fiction, the journey is real."
Her books include: *Grace Restored Series* (5 Books); *Holy Flame Trilogy* (3 Books); *Divine Legacy Series* (4 Books); and *Strength From Within*
For Children, she has started *The Adventures of Chief and*

Sarge Books. Book one *"Cruising"* is out, and she is working on more at this time.

She was also a part of the *'Tis The Season – A Holiday Anthology: 2020 Season*.

You can find out more about Texas Sisters Press online at:
https://texassisterspress.com

Making Waves

By:
C.J. Peterson

10

Making Waves

C.J. Peterson

Welcome to Silver Lake. An area for families to grow together and enjoy what life has to offer. There are some part-time residents as well as full-time residents. There are families with children and without. There are families of higher income as well as lower income. What brings them together is the love of nature. As much as this is a story about heart and family, this story centers on the journey of another.

PART 1
Darren and His Father

DARREN and his father worked on the boat for weeks. His father returned from his tour during World War II about two months prior. At first, his dad was withdrawn. However, when Darren explained his problem to his dad, that familiar sparkle appeared in his eyes. Darren was in love with Sarah. Sarah's family, along with Darren's were the only two families who lived on the lake at the time. Darren and his brothers grew up with Sarah and her siblings. They often walked to school together, and enjoyed each other's company.

Then one day about six weeks ago, something strange happened to Darren. He found himself liking Sarah as more than a friend. Her smile brought him joy. Her laugh made his heart skip a beat. When she said his name, he got butterflies in his stomach. And the best part? She held his hand the other day on the walk home from school. The issue? Silver lake was a large lake. It took him a good thirty minutes to walk to her house.

Darren's dad worked as a carpenter before the war. In his shop in the backyard, he started a boat prior to being drafted into the Army. When Darren told his dad his dilemma, his dad suggested they finish the boat for Darren to use to cross the lake. Darren lit up in excitement!

It took them a good month to complete their project. They worked night and day. They had a mission. It was a mission for love – one of the greatest causes.

WHEN DARREN SAT down at the table for breakfast one morning, his dad said, "Darren, we need to go to town today. We have to pick out the paint for the boat. It's almost done."

"Can we afford it?" Darren asked, concerned. He knew how tight things were for everyone. After all, the depression had been going on for almost ten years by 1939.

"We have to. We need the paint to seal and protect the wood," his dad explained. "As for the color, we'll see what's on sale when we get down there."

AFTER BROWSING through the options at the store for about an hour, Darren and his dad chose teal. While it is not normally a color Darren would pick, his dad liked it because he would stand out on the lake.

After they painted it, they let it dry overnight. Darren was so excited he could hardly sleep. He kept thinking of rowing the boat across the lake to see Sarah! He imagined the smile that would appear on her face, as her green eyes twinkled, and her soft brown hair flowed in the breeze.

———

THE NEXT MORNING, Darren inhaled his breakfast, and then ran for the shed. Opening the door, he gasped. His dad was waiting for him.

"While I know you're excited to take the boat to see Sarah, I want to make sure it's seaworthy," his dad said, leaning on the table next to the paddle. "What do ya say? Wanna go for a ride?"

A grin spread across Darren's face. "Would I ever!"

"You don't mind going with your old man?"

"It's okay, Pa." Darren waved him off. "I like doing things with you."

"Great! Let's go!"

Together, they navigated the bumpy terrain with the boat, careful not to drop the paddle. Once they got it into the water, Darren's dad said, "Stay here and hold the boat. Don't let go."

"I won't," Darren promised.

His dad ran for the shed, promptly returning with the anchor tied to a rope, along with an extra rope. He tied the extra rope to the end of the boat. "This is to pull it up on shore or to tie it to a dock or tree. Hop in. I'll tie the anchor to the back end of the boat once you're safely seated."

"Yes, sir," Darren said. He chose a spot toward the back of the boat closest to the shoreline, leaving the front for his dad.

His dad handed Darren the anchor. While Darren set the anchor inside the boat, his dad ran back to the shed and returned with fishing gear. After handing the gear off to Darren, he climbed in and tied the rope for the anchor to the back end of the boat.

"Okay, row," his dad said, handing Darren the paddle.

Darren raised an eyebrow. "Shouldn't we do this together?"

"Not if you are going to do this to visit Sarah. You have to learn to navigate the boat by yourself, along with someone else in it who is not helping you."

"Fair enough."

Darren and his dad played on the lake all day. Sometimes they fished. Sometimes they just talked.

"You have to take matters of the heart slowly," his dad cautioned that afternoon. "When it comes to love, you can hurry it and get into trouble."

"I know."

"I don't think you do. Things can go as fast or as slow as you want. It is up to the two of you. Don't let your friends pressure you into doing anything. Remember God is a part of both of your lives, and you want to honor Him in all you do."

"I will."

"Good man," his dad said, and cast his line back into the water. "Tomorrow the boat is yours. Be careful and responsible. Don't make me regret giving you this freedom at fourteen."

Darren grinned. "I won't. I promise!"

⊷

DARREN AND SARAH grew close and continued to date all through high school, and into college. Sarah became a nurse, while Darren joined the military. Once Sarah graduated, she and Darren married. Since the boat allowed them freedom and peace to talk whenever they wanted, for the wedding they made sure to use the boat during the wedding ceremony. They parked their car at Darren's parent's house, while the wedding was at Sarah's parent's house. It was a beautiful day that year on June 22. One neither would ever forget. Darren rowed the boat away from the wedding guests toward his parent's house where their car waited for them to take them on their honeymoon. While he rowed, he admired his beautiful bride. Their life with just the two of them was starting!

PART 2
Brielle and Colton

THE DAY BRIELLE and her family moved into their house on Silver Lake in 1975, across the lake was a young man named Colton Marshall. He was sixteen. While he sat on his porch, he could see there were new neighbors moving in. There was a young girl amongst them who piqued his interest, who looked to be about his age.

Being born and raised on Silver Lake, Colton knew the area like the back of his hand. His parents died in a car accident when he was only three. Afterward, he lived with his grandparents, who also lived on the lake. His grandpa was a military man, and often taught Colton survival tactics, as well as simple tools to live in nature. Working with wood was one of Colton's favorite things to do with his grandpa. His grandpa even had a workshop in the back where he made furniture and cabinetry.

As Colton watched the movers empty the truck, he whittled a wooden wolf he was working on for a few weeks. Colton loved to take chunks of wood and turn them into amazing woodland creatures.

His grandma came out to the porch after an hour, bringing

lemonade and cookies with her. Setting the tray on the table between the chairs, she then took her seat in the other chair. "Lemonade?" she asked.

"Yes. Please," Colton said, not taking his eyes off the young lady while he absentmindedly whittled.

"You have been working on that wolf for a while," his grandma said, pouring both of them a glass of lemonade, "it would be a shame for you to cut off a foot or a tail because your interests were elsewhere."

"What do you mean?"

"The young lady across the lake?" his grandma said knowingly. "I recognize the signs. Go talk to her."

"It's a long walk over there."

"Take your grandpa's boat," his grandma said, gesturing toward the teal canoe his grandpa and great grandpa made when his grandpa was in his teens. When Colton and his grandpa were fishing, his grandpa shared stories of courting his grandma. His grandma lived across the lake from him, and he used the boat to see her every day.

Colton raised an eyebrow. "Would he let me take it on my own?"

"For love? Yes. I'm certain Darren would approve! He's working on the Shultz's table. I will let him know I gave you permission. Here. Let me put this plate of cookies in a tin for you to take over as a welcome. That will give you an excuse," she said, getting up. She returned in a matter of moments with the cookies in a tin. "Don't let them fall in the water," she cautioned.

He accepted the cookies, and then set his wolf on the tray for his grandma to take back inside. He gave her a kiss on the cheek and then off for the boat. "Thank you!" he called over his shoulder.

Rowing to the other side of the lake, Colton's heart raced. As close as he was, he could clearly see her flowing strawberry blonde hair and sparkling blue eyes. He could tell by her gait she was energetic and feisty. His grandpa's family was from Ireland, and his grandma's family was from Scotland, so he was used to aggressive temperaments. He was also used to the passion, which was also a sign of both temperaments. Once his grandparents set their mind to do something, it got done. That was one trait he was grateful to have inherited.

When he got to the shoreline, he tugged the boat onto a sandbar and tied it to a tree. Grabbing the cookies, he made his way up to the house. Only the movers were still roaming around outside, emptying the truck. The family had since gone into the home.

Hearing the mother calling out orders to the family, he knocked on the door. "Brielle! Get the door, please!" the mother yelled from the kitchen.

"Got it!" she said. Opening the front door, only a screen door separated her from the boy. Before her stood a handsome young man who looked to be about her age. He had jet black hair, and baby blue eyes. He had a rugged look to him that Brielle found intriguing. "Can I help you?" she asked.

"Hi. I'm Colton. I live across the lake, and saw y'all moving in. My grandma baked some cookies for y'all," he said, holding up the tin of cookies.

"Mom!" Brielle yelled.

"Coming!" she called back.

Brielle was a carbon copy of her mother, and she knew it. She did not mind. She thought her mom was pretty. She was a bit bossy, but pretty nonetheless. "He brought cookies," Brielle said when her mom walked in.

"Well, let him in. Don't make him stand there," her mom said, picking up a box to take back to the kitchen. "You can handle this," she said with a wink.

Blushing, Brielle turned back toward Colton, and opened the door. "Sorry."

"Not a problem. I was fixin' to take a walk. Do you want a break?" Colton asked.

Glancing toward the kitchen, she could hear her mom calling out orders to her siblings and cringed. "Not sure. Just a second," she said taking the tin of cookies. Thinking her mom would be more apt to grant her request if she gave her mom the cookies, she opened the tin, allowing the wonderful aroma of the freshly made cookies to surround her. "Cookie?" Brielle asked her mom.

"Sure. Ooo! Chocolate chip! And they're still warm!" her mom said, accepting a cookie. "Mm! It practically melts in your mouth!"

"Colton is the boy who brought them. He asked if I wanted to take a walk with him."

"Do you?" she asked. "I can give you a reason not to if you want to pass?"

"Actually, he's cute!" Brielle smiled. "I want to go."

"With as much as you have been complaining about moving from the city, if you can make a friend here, I'm all for it," her mom said, taking another cookie from the tin. "You will have to do a fair amount of work before bed, so don't be too long or you will be tripping over boxes to get to bed."

"Got it. Thanks, Mom!" Brielle grinned. Leaving the tin of cookies, she quickly made her way back to the door. "My mom said I could go for a bit. I'm Brielle, by the way." She shook his hand.

"Welcome to Silver Lake," Colton said. "I'm Colton Marshall. Want to take a walk, or head out into the lake in the boat."

Brielle grinned. "Boat! Definitely!"

Seeing her face light up at the boat idea, he happily obliged.

That tiny boat took Colton back and forth between the houses, along with many afternoon boat rides with Brielle through the last few years of high school. Even during breaks at college, he was able to still take the boat to her house.

When he knew Colton was coming home, his grandpa made sure the boat was in perfect working order. His grandpa knew how much the boat meant to Colton, and he would soon be passing the teal canoe onto his grandson.

THE DAY COLTON graduated from college was the most exciting day for him. After the festivities, he and his grandparents headed home. Unfortunately, Brielle graduated from college on the same day, so they could not attend each other's graduation. However, they made plans to meet up later that night. Colton would pick her up with the boat.

"Colton, your Grandpa Darren and I have something we want to give you," his grandma said, sitting him down when they got home.

"We know you got a ring for Brielle. However, we have an alternative if you are interested," he offered.

Blushing, Colton admitted, "I was going to surprise y'all."

"Honey, we have seen this coming a mile away. We knew you were just waiting for both of you to finish college," Grandma Sarah explained. Holding a tiny, black velvet box out to him, she continued, "These are your parent's rings. You can choose to use them or not. It is up to you."

Accepting the box, he opened it to find a his and hers wedding set. His parents had a modest amount of money when they were alive, so the set was stunning. They were definitely not something he could afford right now. Hers was a marquise cut diamond, with tiny diamonds surrounding it and around the band. The wedding band included five perfect diamonds on a gold band. His was a solid gold band.

"These are perfect! They may have to be sized, but they are really pretty. I think she'll like them," Colton said, his face unable to contain the mix of emotions churning within. "*Much better than my simple little stone. Are you sure?*"

"We're positive your parents would want you to have them," his grandpa said. "We're also certain they would approve of the young lady. You have been responsible in waiting until you both graduated. As a couple, you have honored God and all He holds dear. It's time to pass these down to the next generation. Speaking of passing down, you will also be getting another gem."

"What's that?" Colton asked.

"I have been working day and night to make sure it is in the best possible shape it can be. The boat is yours."

"Really?" Colton grinned. "Thank you!"

Grandma Sarah momentarily cleared her throat before she said, "We're not sure what your plans are for the future. Until you figure them out, you're welcome to stay in the guest house after the wedding."

"That would be great! You guys are amazing! Thank you so much!" he said, giving each of them a hug, and then a kiss on the cheek.

"We know you didn't have the benefit of having your parents, but we did our best," his grandpa explained. "We want you to have a leg-up in this section of life. You and Brielle were in love at first sight, much like your Grandmother and I," he said, taking her hand into his. "We wish you both the absolute joy and happiness."

"Thank you. I-I don't know what to say."

His grandma smiled. "You've said more than enough."

"Now, go get that young lady and ask her to be your bride," his grandpa said with a wink.

AFTER HE PACKED A PICNIC BASKET, Colton headed down to the dock to load the boat. Ring box tucked in his pocket, he untied the rope, and began the familiar trek across the lake. Through the years, he saw many fish, turtles, and even a few alligators in the lake. He saw the seasons change. He saw houses torn down and new ones built. He saw many move in, while others moved out. One thing remained the same – Brielle and her family continued to live across the lake, bringing a deeper love to his life than he ever knew.

He dragged his canoe up onto the sandbar, making sure it was far enough no water would pull it back into the lake. His heart racing as it did on the day he met her, he climbed up onto the porch and rang the doorbell.

"Colton!" Brielle yelled. She threw open the door between them and flung her arms around his neck. "I'm so happy to see you!" She kissed his cheek. "Guess what?" she asked, a twinkle in her eyes. "We're officially adults!"

Colton laughed, resting his hands on her waist. "We've been adults for a couple years, honey."

"Yes, but we were student-adults. We're full-fledged adults now!"

"I know," he said, and gave her a kiss. "So, what's the plan?"

"Mom and Dad are in the kitchen. We could go find out?" Brielle suggested.

"Tell you what," Colton said, "why don't you run upstairs and get your jacket? While you're up there, count to one hundred before you come down...and not fast counting either. I mean look at your watch and count by the seconds."

"Why?"

"Please just do it? For me?"

"I will," she said. She kissed his cheek and then ran upstairs.

Taking a deep breath, Colton headed into the kitchen. "Hi," he said to her parents.

"Colton!" her mom gushed as she gave him a hug. "Congratulations!"

"Yes. Congratulations, son," her dad said, shaking his hand.

"Thank you. I, uh, don't have a lot of time, but I wanted to talk to you before Brielle came back downstairs."

"What's up?" her dad asked.

"I wanted to ask your permission to marry your daughter."

When they grinned, Colton breathed a sigh of relief. Unsure how they would take his asking, he was relieved to see the smiles of delight on their faces.

"Let's go talk in the den," her dad said, wrapping his arm around Colton's shoulder to guide him.

Colton gulped, but dutifully followed. *He thought they were excited. Maybe he read them wrong?*

Once seated, her dad started, "You two have been together for six years. I respect that you waited until you both graduated college before you asked. That gave Brielle the confidence of having a degree of her own. Thank you."

"I want to give her everything I can, sir."

"What are your plans?"

"Well, I figure we can talk about that together. However, in the meantime, once we're married, my grandparents have offered to let us stay in the guest house on their property. As for rings, they gave me my parent's rings. I only hope she likes them, that is, if you give me permission?"

Her dad covered his grin. Pride was evident as he beamed at Colton. He cleared his throat, bringing himself back to the conversation. Putting on a stern face, he continued, "Brielle is accustomed to a certain level of lifestyle."

"I understand. However, when you were first married, you were not at this level. She and I have discussed what our life would look like many times. We know getting to the level we both want will take time. We also know we will be eating a lot of hot dogs and spaghetti for a while."

"We ate our share," her dad said, sitting back in his chair, resting his hands on his stomach. "When would you get married?"

"Again, that will be something Brielle and I talk about. Sir, we have been together longer than many of our friends who are married already – some even with a child. We *have* waited. We waited in all aspects. With both of us being Christians, we wanted to make sure God approved and blessed our marriage. We know there is a long road ahead of us. We know things will eventually work out if we only trust in God. A chord of three cannot be broken."

"Agreed."

"We do devotions when we go out onto the boat. We make sure to keep God in our thoughts, especially when we are together. There is a lot of temptation. I'm not gonna lie. However, I have respected your daughter, and she has respected me. We waited to start our lives together. May I please marry your daughter?"

"Yes," her dad said. "I couldn't ask for a better husband for my daughter, or a better son-in-law. I will caution you, though. Do not hurt her. If you hurt her, there is nowhere on this earth you can hide."

"Her brothers have made that abundantly clear over the years. I couldn't hurt her anyway. That would be like stabbing myself in the chest. She is my heart."

"I know. And, I appreciate it. Go make my daughter a happy young lady."

"Thank you, sir!" Colton said, standing, shaking her father's hand.

—◆—

BRIELLE AND COLTON rowed into the middle of the lake before either said anything. "You're being awful quiet," Brielle finally pointed out.

"I have a lot on my mind," Colton said.

Brielle raised an eyebrow. "Good. I hope."

"With you? Always."

She smiled shyly.

Colton reached behind and dropped the anchor into the water. Turning back toward Brielle, he opened the picnic basket. "Dinner?"

"Of course! I'm always up for food!"

He grinned. "I know."

They enjoyed a wonderful meal of fried chicken and coleslaw, with apple pie for dessert. All were her favorite foods and he knew it. He wanted this moment to be special. He wanted to please her and make a memory they both would cherish forever.

"All my favorites!" Brielle said, finishing her apple pie. Wide-eyed, she looked up and asked, "I'm not dying, am I?"

"No," Colton said in a chuckle, appreciating her sarcastic humor. Taking her empty plate, he set it in the plastic bag before resting it in the picnic basket. Then he took both her hands into his and explained, "Brielle, from the first day I saw you move in, you changed my life forever. Your smile lights up my day. Your heart never ceases to amaze me. Your endless patience with me and my schedule and volunteer work at the fire station boggles my mind. Thank you for loving me."

"Of course! How could I not?"

Carefully kneeling onto the floor of the boat, he saw her looking at him wide-eyed. "Brielle, my grandparents used this boat to see each other over the years until they were married. During their marriage, they took this boat out, enjoying many lake days together. When my parents started dating, they took this boat out all the time. The day they got married, they rode the boat to the other side of the lake to get their car for their honeymoon, same as my grandparents. It's almost a tradition at this point. Today, I wanted to be in this boat when I asked you to be my bride. Brielle Marie Flannigan, would you marry me and make me the happiest man alive?" he asked, pulling out the black velvet box with his parent's rings inside. Opening it, he presented the rings to her.

She looked from the box to him, multiple times. She looked him right in the eyes, and nodded. "I would love to be your wife. It would be my honor."

Hands shaking, he placed the engagement ring of the set on her finger. It was slightly too big. "We will get them sized."

"That's fine. It's stunning! How did you afford these?"

"They are my parent's rings," Colton explained. "I hope you don't mind that they're not new."

Tears in her eyes, she said, "That means even more to me than if you bought new. These are the rings your mom and dad wore. They are something I will cherish forever."

He leaned forward and gave her the most passionate kiss to date!

———

THE DAY OF THE WEDDING, Brielle, her mom, and Colton's grandma decorated the boat. Brielle and Colton would be taking the boat across the lake to where Colton's car was parked. From there, they were to head to airport to fly to the Bahamas for their honeymoon.

The gazebo was already decorated, and the chairs were already set up in the backyard of Colton's grandparent's house. In case of rain, they would move the wedding indoors. The wedding would have their pastor marrying them, Brielle's best friend Maggie as the maid of honor, and Colton's best friend Scott as the best man. Otherwise, those in attendance would consist of youth group members, church members, and family members. Per the RSVP's there would be fifty in attendance.

THE WEDDING WAS BEAUTIFUL. As Colton rowed the boat away from the shore, those in attendance threw bird seed.

"Hello, Mrs. Marshall," he said with a grin.

"Hello, my loving husband."

"We're actually married!"

"I know!" She giggled. Looking back toward the shore, seeing their friends and family, she then turned back and said, "It was absolutely beautiful."

"It was. And, heading into our lives without a lot of debt will make things easier."

"Outside of our school loans, I think we're doing really well."

"I'm glad we were able to find work around here. That will let us pay off those loans by not having to pay rent to my grandparents as well."

"So, when are we going to want to start for children? I know that will be the first question our families will ask when we get back."

"If they wait that long," Colton said, rolling his eyes.

Brielle laughed. "Things could be worse. At least our families get along and love each other."

"I know. God worked everything out."

"I can't wait to see what else God has in store for us."

"I keep ahold of Grandpa Darren's favorite verse. He said it helped him through the war. It's Jeremiah 29:11, which says, *'For I know the plans I have for you,"* declares the Lord, *"plans to prosper you and not to harm you, plans to give you hope and a future.'* We need to trust in Him, and keep Him in the center of our family. This verse reminds me He does have a plan for each of us, and it's one of hope. I think it needs to be our family verse. What do you think?"

"I think it's perfect," she agreed.

Once to the other side of the lake, he climbed out of the boat and pulled it up onto the sand bar. Knowing his grandpa would be picking up the boat later, he didn't worry about tying it off. He helped his bride out of the boat, and they headed off to their honeymoon!

PART 3
Emma and Flynn

ONCE THEY HAD ENOUGH MONEY, Brielle and Colton bought their own house on the lake. Over the years, they had three daughters: Emma, Makenna, and Jenna. These three lovely young ladies enjoyed growing up on the lake growing up. The girls learned everything Colton's grandpa taught him, as well as everything Brielle's parents taught her.

One day, Colton had Emma on the lake. It was their day to go fishing. While out there, Colton asked Emma, "Sweetheart, you are going on thirteen now."

"Yep. That's what they tell me," she said with a smirk. With her mom's strawberry blonde hair and blue eyes, she was the spitting image of her mother.

"You have grown up in church, but I have yet to hear you mention being a follower of Christ."

"Dad," she said, rolling her eyes, "I'm a good girl. You know I'm fine."

"Emma, if you were to die today, and were to stand before God, and He asked you why He should let you into His Heaven, what would you say?"

Emma pondered the question for a moment before she answered, "I have grown up in church, like you said. I have also been a good girl, and don't intend on doing anything bad."

"That's your answer?"

"Yes," she said firmly.

"Well, you've gone to Uncle Mark's auto shop for most of your life, but that doesn't make you a mechanic. You're learning many things, but you are not a certified mechanic. Correct?"

"Yes."

"Then, why would going to church make you a Christian?" he asked.

Emma narrowed her eyes as she crossed her arms. "Fair enough. What about the other portion of my argument?"

"Well, that's an easy one. Ephesians 2:8 and 9 says, *'For by grace you have been saved through faith. And this is not your own doing; it is the gift of God, not a result of works, so that no one may boast.'* You see, the only way to Heaven is the gift of Jesus's sacrifice. You cannot be good enough to get to Heaven. No one can. That's the reason why Jesus came from Heaven and died on the cross. He shed His blood, paying the ultimate price for our sins."

"Dad, I have heard this all before."

"You've heard it, but it doesn't seem to be sinking in. If it did, then you would have a different answer to my question."

"I get it," Emma said. "I hear this every Sunday and Wednesday."

"I'm not going to push this on you. However, it *is* my responsibility as your dad to make sure you have a clear understanding of what Christ did. Afterward, it's up to you. I won't mention it again. Agreed?"

"Agreed. Go ahead."

"Okay. You are at an age to make a knowledgeable choice. This decision is yours to make. It's a decision only you can make for yourself. We both know John 14:6 says, *'Jesus saith unto him, I am the way, the truth, and the life: no man cometh unto the Father, but by Me.'* And in John 3:16 and 17, it says, *'For God so loved the world, that He gave His only begotten*

Son, that whosoever believeth in Him should not perish, but have everlasting life. For God sent not His Son into the world to condemn the world; but that the world through Him might be saved.' God doesn't want to make you feel bad. He wants to save you. Jesus came here to give you the opportunity to have the choice between Heaven and Hell. He gives us all the free will to choose. If you choose to make the choice to follow Jesus, you have an opportunity to fulfill the plan God has for your life. Whether it's raising children for Him, like we are doing, or spreading His word a different way. Your job will be to tell others about Him."

"I understand."

"When or if you want to accept His gift, you know you only need to pray and ask Him. Romans 10:9 says, *'That if thou shalt confess with thy mouth the Lord Jesus, and shalt believe in thine heart that God hath raised Him from the dead, thou shalt be saved.'* All you have to do is trust Him and pray, asking Him to forgive you of your sins and help guide you in your life. Do you understand what I'm saying?"

"I do. Thank you. I know all of this. I'm just having a difficult time processing and thinking about it."

"Not pushing, but can I ask what's holding you back?"

"Well, I don't know if I want some guy from a long time ago telling me how to live my life. I don't know what to do."

"The choice must be yours. However, let me tell you what I know. I know He walked beside me when my mom and dad died. I know He was with me when I met your mother. He was also with me when I graduated high school and college, and got married to your mom. I know He was with me when Grandad died a couple years ago, and still walks with Grandma Sarah right now. She relies on her prayer time with Jesus. She knows God is looking out for her. She's at peace. He is and has been there through all of the good and the bad. He's not leaving us. He gives us peace to face everything this life throws at us."

"I see that. I want that peace. I feel on edge a lot," Emma admitted.

"What do you want to do? You know the information. You know the verses. We've taught it to you all your life. If you want time to think about it, take the time."

"I don't need time." Emma shook her head. "I see God in nature. I know He's here with us right now. I also know what Jesus did and what He taught. I want to accept His gift."

"Really?" Colton's heart leapt.

"Yes. Right here. Right now."

They took the time and prayed together. Emma accepted the gift Jesus gave in salvation.

EMMA GREW STRONGER in Christ each year. When she turned seventeen, her Grandma Sarah passed. On that day, she and her dad took some time on the lake. Emma and her great-grandma were close. Colton understood that bond. When his grandpa passed, Colton was crushed.

When they were in the middle of the lake, Colton set the paddle aside and dropped the anchor. "We can just sit here quietly or talk. It's up to you. We'll do what you want."

Emma rested her chin on her hand and sighed.

"Ooo." He cringed. "The heavy sigh. Haven't heard that in a while."

Emma rolled her eyes.

"Oh no! Am I in trouble? A sigh *and* eyeroll?" he said, trying to make her smile. The most she gave him was a smirk. Concerned, he asked, "What's going on in that head of yours?"

Resting her hands in her lap, she explained, "I know I'm supposed to be happy for Grandma Sarah."

"Who said that?"

"It was a celebration of life."

"Of course it is. Grandma Sarah had a beautiful life. She and Grandpa Darren lived full lives. The celebration of life portion is to celebrate that they are now at peace, together, with the Lord. That doesn't mean there isn't a hole in our hearts from the pieces of our hearts she took with her. It's okay to love her. It's okay to miss her. It's okay to be upset."

"Is it okay to be angry?" she asked, tears in her eyes.

Darren's heart broke. Cocking his head to the side, he asked, "Why are you angry?"

"I'm mad God took her."

"God didn't take her. He allowed her to come home. She lived her life. She lived it to the fullest. She lived it with true joy and pure love. God allowed her to come home as a reward for a life lived for Him."

"But she's still gone."

"She's gone from here, but she's in Heaven with God, Jesus, my parents, and Grandpa Darren. They're together."

"It hurts, Daddy," she admitted.

"Trust me. I know. I lost them too. They took the place of my parents when they died. I basically lost two sets of parents in my life. I feel your pain. I get it."

Tears rolling down her cheeks, Emma begged, "Make it stop. Make the pain stop! Please?"

Colton wrapped his arms around his daughter, allowing her to cry. "Go ahead and cry. We all miss her."

For a few hours, they shared stories about his grandparents. They laughed and cried. They talked and got angry. Finally, they cried it all out, and headed back to the house.

THE NEXT DAY, there was a knock on the door. Emma answered it to find two boys her age standing there with a casserole. "Can I help you?" Emma asked, studying them. The boys were identical twins. She struggled to find something different between the boys, aside from a slight height difference.

"Our parents found out about your grandma passing, and made a casserole," one of the boys said as he held it up.

"I'm Flynn, and this is my brother, Wynn," the other brother introduced them. "We moved in a few months ago. We started going to your church last week, and our mom saw the notice in the bulletin on Sunday. We're really sorry about your grandma."

"Come on in," Emma said, opening the door, standing aside. Her parents and sisters were in the dining room eating lunch. When they walked into the dining room, Emma explained, "This is Flynn and Wynn. They moved here a few months ago, and found out about Grandma Sarah last week at church. Their mom made a casserole." She gestured toward the casserole in Wynn's hands.

"Thank you for your kindness," Brielle said, grateful.

"Which house do y'all live in?" Colton asked.

"The brown and green one five houses down," Flynn said.

"How are you liking it?" Makenna asked.

"It's nice. We'll probably like it better once school starts next week," Wynn said. "Nothing personal, but there isn't a whole lot to do around here."

Colton chuckled. "No problem. I grew up on this lake. I get it. There are a few places to hang out, but honestly, the youth group will be your best bet in connecting."

"We're going to branch out into the youth group next Sunday," Flynn said.

"Great!" Emma grinned. "Well, you already know me and my sister, Makenna."

"If you don't mind my asking how old are you two?" Flynn asked.

"I'm seventeen, and she's sixteen," Emma said. "That one is Jenna, who is fourteen."

"We have a sister who's fourteen," Wynn said. "I'd be happy

to introduce you to her. She is bored out of her skull!" He rolled his eyes. "And taking it out on us."

Jenna laughed, and then added, "That would be great. May I be excused?"

"Go ahead," Brielle said. "Just be home for dinner."

"Come on," Wynn said.

"Um, we have a boat if you'd like to see it," Emma offered. Glancing toward her dad, Emma was relieved to see him nod.

"Why don't you two go," Flynn said to Wynn. "I'd like to see the boat."

Wynn smirked. "I'll let Mom know."

"You know the boat rules," Colton mentioned.

"Thank you!" Emma said, unable to hide her excitement.

Makenna left with Wynn and Jenna, while Emma and Flynn headed out to the boat. "Wow. This looks old," Flynn said, admiring the boat, "but in excellent shape!"

"My Grandpa Darren originally made it with his dad back during World War 2."

"Really? History fascinates me. I would love to hear the story."

Climbing into the boat, Emma started the story. As they headed out into the lake, the pair talked, engrossed in each other, not even seeing her parents walk out onto the porch.

"Well, that looks familiar," Brielle commented, as they each sat in a rocking chair.

"That boat has facilitated many relationships through the years," Colton said, reaching over, taking Brielle's hand into his.

"Yes. That little boat has made waves in the love lives of this family. As a matter of fact, it has made waves by fostering quiet moments for many important events in this family's life. I pray it stays in as good a shape as you have kept it. I would love to see the girls use it for their weddings."

"I will make sure of that," Colton promised. "That little boat has seen a lot over the years. It helped the love of my grandparents, my parents, us, and now it looks like Emma's life as well. There have been many lake days where heavy talks occurred, as well as some pretty prominent events too. I'll teach Emma how to care for it and keep it up."

Turning her head toward Colton, Brielle said, "I know we're not supposed to have favorites, but pretty sure Emma is yours."

"She is," he admitted.

"So, am I assuming correctly that *she* will be the next to inherit the little blue boat?"

"She will. And then she will pass it onto her children."

"You know, in eighteen years, that little boat will be a hundred years old. Your Grandpa Darren and his dad made it in 1939," Brielle pointed out. "It's crazy how many years that little boat has held on."

Colton smiled, remembering he and his grandpa working on the boat. "And she doesn't look a day over twenty," he said on a sigh.

Author - Richard Schwindt

Richard Schwindt is a writer and psychotherapist in Kingston, Ontario. He has been shortlisted twice in the International 3 Day Novel Contest, and won the outstanding book (self-help,) and Book of the Year (3rd,) in the 2016 Independent Authors Network Book of the Year Awards, for **Emotional Recovery from Congenital Heart Disease.** He is also author of **Emotional Recovery from Workplace Mobbing**, and a short story collection, **Dreams and Sioux Nights**. He has been married forty years, and has two children and two grandchildren.

You can find him online: www.richardschwindt.ca

His Amazon Page is:

https://www.amazon.ca/Richard-Schwindt/e/
B00RDF3NX6/ref=dp_byline_cont_pop_ebooks_1

Roses for Grant

By:
Richard Schwidt

11

Roses for Grant

Richard Schwindt

When the plane touched down Pam gave a small cry. Craig, who had been looking out the window, turned towards her. "Still hurt?"

"It's nothing," she said.

Both waited until the plane arrived by the gate then joined the crush, stepping out, blinking, into the heat. Herded towards the terminal, they fell into line for processing and picked out their luggage-Craig had tied a red ribbon on each bag-then exited the gate in search of the resort bus.

A tropical vacation had been Pam's idea, though it was late in the season, and they would miss the first week of spring. Cleaning out the sticks and old leaves from the garden would have to wait.

The beauty surrounding them felt invigorating, despite the torpid humidity. They looked out the window at the countryside during the ride to the hotel. Craig bought a beer from the tour guide.

They and their fellow passengers still wore cold weather clothes, sweated, and patiently waited, again in line, sipping thin rum punch from plastic cups. Birds shrieked from coconut palms outside an expansive Moorish atrium.

Later, as Craig fumbled with the door key, the couple in the next one over arrived, back from the beach.

"Hello," Pam said.

Their neighbors looked up, a little stunned to be addressed. Handsome and tall, he wore a bathing suit, and a plain grey tee shirt. She was blonde, attractive and, in the presence of Craig, only just remembered that she wore a bikini.

Pam looked at Craig, who tried not to do more than glance at the woman. "It's okay to ogle a little," Pam said, once ensconced in their new space.

Craig smiled. He checked to see if the small fridge contained cans of beer. "I only have ogles for you."

She rolled her eyes, then directed them down to the bed; an old ritual.

"Really?" Craig was game. He briefly considered putting it off, then said, "I need a shower first." Pam watched him disappear and shortly thereafter heard a brief yelp. Was it the hot or cold tap?

Later, as they laid side by side, Craig considered, and rejected a number of comments, thinking they would sound stupid.

Instead, he leaned in, brushed some of her white hair aside, and provided a quick kiss on the lips.

She smiled, and briefly wondered if her figure had blown right past curvy, and into lumpy.

"Has it been three months?" she said.

"Feels like four," he replied, introducing some levity. It worked. She laughed.

"You're out of practice," she said.

"I need practice."

"The tumor was benign," Pam said, "but it was an intruder too. I need to make space for you now."

"And when we get back I'm going to call Dr. Da Silva, and get some of those blue boner pills." Craig paused, but didn't leave time for her to respond: "Did you know Jeff Saunders takes them?"

"No! Really?" She recovered quickly. "He's younger than you. How do you know?"

"He told me." Craig took a moment to let this bit of rare gossip sink in. "He says they really do the job."

"Jennifer works at the pharmacy."

"Yeah, Reverend Jeff said the first time he picked them up everyone stopped joking, and suddenly got all professional and serious."

This triggered some instinct for justice in Pam.

"Everyone has a right to a love life," she said, walking into Craig's trap.

"Yes they do."

Her memory was triggered too. "Didn't they give, what's his name, the accountant… right, Nick Rivette, headaches?"

Craig slowed and deepened his voice: "I'm prepared to take that risk."

Both loved the beach, and the next morning found Craig showering again, and Pam packing the beach bag. When he emerged she said: "Remember to either wear a hat today, or put sun screen on your bald spot. Do you remember last year?"

They spent the day wandering the expanse of sand, lounging with paperback mysteries, and drinking thin beer. The clouds were mere wisps, and heat from the golden sun only mitigated by shade from a coconut matting umbrella, and a saline onshore breeze.

They hadn't taken a vacation since the operation. Jeff was entranced with the waving palm trees, and the moving spread of cerulean sea over the bay, and beyond.

Tourists and locals waded through the water, Pelicans skimmed the waves, and lifeguards patrolled in powerboats.

Vendors sold cigars, crafts, or took your picture with a large parrot. Snow white sails appeared on the far horizon.

Craig jumped into the water at intervals to refresh his body from the heat, but also, a little guiltily, to pee.

Later in the afternoon they took a walk along the beach. The water had calmed, and as they passed a squat grassy dune, they discovered a small boat, with flecked blue paint, pointed bow, and narrow stern. "Someone left it here." Craig stated the obvious.

They had turned round a point, and no one was in sight. Pam thought they must have passed the boundary of the resort. From their vantage point the beach continued; empty, except for a few neglected shacks and broken chairs. "I'm sure it's not abandoned," Pam said, "See, there's a paddle."

Craig looked down, and then up. One look at her face, and he could read her mind. "No," he said. "This is somebody's boat."

"We won't go far. C'mon, it will change our perspective." Craig frowned then pulled off his sandals. They awkwardly dragged the boat to the water, then he held it as still as he could while she stepped in.

Craig, up to his knees in water, gingerly pulled himself onto the tiny vessel.

"Ouch! This is going to kill my rotator cuff." He was expected to paddle, and attempted first to push them out, then steer a straight line for the open sea.

"I can see the resort now," Pam said. She looked down the beach, but Craig was trying to figure out how to navigate the blue boat.

"Do you think there are rip tides?" Craig found the boat hard to direct. He thought it would be like a canoe. But the design was different. And the paddle too long. Surely you weren't supposed to stand up in it?

He tried another line of conversation when his wife failed to answer: "Did you ever see one of those pictures; I think they take them from drones or something, where there's a little boat, and the people don't know that there's a giant shark right under them." This captured her attention.

"That's ridiculous," she said, then looked over the side, cupping her eyes from the sun.

"Do you see a shark? Some of the pictures show huge whales."

"No," she said. "But I think this is far enough." They had drifted farther out than anticipated.

The water below them darkened, and an unexpected wave tossed them against the corner of a coral reef.

"You okay?"

"Yeah, I just need to push a bit to get us out of this stuff." Pam had hoped for a pleasure cruise, but Craig was gingerly poking at the reef when a second wave arrived, bigger than the first.

They stayed onboard, but the paddle was wrenched out of his hands, even as the boat was propelled back into open water.

They sat for a moment, clutching the gunwale, and catching their breath. Pam spoke first.

"Is the boat leaking?" They examined the insides, still holding on, despite the now calm surface.

"No, there's a little bit of water, but I think it's from the splash." Craig released his grip, and sat up in his seat. "We have another problem."

"What?"

"Paddle's gone." Pam looked out over towards the reef. The paddle was nowhere to be seen.

"That's great." They looked again. Still no paddle.

"We could try sculling with our hands," he said. What else could they do?

"We can try. It's going to hurt your rotator cuff."

"It's already hurting, but we need to get back to shore. The boat's pretty small, we can probably do this. We will have to work as a team to keep it straight though." He dipped in a finger into the tepid water. "At least we won't freeze our hands."

After a few minutes work, little progress had been made. They hoped sculling would work, leaving them with only a few sore muscles, and a walk back to the resort. Pam looked up sharply. "Craig. Craig! Look!"

A fin split the surface of the water, maybe ten feet from their boat. "It's a shark." Something grey elided through the surf.

Both of them lifted their hands and sat back.

"Oh my God!"

"It's okay, we're in a boat," Craig tried to sound a positive note, but failed.

"The shark could butt us with its nose or something. It's just a little boat," Pam said.

"Most sharks are friendly." That comment, possibly true, made neither of them feel better. It is hard to think of sharks as friendly, and who knows the difference?

"Oh my goodness, there are two of them." Another fin split the surface. "It's a shark thing, a shark orgy!"

"Frenzy." They clutched the gunwales again, prepared for the worst.

But Pam got a better look. "Hey, the two fins are together, I think it's a Manta Ray." Craig leaned over, and the boat leaned too.

"Hey."

"Sorry. That's good, Manta Rays aren't aggressive." It drew closer to the boat.

"Are you sure? It's huge. Didn't one of them kill that Australian guy? They have big stingers." The Ray passed a lazy circle around their fragile vessel.

"He got right in its territory. It was scared."

"Territory? You mean the ocean? What if this one is scared?"

"We need to paddle back to shore," he said.

"And who puts their hands back in the water first?" The

Manta Ray pivoted, then continued its journey, running a parallel line with the beach, and soon it was many yards away. Pam and Craig were left in their little boat, further out than before.

Pam reached forward and tapped him on the shoulder. "Look this way," she said.

He turned and saw a silver power boat headed towards them. They yelled and waved, as if they had been adrift for months. The power boat didn't turn because it had been headed their way the whole time. Another tourist walking the beach had noticed they were adrift.

When the vessel pulled alongside them, everyone became aware of the language barrier. But the driver and the lifeguard threw a rope for Craig to tether their boat to the larger craft.

Then they crawled over the higher gunwale and sat, wet and a little despondent, in the rescue craft.

The driver impassively guided it away from the reef towards the resort, then, turning in, tilted his engine so both vessels could drift with the last bit of thrust into the sand.

The remaining resort beachgoers watched Pam and Craig climb down. Craig had twenty dollars in his pocket.

He passed the money to the skipper, or whoever he was, and said, "Thanks." The skipper gave him a curt nod.

"I need a drink badly," he said.

"The maid left miniatures of Rum in the room before we left this morning. And more beer. Let's go back. We can change our clothes, and sit on the balcony." The sun lay close to the horizon now, and the wind had cooled. They were grateful to be returned to safety.

"I need to report the boat," Craig said. "Somebody is missing his boat."

They entered the atrium and approached the desk clerk. Craig felt fatigue catching up with him. The woman at the desk looked up from her computer.

"Hi, the lifeguard just brought us in. We took a boat from

down the beach, and we don't know who owns it. It's on the resort beach now and we want to make sure the owner gets it back." He had no idea if she understood.

"Just a small boat?"

"Yes."

"Blue?"

"Yes."

"That belongs to the resort. It is for staff. Someone must have left it down the beach."

"Okay, thank you." She nodded. Someone else approached the desk. He briefly wondered if he should mention the paddle, then decided to let everything be. Maybe it would drift in or something.

"So?" Pam said, when he stepped away, back into the lobby. He took her shoulder and steered her towards the elevator.

"The boat belongs to the resort. It seems we did them a favor."

"Did you mention the paddle?" This question seemed, to Craig, unnecessary. He dismissed it.

"I'm sure they have lots of paddles around."

Later, they sat on the balcony, with drinks. The last sliver of blood orange sun disappeared into the west, over the ocean. Jaunty music rose from the lower deck.

"Did today trigger anything?" Craig asked. "Any memories?"

"I think it happened in front of the resort, not where we were."

"I know, that's not really what I meant." Craig sipped some of the pungent rum from a water glass and made a face.

"Okay, I did wonder if Grant was scared." After a pause. "Maybe you would have liked a beer more."

"Were you scared today?"

"A little. That boat was so small. I kept imagining what

would happen if we just drifted out to sea, or were butted by a big shark."

Craig saw her index finger tap a few times on the glass table between them; a sure sign she was fighting off tears. He covered her hand with his.

"He probably was scared," Craig said, "But it was a heart attack, in the water. It was over pretty quick."

"Grant raised me. He was always there for us. He took me to the beach when we were kids."

"Your brother was eighty years old, at a resort." They both paused as a few tears appeared on Pam's cheek. "He was probably full of rum and blue pills."

Pam turned her head to face him. "What a terrible thing to say! Really Craig?"

He pushed back. "Grant was a great guy. I loved him, Pam. And for a really good man he was all kinds of fun. So he came for his honeymoon, at a resort, with his new bride – a young chick…"

"She was seventy."

"Well, a young chick to him. It's sad, really sad, and I know you miss him a lot, but he more or less went out on his own terms."

Pam sniffled, but she giggled a bit too.

"You are so bad."

"You know I'm right."

The sound of raised voices came from the room next door. The young couple seemed to be having an argument. Something shattered, a glass or vase, then: "Look what you've done!"

Shortly after, even on the balcony, they heard the door to the room being slammed as someone exited. "Trouble in paradise," Craig said.

They lingered on the balcony for a while before he asked: "What time is supper?"

Pam stood up. "My watch and the info are inside. I think it's soon." She shouted out the door to him a few minutes later: "Dinner's at 7:30."

"Where?" Craig pulled himself to his feet. His whole body ached. It was going to be an early night. He would feel his right shoulder tomorrow.

"The Japanese restaurant."

"Hmm, do you know where it is?"

"No, so we had better get going now, or we're going to be late."

In the restaurant, over a plate of Teriyaki Salmon, Craig said, "Maybe Manta Ray sushi would be more appropriate."

Pam rolled her eyes. "It didn't do anything to us. It just visited for a moment, then went on its way."

"It scared you."

"I didn't see you putting your hands in the water after it appeared." She had a point. "It was in its home. We were the interlopers."

"I wonder if Grant ate here the night before he died." Craig was musing. He couldn't say it, and he didn't even like to think it, but he kind of wished it had been Pam's other brother, who was an obnoxious bigmouth.

"Oh, I know the answer."

"How on earth would you know that?" They paused while the waitress, lovely in an emerald kimono, stopped by to fill their wine glasses.

"I asked Alice at the funeral."

"Why?" Craig took a sip from his glass. He made another face.

"You shouldn't drink the wine if you don't like it."

"Why did you ask her where they ate the night before?"

"I wanted to know if maybe indigestion or something caused the heart attack."

"Well?"

"They didn't eat here; he had a bad stomach and thought MSG made it worse. She didn't know about that."

"Pam, she only knew him for a few months before they got married."

"Exactly!" She tapped the table again, this time with frustration. "Alice got quite shirty. You would have thought I'd accused her of murder."

"You were thinking it." Pam laughed. "And it wasn't the MSG." She laughed again, this time loud enough to attract the attention of the diners at the adjacent table, who glanced up from their Miso soup.

The following morning, after breakfast, dressed for the beach, they picked up a delivery from the front desk, then made a diversion to the lobby bar.

At the beach, they found lounging chairs, laid down their beach towels, Pam's Macramé beach bag, organized the other items, and turned towards the water. Craig carried the roses, and each held a plastic wine glass with some kind of sparkling wine, already flat.

Other tourists looked at them and didn't understand. But eccentric behavior on the beach was hardly unusual. If this couple wanted to swim with flowers and wine, why not?

Pam's speech was short and heartfelt. "Grant, mom and dad left us when I was eight years old, and you were twenty. You put your life on hold to raise your little sister and brother. You missed much of your young manhood caring for us.

"But you never acted like you resented it, and you never stopped enjoying life. Miss you, best of brothers. I loved you so much."

They raised their glasses and took a drink. Craig then handed the roses gingerly to Pam who tossed them into the ocean. They stood and watched the flowers scatter, briefly floating on the water.

A large wave appeared and tossed the flowers behind them, back towards the beach.

"We better pick them up," Craig said, tracking their progress. "We don't want people stepping on the thorns. We can take them back to the room."

"Won't they be all salty or something?"

"They'll look pretty for the rest of the vacation." His pragmatic streak asserted itself: "And they were expensive."

"Then we'll be gone."

Craig raised a hand and waved to the sky. "Thanks Grant, we're going to enjoy your roses."

Another wave arrived and pushed them both backwards, but not quite off their feet.

Pam laughed one more time, before they turned away from the horizon, and started to wade towards the shore.

Author - Ronald E. Yates

Ronald E. Yates is a multi-award winning author of historical fiction and action/adventure novels, including the highly-acclaimed *Finding Billy Battles* trilogy. His extraordinarily accurate books have captivated fans around the world who applaud his ability to blend fact and fiction. Ron is a former foreign correspondent for the *Chicago Tribune* and Professor Emeritus of Journalism at the University of Illinois where he was also the Dean of the College of Media.

The Lost Years of Billy Battles is the final book in the trilogy and won Best Overall Book in 2019 and the Grand Prize in the Goethe Historical Fiction Category from Chanticleer International Book Awards.The first and second books of the trilogy have also won multiple awards.

As a professional journalist, Ron lived and worked in Japan, Southeast Asia, and both Central and South America where he covered several history-making events including the fall of South Vietnam and Cambodia; the Tiananmen Square massacre in Beijing; and wars and revolutions in Afghanistan, the Philippines, Nicaragua, El Salvador and Guatemala, among other places. His work as a foreign correspondent earned him several awards including three Pulitzer Prize nominations.

Ron is a frequent speaker about the media, international affairs, and writing. He is a Vietnam era veteran of the U.S. Army and lives just north of San Diego in Southern California's wine country.

Links to social media etc.

Website: https://ronaldyatesbooks.com/

Facebook: https://www.facebook.com/ronaldyatesbooks/

Twitter: https://twitter.com/jhawker69

LinkedIn: https://www.linkedin.com/in/ronyates/

Amazon: https://www.amazon.com/-/e/B001KHDVZI/-/e/B00KQAYMA8/

Goodreads: https://www.goodreads.com/author/show/77404.Ronald_E_Yates

Barnes & Noble: https://www.barnesandnoble.com/s/Ronald%20E.%20Yates/_/N-8q8

Authors Guild: http://www.ronaldyates.com/index.htm

The
Encounter

By:

Ronald E. Yates

The Encounter

Ronald E. Yates

Millennia ago, in what is now the Indonesian province of West Papua New Guinea, something inside a seven thousand foot jungle mountain flashed to life, pulsed, and sent a powerful surge of energy into the cosmos.

You wouldn't have noticed it unless you were standing within a few hundred meters of it—and if you were standing anywhere near it when that intense cobalt hue flared it would have been the last thing you did. The energy coming from what was deep inside a crevice would have vaporized you within a millisecond, leaving no trace of your existence anywhere on the mountain.

The primitive people who lived in a handful of villages hacked out of the ancient rain forest at the edge of the Foja Mountains acknowledged the spirit that lived there—a deity that could not be seen, but whose terrifying wrath could make you vanish faster than you could blink an eye.

"Never go to that mountain," tribal shamans regularly warned the villagers. "If you do, you will never come back."

There were plenty of stories about those who ventured into the mountains and who witnessed people vanishing before their eyes in a flash of blue light. Those accounts had been passed down from one generation to the next.

Nobody dared to venture into those mountains now, not in countless generations. The shamans warned the few outsiders who stumbled upon their village about venturing into the mountains and most heeded their warnings. Others didn't, and they never returned.

That's the way things remained for thousands of years until a world war erupted and soldiers arrived from a far-away place called Japan.

Now, nothing would ever be the same.

WESTERN NEW GUINEA: 1942

Colonel Koichi Usami was not happy with his orders. He was to establish a base far to the west in the inhospitable interior of Netherlands New Guinea. That meant he and his battalion of eleven hundred men would miss the impending attack on Port Moresby on the east coast of the New Guinea mainland. The capture of Port Moresby was critical to Imperial Japan's strategy to cut the lines of communication between Australian and American forces in the Pacific and thereby capture and fortify the chain of islands between New Guinea and Samoa.

The colonel was a wiry man with high cheekbones that seemed on the verge of poking through his skin. His eyes were dark and intense, and a thin black mustache flourished above his lip.

He couldn't help wondering why he and his men were given such an unimportant task in the backwater of Western New Guinea. After all, they had acquitted themselves well during the invasion of the Philippines. But what could he do? The order to make the landing along the coast one hundred miles north of the Dutch port town of Hollandia had come directly from Lieutenant General Hatazo Adachi, commander of the Eighteenth Army.

You are to establish a base of operations and then push inland into the Foja Mountains, General Adachi's orders said. *We have picked up some kind of beacon coming from there. I want you to find it and destroy it. Intelligence believes it may be a communication post designed to assist enemy ships and planes.*

Now, with a base established in the forest just beyond the beach, Colonel Usami was preparing to send a company of one hundred men deep into the uninhabited interior in search of the mysterious beacon. Fifteen of the men were trained in the use of radio direction-finding and radio fingerprinting equipment. Direction Finding, or "D.F." and Radio Finger Printing, or "R.F. P." were technologies about which Usami knew little.

He asked Lieutenant Ota, who was in charge of the special unit, how D.F might help them locate the mysterious beacon, and the answer he got was not helpful.

"I am not sure. The transmissions we are picking up are very strange," Ota said. "Unlike most radio signals, there doesn't seem to be any logical pattern. It appears to span several very high frequencies, and it definitely is not Morse code."

"I see, but can you pinpoint where it is coming from?"

"Once again, I am not sure. The signal is erratic and intermittent. One minute we think we have a fix on it, and the next it seems to have drifted through several frequencies. And frankly, I'm not even sure if the signal is coming from a radio transmitter. It seems to be something else."

"Something else? Do you think it is a new kind of radio or secret code the Americans have created?"

"I don't think so, Colonel. As I said, it doesn't use a series of dots and dashes the way Morse code does. There are long bursts of noise, almost like an echo, then a hum, then silence, then something that sounds like wailing, followed by a silence that sometimes lasts several hours. We don't know what to make of it."

Usami sighed. "Then I wonder if we are being sent on a fool's errand."

Ota wasn't about to question the mission. "All I can say is that I have never heard anything like it."

"No matter, Lieutenant. Make sure you have all the equipment, ammunition, and rations you need. You will leave at 0500 tomorrow."

Usami knew it would be a difficult trek into the Foja Mountains. It was an area so remote and unmapped that even the indigenous people had never ventured into the trackless tropical rainforest that covered some three thousand square kilometers north of the Mamberamo River basin. Not only was it the largest and most impenetrable tropical forest in the Asia-Pacific region, there were no passable roads. To make matters worse, the unexplored Foja Mountains soared to more than seven thousand feet. And then there were the stories Usami was hearing from local natives about bizarre incidents in the mountains. Of course, they were just superstitious nonsense, like the stories of spectral samurai that roamed the forests of his home in the Ise-Shima region of Japan.

The terrain in this part of Netherlands, New Guinea was a soldier's nightmare. As much as three hundred inches of rain fell each year making passage through mangrove swamps almost impossible. Monsoon rains of ten inches a day turned tiny streams into raging, treacherous rivers. After the rains, what few footpaths there were dissolved into tracks of calf-deep mud. Exhausted soldiers were reduced to lurching over viscous ground that pulled at their soaked boots. Disease thrived, with malaria the greatest threat. But dengue fever, dysentery, scrub typhus, and a host of other tropical illnesses awaited unwary soldiers in a dense, impenetrable tropical jungle that devoured men and equipment.

Such a waste of good men and critical resources, Colonel Usami thought.

Of course, he couldn't share those thoughts with the two subordinate officers who would be leading the expedition. To Major Imai, Captain Nakano, and their men, this was a reconnaissance mission in search of an enemy communications center —though Major Imai had wondered out loud why the enemy would establish a base in such a remote area of the world.

"Precisely because it is so remote, Major Imai," Usami had responded with minimal conviction. "The enemy presumes they would be safe from assault in such an inhospitable place. In any case, make sure you have enough rations and supplies for at least two weeks. And remind the men to take good care of their feet. Keep them powdered and dry. You don't want them getting jungle rot. You have a long march ahead of you."

Several days later, when Major Imai and his men stopped at a village looking for guides to take them into the mountains, they were emphatically rebuffed.

Imai was at a loss. He couldn't offer the villagers money. They were a primitive barter society and didn't even know what money was. Instead, he provided them things like matches, cigarettes, boots, clothing, and coffee—all to no avail. They were an aboriginal, superstitious tribe in which half-naked men wore traditional penis gourds and the women wore dresses made of tree bark.

"I wonder if they are cannibals," Major Imai asked Captain Nakano and Lieutenant Ota. "They aren't very friendly."

"These people are prehistoric," Captain Nakano said. "It's as if we have walked thousands of years back in time."

Major Imai nodded. "It seems so. We can't force them to guide us, but we could punish them for refusing. We could shoot all of them and burn their village."

Captain Nakano regarded the major for a moment. *Did he mean it?*

"That might not be a wise thing to do," Nakano said. "It would attract attention and, after all, this is a covert mission."

"Quite so, Captain Nakano. It was my frustration talking."

The villagers allowed Imai and his men to camp next to their hamlet while Lieutenant Ota and his D.F. crew set up their portable transmitter and rhombic antennas and waited to get a new fix on the beacon, which had been dormant for the past eight hours. While they waited, their aboriginal translator spoke a spattering of Dutch, English, and a few native dialects and used sign language to communicate with the villagers. He was cautioned again and again about venturing up into the mountains. But these strange outsiders who all wore the same clothes and spoke a perplexing language discounted the warnings.

"We have no choice in the matter," Major Imai told his men. "Our orders are to find this beacon. And we will do it, or perish in the attempt."

Early the following day, an excited Lieutenant Ota ran into Major Imai's tent. "We have picked up another transmission, and pinpointed it to this general area," he said, pointing his finger at a spot on one of the ambiguous maps Colonel Usami had given him.

"That doesn't seem very precise, Lieutenant. If the scale of this map is anywhere near accurate, it looks like that could be anywhere within a fifty square kilometer area."

"Yes, Major, I know. But the map you have of this area is extremely inadequate. We have no way to determine exact coordinates."

"It's the only map we have. It was taken from the Dutch colonizers. We are fortunate to have it. At least it shows the rivers and a few streams."

Lieutenant Ota nodded. "I will do my best to set a course to the general area. Maybe as we get closer we can zero in more accurately on the beacon."

At 0800 the next morning, Major Imai's men broke camp and began slogging toward the southwest and the Foja Mountains whose olive green peaks were shrouded in a heavy pasty mist.

Before they left the village Major Imai sent a coded message to Colonel Usami at his beachhead headquarters telling him of their progress.

As the outsiders marched toward the mountains, a few dozen members of the village lined up and chanted what the Japanese soldiers took to be a farewell refrain. The soldiers waved in appreciation. But it wasn't a simple parting incantation. It was the tribe's death song.

———

A LITTLE LESS THAN four weeks later, Major Imai and a corporal named Nakamura were met by a reconnaissance patrol. The two had just pulled a blue pirogue onto a sandy beach a few miles from Colonel Usami's beachhead headquarters. Once back at the camp, the two men were treated for exposure, exhaustion, fever, and insect bites, then, a few hours later as they lay on cots in the medical tent, they were visited by the colonel.

"What happened? Where is the rest of your company, Major Imai?" the colonel asked as calmly as he could.

"Gone," Major Imai wheezed. "All gone."

"What do you mean? You had more than one hundred men with you. Were you ambushed? Were some of your men captured?"

Major Imai pulled himself up on one elbow and motioned for Usami to come closer. "They are all gone, Colonel," Imai rattled. "And I can't tell you what happened."

Usami pulled back in exasperation. "What do you mean, you can't tell me what happened? Did you encounter Americans or Australians? Was there a battle? Did they rebel? Run away?"

Imai shook his head and crumpled back onto the bed, his eyes closed and his face contorted with exhaustion. "Nothing like that," he whispered, then he passed out.

Usami studied Corporal Nakamura, who was lying on the

next cot, unconscious and battling a fever. *Major Imai isn't making any sense,* Usami thought. *He must be delirious.*

Then, turning to one of the physicians, he said, "Let them sleep. I will return tomorrow morning when they are more rested."

As Colonel Usami entered the medical tent the next morning, he was met by Major Imai wearing a clean uniform. He was doing his best to stand at attention, but he was trembling and swaying.

"Shouldn't you be in bed, Major?" Usami asked.

Major Imai bowed deeply. "I am sorry I was not able to answer your questions yesterday, Colonel Usami. Now I am able to report what happened on the mountain."

Usami acknowledged Imai's bow with a token bow of the head. "Let's go to my tent where we will have more privacy." He looked at Corporal Nakamura, who was still lying unconscious on his cot. "I will talk to the corporal later."

Imai, still weak from his ordeal, lost his balance a few times as he tottered next to Usami. Once in the tent, Usami motioned for Imai to sit in one of the folding camp chairs arrayed around a small desk. He was eager to hear how more than one hundred men could have been lost.

"You said what happened wasn't a battle," Usami said. "If it wasn't a battle, then what was it? A contagious disease of some kind? An earthquake?"

Imai cleared his throat. "Let me explain. We located the source of the beacon at about two thousand meters up a mountainside. As we drew near, we could see something glowing. It was coming from a fracture in the earth. At first I thought it was a volcano, but the color was wrong. It wasn't red or orange like lava. It was a brilliant blue color. As we approached, the glowing stopped."

"Where were the men operating the signal or whatever it was?"

"There was nobody. No Americans, no Australians, no Dutch. Nobody."

"I don't understand. There had to be somebody producing the light you describe."

Imai, still feverish, wiped perspiration from his forehead. "I sent a squad of men into the crevice to find the source of the beacon. They climbed down and after about twenty meters they located something. They called me and I joined them. I saw a sphere that was about twice the size of a naval mine. It was inside of a rectangular translucent shell that looked like it was made of glass."

"Glass? A sphere twice the size of a naval mine? In the heart of a primeval jungle?" Usami was having trouble envisioning what Imai was describing.

"Except, the shield that surrounded the sphere was not glass. It was something...a substance I have never before encountered. When you touched it, it gave way, like putting your hand into a transparent wall of warm gauzy wax. No matter how hard you tried, you couldn't penetrate it with your hand. I stabbed at it with my sword, but I was only able to push the tip of my blade into the substance. Then, I ordered two men to fire their rifles into it." Imai paused. He seemed to be pondering whether he should go on.

"Well? What happened?"

Imai, looked squarely at Usami. "The bullets tore maybe a quarter meter into the substance, stopped, and then fell to the ground. They never got close to the sphere."

"What? That's not possible. Neither the Americans nor the Dutch have a defense system like that."

Imai looked at the ground, contemplating how to describe what happened next.

"And the rifle fire didn't attract the enemy?"

Imai shook his head. "As I said, there were no Americans, no Australians, no—"

"Yes, yes, I heard you. But somebody had to put this thing, this device inside that mountain. It didn't just grow there."

Imai remained silent for a moment. "Yes, somebody, or something put it there."

"Something? What are you saying, Major?"

"I don't believe it is of this earth."

Colonel Usami studied Imai's drawn face. "What makes you say that?"

"Because of what happened next." Imai paused and pulled himself forward in his chair.

"And what happened next?" Usami regarded Imai the way he might a child with a vivid imagination.

Imai cleared his throat. "The sphere began to make a noise… a low humming, pulsating sound that hurt our ears. We scrambled out of the opening and ran down the mountain about one hundred meters away. Then we waited, holding our ears. A while later, the vibrating sound stopped, and we returned to the opening and looked down. The sphere was a bright blue color, and it was glowing and pulsing and seemed to be growing stronger. The light it produced was so intense we had to cover our eyes."

"Bright blue, glowing and pulsing, eh?" Usami repeated Imai's words. He wasn't sure what to make of Imai's report. "Then what?"

"I ordered my men to stay away from the fissure and to set up a bivouac some one hundred meters away from it. Then I took a squad of men and began to reconnoiter the immediate area. I wanted to make sure we hadn't walked into an enemy trap of some kind."

"I see. Well, that was the proper military procedure, Major. What did you find?"

"After about an hour we had found nothing. No sign of human life anywhere. No evidence that anybody had ever been in the area before us." Major Imai stopped talking and slumped back in his chair. "That is when it happened."

"When what happened, Major?" Colonel Usami was annoyed with Major Imai's methodical way of relating his report even though he was being appropriately detailed.

"We had just about completed our inspection of the perimeter when a loud blast...a sound like I have never heard in my life—It was both shrill and deeply resonant and the shock waves from it knocked all of us to the ground. Then, as we lay on the ground looking in the direction of our camp, the brightest light I have ever seen enveloped and shrouded everything above us. We were maybe five hundred meters below it in the forest. After maybe ten minutes both the light and the terrible sound stopped, and we dashed up the mountain to our camp."

Major Imai stopped and cupped his head in his hands. Then he leaned forward. Colonel Usami's eyes focused on Imai's face, which was pinched as though he was in physical pain.

"Take your time, Major."

"This is difficult," he rattled. "When we got back up the mountain to where the rest of our men and our camp were, there was nothing. Nothing. No sign of anything. No equipment. No tents. Nothing."

"And your men?"

"Gone. It was as though they had never been there at all."

"You mean there were no wounded? No bodies?"

"Nothing. Not one shoe or belt buckle or rifle. Nothing."

Usami stood and walked to the open flap of the tent. He looked up at the misty, jungle-veiled Foja Mountains and stood there for a moment, rocking back and forth, his hands behind his back. Imai turned in his chair until he could see the colonel.

"I know it all sounds so incredible, so unbelievable," he said, his voice barely above a whisper.

Usami walked back to his chair. "You said you took a squad

of men with you to reconnoiter? That's twelve men. Yet only two of you came back. What happened to the other ten?"

"It took two weeks to find our way back from the mountain because everything in our camp—our rations, water, medical supplies, weapons, ammunition, clothes, tents—all vanished along with my men. We only had what we had when the beacon erupted. We had to live off the land. We did our best, but every day one of the men either got sick, or died from hunger or lack of drinkable water. Then there were poisonous snakes and insects I had never seen before. It was as if the mountain was trying to keep us from leaving."

Colonel Usami frowned at Major Imai. "How is it that you and Corporal Nakamura managed to return while the rest of your men didn't?"

"We were lucky, Colonel. There were times when I didn't think I could go on. Nakamura was bitten by a snake, and I was half-carrying him when quite by accident the four of us still alive came upon the village where we had stopped on the way up the mountain. The natives treated Nakamura's snakebite with some kind of poultice and gave us several gourds of water along with some dried monkey meat.

"Two days later, just before we left, Private Abe died of malaria. Then, as we walked through the mangrove swamps, Private Murakami was attacked and killed by a crocodile. As you can see, Corporal Nakamura still is not fully recovered from his snakebite. We eventually came to a river and found a small native boat. I decided, rather than to walk back to the base camp, we would use the boat and follow the river to the sea. After three days, the river emptied into the sea, and from there we rowed south toward your encampment. When I calculated that we were close, we beached the boat and began moving inland. That's when the patrol found us."

"I see," Colonel Usami said. "You were quite fortunate,

Major Imai. You seem to have come through the ordeal in relatively good condition."

"Yes, lucky. Except for these." Major Imai raised his pant legs to reveal several golf-ball sized cysts on his calves.

Colonel Usami clicked his tongue. "I am left with a dilemma, Major Imai. How am I to report this to General Adachi? He will think I have lost my mind. There was no encounter with the enemy, no battle, yet we have lost an entire company of men to what? To some unknown force that presumably gobbled them all up?"

"Yes, I am very sorry."

"I don't need an apology. I need an explanation. I need to understand what happened."

Major Imai stood up from his chair. "Then, Colonel Usami, may I suggest that you go up the mountain yourself. I will take you there so you can witness what I did."

"That, Major Imai, is the most reasonable thing you have said today."

Two weeks later, Colonel Usami set off for the mountain area with Major Imai and a platoon of men. After several days of trekking through the dense forest and using some rough latitude and longitude coordinates that Major Imai had created, the party managed to arrive at the mysterious crevice on the mountain.

When they got there, Major Imai insisted the group make camp further down the mountain. "We shouldn't get too close," he warned.

Sure enough, two days later, whatever it was inside that mountain crevice sent an intense cobalt beacon into sky along with an ear-splitting wail. It lasted no more than twenty seconds, but it left the colonel and the other men in the platoon terrified.

"That is not something created by the Americans or the Australians," Usami gasped as he removed his hands from his ears. "It is...uh...something else."

"Yes, something else," Major Imai repeated. "Something not of this world. Something made by the gods."

"The Gods? I doubt that," Colonel Usami said. "This is a device for physicists or engineers to investigate, not for me. I am a soldier, not a scientist."

Major Imai nodded.

Nevertheless, the temptation and the allure of the unknown prompted Colonel Usami, Major Imai, and five of their men to slither up the mountain to the crevice that held the source of the beacon. Just as before, Major Imai pointed out the translucent sphere inside of a gauzy formation. Once again, soldiers attempted to breach whatever it was that surrounded the sphere, but were unable to get inside the viscous cocoon that enveloped it.

After several minutes, Major Imai urged the men to stop and advised that they retreat back down the mountain. Colonel Usami agreed, but before he did, he snapped several photos of the sphere.

"I will send the film back to Tokyo and let the doyens figure it out," the colonel said.

"Do you think they ever will?" Major Imai asked.

TOKYO: 1946

Colonel Usami sat in an office inside the Dai-ichi Semei Building, which served as General Headquarters (GHQ) for General Douglas MacArthur, the Supreme Commander for the Allied Powers—otherwise known as SCAP.

Colonel Usami no longer wore the Japanese Imperial Army uniform. Instead, like a lot of destitute Japanese following Japan's surrender in August 1945, Usami wore civilian clothes that were a bit frayed and tatty. His dark blue suit was one that he had purchased in 1935, almost six years before Japan had attacked the U.S. Navy fleet at Pearl Harbor. He was fortunate to have it. His wife had kept it boxed in mothballs during the war.

Usami was almost thirty pounds heavier in 1935 than he was today and, as a result, the suit drooped over his thin frame like a poorly pitched dog tent. Nevertheless, he had been more fortunate than many of his fellow officers. He had not been arrested by the occupation authorities, nor had he been questioned extensively. In fact, this was the first time he had been summoned to GHQ and he was plainly uneasy.

Behind a desk sat an American colonel named McGrath who looked to be in his early sixties. The American colonel was with the Office of Strategic Services, and he was holding a sheet of paper filled with Japanese hiragana and kanji characters.

"Do you know what this is, Colonel?" he asked, speaking almost perfect Japanese and waving the paper in front of Usami.

"No, I do not," Usami said.

"It is a letter we received from a Major Imai telling of a secret base in Western New Guinea that you were in charge of. It also talks about a powerful weapon hidden in the mountains there. I would like to know more about this secret base and this weapon the major refers to. Are you familiar with those things?"

"Yes."

The American colonel was noticeably surprised by Usami's answer. He expected him to deny any knowledge of the base or the weapon.

"And are you familiar with Major Imai?"

"Yes, he was under my command in Western New Guinea in 1942."

"Major Imai sent this letter to GHQ about six months ago. We tried to interview him but when we tracked him down in Kyushu we discovered that shortly after mailing this letter he shot himself. Do you know why he might have done that?"

Usami was perceptibly stunned. "Shot himself? I have no idea why he would have done such a thing. He was a fine officer who only did his duty as ordered. Of course, it has been four years...."

"Yes, yes, war changes people." Colonel McGrath produced a file, opened it, and ran his finger down a few paragraphs. "Says here you were in charge of a secret base in Western New Guinea called Aoi Yanagi. Is that correct?"

"Yes."

"It also says that the purpose of that base was to deal with some kind of a new weapon that you had stumbled onto somewhere in the Foja Mountains. Is that correct?"

Usami, looked at the floor. "Yes, but we were never able to comprehend or work out what it was. I concluded it was not a weapon, but something else. It possessed power I have never seen before. The local natives claimed it had been in the mountains for a thousand generations—maybe longer. They told us it was a spirit and by disturbing it we were making it angry."

"And did you believe all of that?"

"Of course not, but I did see the kind of power the device, or whatever it was could unleash, and I know that I lost more than one hundred men when they ventured too close to it. Frankly, I don't think it is of this earth."

The American colonel's mouth curled into a skeptical smirk. "Really? I find it very curious that none of Japan's military leaders ever mentioned this weapon or whatever it is. It's as if they were trying to hide it from us."

Usami cleared his throat. "They were not trying to hide it from you, Colonel. They knew nothing about it."

"They didn't know about it? How is that possible?"

Usami leaned forward in his chair. "Because I never informed them about what we found."

"Why not?"

"By that time, Japan had been defeated at Midway and any reasonable person could see that continuing the war against the

United States and its allies was futile. Why should I do anything to prolong the conflict? Not even General Hatazo Adachi, who ordered me to set up the Aoi Yanagi base, knew of the discovery."

"Are you aware that General Adachi is in custody in Australia, charged with war crimes?" Colonel McGrath asked.

"Yes, I know."

The colonel studied Usami for a moment. "That brings us to Major Imai. Why do you suppose he alerted us to what you found in New Guinea the way he did?

"As I said, whatever it is possesses incredible and highly dangerous power we were never able to control. Major Imai was convinced that whatever it is was not created by man. And I agreed with him. In my opinion, whatever it is should be avoided and forgotten. Major Imai disagreed. He felt it should be investigated further. I assume that is why he wrote the letter. I took some photos when I returned to the mountain with Major Imai, but I lost the film and my camera on our trek back to my headquarters camp."

The interview continued for several more minutes, then the colonel called another officer into the room. "This is Captain Niejahr. I want you to return to New Guinea with him and show him this new weapon, or whatever it is."

Usami watched a tall man in his mid-forties with captain's bars on his shoulders enter the room and settle on a leather couch.

"Captain Niejahr is a physicist from the Massachusetts Institute of Technology. We want him to examine this object or device and resolve this mystery once and for all."

"I see," Usami said. "And you are ordering me to go with him?"

"Yes, it's an order," the colonel said. "And, by the way, it's entirely off the books. Nobody but the three of us in this room is to know the objective of this operation. Is that clear?"

Usami assented with a nod and a deep breath. His war was not over, after all.

Three weeks later, Captain Niejahr, Usami, two squads of American Rangers, a four-person camera crew, and a half-dozen native guides headed into the uninhabited Foja Mountains of Western New Guinea. Their top-secret mission was to find, monitor, and, if possible, take possession of the device.

They never returned.

GHQ's official explanation was that the airplane carrying the men crashed somewhere in the Foja Mountains, and a search for the wreckage and survivors was unsuccessful.

However, six weeks after the group's disappearance, a six-inch round metal canister of 16mm color film packed in a box arrived at GHQ in Tokyo. Somebody had addressed the package to Colonel McGrath.

"What the hell is this?" the colonel asked his adjutant as he turned the canister over and over in his hands.

"I don't know, Colonel," the lieutenant adjutant replied. "It came in the morning mail pouch. There was no return address."

"Wasn't there a letter or a note?"

"No, sir. Nothing. Just the canister with the film."

A few hours later, the colonel loaded the film into a projector, lit a cigar, settled back in his chair, and watched the movie alone. The film began with a short title page that read: *Top Secret. Foja Mountains, Western New Guinea. Unexplained Beam of Light or Weapon.*

The film ran a total of eight minutes and twenty-six seconds, and by the time it had worked its way through the projector's sprockets and onto the take-up reel, Colonel McGrath was sitting forward in the chair, incredulous. His heart was pounding, and beads of sweat had formed on his forehead.

"Son of a bitch," he said out loud. Then, he thought: *What in the hell did just I see? Incredible.*

He rose unsteadily from his chair, rewound the film, and

hastily replaced it in the canister. He stabbed out his cigar in a metal ashtray, picked up the canister, and bolted past the startled adjutant in the outer office. Then he sprinted up the stairs that would take him to General MacArthur's office.

Halfway up three flights of stairs, the colonel's chest tightened. An intense pain raced from his shoulder, neck, and jaw through his left arm and hammered him to the floor.

As he rested on his knees, gasping for air, the canister fell from his hand and trundled down the steps. He reached hopelessly for it as he collapsed.

The last thing Colonel McGrath saw before the life light in his eyes permanently flickered and died was the canister rolling between the grills of a ventilation grate on the floor and vanishing —and with it, all evidence of The Encounter.

The End